# Praise for

## *The Forbidden Temptation of Baseball*

—◇·◇— ◈ ◇◈◇ ◈ —◇·◇—

★ Winner, 2017 USA Best Books Awards, Children's Fiction

★ Gold Medal, 2017 Moonbeam Children's Book Awards, Pre-teen Fiction: Historical/Multicultural

"Through the eyes of the ever-curious 'Leon' (Woo Ka-Leong), America is a play of both dazzling light and layered shadows. *The Forbidden Temptation of Baseball* turns our assumptions of America, and the Chinese impact on our history, upside down. A riveting and revealing story for the ages."
— CONRAD WESSELHOEFT, AUTHOR OF *DIRT BIKES, DRONES, AND OTHER WAYS TO FLY*

"A smart, authentic, and engaging look at the Chinese experience in America through the eyes of an adventurous and loyal boy who journeys into the sometimes welcoming, often hostile environment that was nineteenth-century America. You'll be drawn in by the absorbing history (which is little-known but true) but stay for the characters—and the story that brings them to life."
— DAVID PATNEAUDE, AUTHOR OF *THIN WOOD WALLS*

"Set against the backdrop of the true story of 120 Chinese students sent to New England by their government to study, Dori follows the lives of Woo Ka-Leong (Leon) and his brother Woo Ka-Sun (Carson), their time with the Swann family of Suffield, Connecticut, and their conquest of baseball in a thoroughly satisfying book that will teach young readers about the Chinese, and to see their own culture through foreign eyes."
— SCOTT D. SELIGMAN, AUTHOR OF *TONG WARS* AND *THE FIRST CHINESE AMERICAN*

"The story shows what it feels like to move to a different country, and how frustrating it is when you have limited language skills. It illustrates the contrasts between the American and Chinese cultures—and how conflicted you can feel when two cultures collide and you're caught in the middle."

—ANNA X., AGE 11, MERCER ISLAND, WA, DESCENDANT OF ONE OF THE 120 SCHOLARS FROM THE CHINESE EDUCATIONAL MISSION

"The much-published Dori Jones Yang, in writing this novel, has drawn on historical accounts of the 1870s Chinese Educational Mission, as well as her own extended residence in China as a foreign correspondent. She knows whereof she writes."

—EDWARD RHOADS, AUTHOR OF *STEPPING FORTH INTO THE WORLD: THE CHINESE EDUCATIONAL MISSION TO THE UNITED STATES, 1872-81*

"My great grandfather, Wen Bingzhong, was one of the 'First 100' and I often wondered about his experiences in America. This was a fascinating period in modern Chinese history, and Dori Jones Yang has written a story which describes how this group of young Chinese males might have felt."

—MARTIN TANG, RETIRED CHAIRMAN, ASIA, SPENCER STUART & ASSOCIATES

"Although the book takes place in 1876, the conflicts and issues raised are completely modern and relevant today as communities wrestle with the integration of traditional values and changes in technology, job requirements, and evolving social mores. As Dori Jones Yang brings these characters to life, they spark lots of thought-provoking questions – fantastic for school or home."

—NANCY KENNAN, MOTHER OF A MIDDLE SCHOOLER, AVID READER OF HISTORICAL FICTION, AND INVESTMENT BANKER IN NEW YORK CITY

*The*

Forbidden

Temptation

*of* Baseball

# The
# Forbidden
# Temptation
# *of* Baseball

## DORI JONES YANG

SPARKPRESS

Published by SparkPress, a BookSparks imprint,
A division of SparkPoint Studio, LLC
Tempe, Arizona, USA, 85281
www.gosparkpress.com

Published 2017
Printed in the United States of America
ISBN: 978-1-943006-32-8 (pbk)
ISBN: 978-1-943006-33-5 (e-bk)

Library of Congress Control Number: 2017936148

Interior design by Tabitha Lahr

—◇·◇—◇—◇◇—◇—◇·◇—

Dedicated to my friend,
Peter Tonglao,
1931–2016,
whose grandfather was one of the real
one hundred and twenty boys
of the Chinese Educational Mission
to the United States

—◇·◇—◇—◇◇—◇—◇·◇—

# Contents

# CHAPTER ONE

# Can This Be America?

—◇·◇—◇◇◇—◇·◇—

*E*ven after four days on the train, Woo Ka-Leong marveled at how fast it zipped along the smooth rails. Outside the windows, the snowy American prairie sped by, flat and white as a big silk quilt, and occasional craggy trees whizzed past like a flock of swallows. Brown lumps in the distance, he had learned, were herds of what appeared to be wild water buffalo but bulkier and hairier. Thick black smoke from the engine poured back over the passenger car, far darker than the wisps from his mother's cooking fire.

Metal wheels clacked in rhythm louder and more insistent than banging cymbals, but you couldn't cover your ears every minute for the seven days it would take to cross this huge continent. Even though the windows were shut tight against winter winds, all the passengers stayed bundled up in layers of clothing. Leong's nose wrinkled from the smell of burning metal, unwashed bodies, and the pungent sharpness of a hot black drink that was definitely not tea.

Next to him, Elder Brother was sleeping, again. How could anyone stay still for so long?

Leong wished he could be exploring the locomotive, figuring out what made this "Iron Horse" gallop. One time, during a mail stop, he had climbed up into the locomotive, where he examined the levers and valves and gauges, guessing how they worked. The engineer greeted him with a friendly smile, half hidden by a bushy red beard, and then tugged on a small bar near the roof of the cab. The whistle blew! As if responding to a warning signal, Elder Brother had come rushing in and dragged Leong back to their car.

"You can't just run around like that," Elder Brother had said. "Don't you ever *think* first, before you run off? What if I lost you? From now on, just behave. You hear?"

Leong had nodded. He didn't want to get lost, but he hated behaving. Besides, he was raring to learn everything he could about trains and about this new railroad that ran all the way across America. It was one of the wonders of the world. About nine thousand *lei,* from coast to coast. Unbelievable.

Quick movements in the aisle caught his eye. Tik-Chang, his best friend, was waving his arms to get his attention without waking Elder Brother. He and Tik-Chang, at age eleven, were the youngest in their group of thirty boys traveling together, and both of them hated sitting still. Now Leong noticed that Tik-Chang was waving a piece of rope.

Leong carefully squeezed past his brother and joined his friend in the aisle. "Where did you get that?" he whispered in their native variation of Cantonese.

"At the last stop. I have an idea. Watch."

He held on to the back of a seat and watched as his friend touched his ankle against Leong's and then tied the rope around their two legs. "What are you doing?"

Tik-Chang laughed and grabbed a seatback as the train jerked. "Let's try to walk like this. It will be fun."

It was fun. When they started to move their legs, they

wobbled and tipped and almost fell. Then they hopped and stumbled toward the back of the car, jerky and awkward. As the train swayed, they grabbed seatbacks as they went. Some of the other boys grinned as they passed, although a few older ones frowned. At the back, they collapsed into a jumble of laughter.

Suddenly, with no warning, the brakes squealed. The train lurched. A sickening crash reverberated. The whole car shuddered. The two friends grabbed each other and skidded along the floor back to the door, then forward. Jolted with fright, Leong lowered his head into his friend's jacket and grasped him tighter. Shrieks and shouts filled their ears.

The two friends pulled themselves up and looked out the window. Six masked men burst out of the snowy bushes, brandishing some kind of weapon. They fired into the air and let out a chilling yell, like wild dogs. Leong bit his lip. His stomach lurched.

"Bandits!" someone shouted in Chinese. "Heads down!"

Leong ducked his head and grabbed his friend's hand, which was shaking. "We'll be fine," he whispered. Then he poked his head up just enough to see out the window, curious to learn what those weapons looked like. His great uncle had an old rifle, left over from the Taiping Rebellion, but these men held shiny metal guns that fit squarely in just one hand. Their shots sounded like firecrackers.

The bandits were running toward the front of the train, where the baggage car was. People were shouting and screaming up there.

Teacher Kwong rushed up the aisle with a metal box, which he handed to Elder Brother, who was obviously now wide-awake. Elder Brother accepted it as if he expected this. Then the teacher returned to the front of their car and faced the boys. "Sit tight! Keep order!" he barked.

Elder Brother twisted in his seat and looked back, scowling. "Little Brother! Come here!"

Leong slipped the rope off his leg and, ducking his head as he ran, returned to his proper seat, next to Elder Brother. Tik-Chang went back to his assigned seat, too, across the aisle. They exchanged frightened glances. This could not be happening. After nearly a year of studying English in Shanghai and one month of pitching and rolling on the high seas, they couldn't die on this train, three days before reaching their destination.

Elder Brother sat perfectly still, his hands tucked into the sleeves of his padded jacket, his feet resting on the metal box. He looked stunned. All thirty of the boys, their braids hanging neatly down their backs below their skullcaps, sat quietly and in order. Leong stuffed his hands into his sleeves and grabbed his elbows to keep from shaking. Maybe the robbers would get what they wanted and leave them alone.

They didn't. Two bandits burst into their car. The ladies shrieked. One masked man carried a half-full sack. "Gold! Money!" they shouted in English, waving their guns in front of the chaperones. Leong knew the meaning of those words.

A shot rang out, and Leong ducked. He knew that the Chinese Educational Mission leaders were carrying many bars of gold, to finance years of education for the boys in his group. The emperor himself had sent them to America to learn about technology so they could one day return to modernize China.

Some of the boys wailed in panic. Tik-Chang heaved with sobs. Leong held his breath.

The group's top leader, Commissioner Ngeu, called out to the Chinese goddess of mercy, begging for protection. He hugged his wives close to him. A bandit jabbed Mr. Ngeu in the back with the butt of a gun, again demanding "Money! Gold!" but Mr. Ngeu didn't understand any English. Teacher Kwong, who did, stood up and handed the bandits his watch and some American cash. Then he raised his empty hands in the air. "No more money! No gold!"

One of the robbers grabbed Commissioner Ngeu and Teacher Kwong by their arms and pulled them into the aisle. Another robber patted them down and rummaged through their hand luggage, pulling things out and scattering them. If these robbers stole their gold, thought Leong, what would become of them all? Worse yet, if the bandits killed their chaperones, what would become of the boys? Would they be kidnapped and forced to live in the wild?

One robber loped down the aisle toward the boys, waving his gun. He stopped and aimed his pistol at Elder Brother. "What's in that?" he said, pointing at the metal box. "Open it!"

Without thinking, Leong jumped up and pushed the man's gun downward. The bandit grabbed Leong by the braid and knocked him off his feet, dangling him by his hair. Leong yelped in pain.

Elder Brother jumped up and grabbed the robber's hand, shouting, "Let go of my brother!" in Chinese.

The outlaw swung his gun and whacked the side of Elder Brother's head, hard enough to knock him back into the window. Leong gasped in horror.

Above the din, another gang member shouted. The robber released Leong and raced back up the aisle. In seconds, all the attackers jumped off the train. They mounted their horses, and, with another barbarian yell, disappeared into the woods.

For a long moment, everyone was silent. Leong touched the back of his neck, where his braid was still attached. Then he turned to his brother, his heart still thumping with fear.

Elder Brother was holding his head in his hands, moaning. One hand had blood on it. "He's bleeding!" Leong shouted. What if Elder Brother died, right then? It would be his fault. Why had he been so stupid as to jump up like that?

Teacher Kwong gently pulled off Elder Brother's skullcap and examined the wound. The gun had scraped off a patch of skin above his ear, bringing out an impressive splurt of blood. The teacher took off his own scarf, tied it around Ka-Sun's head, and pressed it firmly.

"Don't worry," the teacher said. "It looks like a superficial wound." Leong wondered what that meant. He sidled up to his brother, still shivering at what might have been.

Mr. Ngeu strode down the aisle toward them, counting the boys as he went. When he saw Elder Brother, he looked alarmed. "Are you all right? Did they take it?"

Elder Brother reached down and slid the small box into the aisle. "I kept it safe."

Mr. Ngeu lifted it in his hands and hugged it to his chest. "Woo Ka-Sun, today you are a hero. You saved our Chinese Educational Mission."

Leong couldn't believe it. Their gold! Why had the leaders asked Elder Brother to look after it? They must have had this plan all along, should something like this happen, should the group come under threat. Of course, they had chosen Elder Brother as the most responsible.

The other boys gathered around them, complimenting Ka-Sun for his heroism. Elder Brother accepted their admiration with a manly nod. He didn't look too badly wounded.

"It was Leong who went after the bad guy," Tik-Chang said in a small voice. No one seemed to hear him. Leong smiled but shook his head at his loyal friend. It was Elder Brother who took the blow, so he deserved the credit.

"We'll take you to a doctor at the next town," Teacher Kwong promised.

Everyone had to get off the train while the crew assessed the damage. Despite all the gunshots fired, only one man, the conductor, was wounded, and only in the leg. A gentleman in the smoking car tied a tourniquet around the conductor's thigh.

At the front of the train, two thick logs had been placed on the tracks to stop the train, which had resulted in the screeching halt they'd all experienced. The metal bars of the V-shaped cattle catcher on the front of the locomotive were bent, but the thick metal hooks and links connecting the cars seemed strong.

Leong watched as the crew cleared the track and repaired the damage. It took several hours, but he barely noticed the cold. He held his breath as the engineer started up the steam engine. If it didn't work, they might be stuck here for days.

After a splutter and a cough, the locomotive roared to life. Everyone breathed and smiled. They had all survived.

Once the train was running again, Leong sat quietly next to Elder Brother. The bleeding had stopped. "It's just a scrape. Don't worry," he said to the others. But for Leong, he had a sharper point: "I worry about you. You're always running off. America is . . . dangerous, full of . . . crazy people." His words sounded muddled. "From now on, you must obey. Stay by my side."

"I promise," Leong said. Before they'd left China, Father had warned him about his impulsiveness and ordered him to obey Elder Brother.

But he disagreed with Elder Brother; he thought America was marvelous—full of mighty machines and stunning surprises. The train robbery wasn't so terrible. It was exciting, and nobody was killed or hurt too badly. Still, Leong knew better than to write home about it. No need to scare their parents.

How could he learn about America if he did nothing but sit quietly at his brother's side?

# CHAPTER TWO

# Arrival Disaster

—◇·◈—◈—◈·◇—

*A*aiya! Leong's nose smashed into a lady's bosom. This was not the greeting he expected when he got off the train in Springfield, Massachusetts, after his long journey from China. The lady planted her lips firmly on his forehead. Leong had not been kissed since he was a baby, and nobody in China hugged like this—especially a stranger. Teacher Kwong had taught them that Americans always shook hands when they greeted strangers, instead of bowing.

He recoiled in surprise as the lady pushed him back and gazed down into his face with a half smile. Her eyes were an odd blue-gray color, and her hair was a jumble of yellow and white frizzy curls. Her eyebrows faded into her forehead, now wrinkled in concern. "You're so teensy!"

This was not an English word Teacher Kwong had taught them, so Leong couldn't guess how to respond. He just smiled uncertainly.

This greeting was quite a contrast from the way he had said good-bye to his mother, back in his village in southern

China. On his knees, he had bowed to Ah-Ma three times, his head tapping the ground, as she sat, teary eyed, on a wooden chair. For the first time since arriving in America, he felt a lurch of homesickness.

Next, the large lady lunged toward his brother, standing beside him. Elder Brother's bruise was invisible, hidden under the black silk band of his skullcap. He leaned back and thrust out his hand to shake, as their teacher had taught them during their training in Shanghai. The lady paused and then grasped his hand, as if realizing that, at fourteen, Ka-Sun was a man now.

Dressed in official scholar's robes, with an ankle-length silk gown and a jacket with sleeves so long he had to push them up to shake hands, Elder Brother did look like a Chinese gentleman. But Leong just felt foolish in these grown-up clothes. They were meant for dignified gentlemen who sat at their desks and did calligraphy all day.

Leong wished he had remembered to offer his hand, too, and to greet the lady by name. Clearly, she was Mrs. Swann, the mother of the family with whom he and his brother would be living for the next who-knows-how-many years. He had been practicing how to say Swann, which sounded like the Mandarin word for *sour*.

Inside his own long sleeves, his fists flexed as he stood straight, trying to look taller and more grown-up. Although he was nearly twelve, he was small for his age and felt tiny among these towering foreigners with their gigantic skirts. Where were the men of the family?

Mrs. Swann said something in rapid English and gestured to a young woman next to her. This younger, thinner lady wore a fur coat and a tiny hat with a loose green feather sticking out the top. He wondered how that hat could possibly keep her head warm.

"How do you do?" the young woman said, looking at Leong with serious, pale eyes. She spoke slowly and clearly enough for him to understand. The feather shimmered like a peacock's tail as she offered her hand.

"How do you do," Leong repeated, pumping her gloved hand. Here was one American who acted the way he had learned in the classroom.

"How do you do?" the young woman repeated to Ka-Sun, who should have been addressed first, since he was the elder brother. Such bad manners.

"My name is Julia," she said. Here was another sentence he could understand. "You are Ka-Sun?" she said to his brother, who offered his hand reluctantly. Touching a lady was wrong in China, especially if she was unmarried.

"And you are Ka-Leong?" She pronounced his name in an odd way, Ka Lee-ong, not at all the way anyone back home would say it.

Should he call her Miss Julia? Or Miss Swann? Or Mrs. Julia? Or—

Before he could reply, Teacher Kwong introduced himself in English to Mrs. Swann and Julia and shook their hands. Then he shepherded all the boys to a place on the snow-covered part of the platform where their baggage was being unloaded and piled in rows. The other Chinese boys in their group, also surrounded by strange Americans, were busy pointing out their trunks. Leong found Tik-Chang and patted him on the back, but he didn't have time to say good-bye to the other boys before they all parted ways to live in different homes.

Many of his companions had become his good friends after nine months of training together in Shanghai, a one-month journey by ship across the Pacific Ocean, and a seven-day train trip across America. They had shared an adventure together, and now he wouldn't see them again for months. His heart drooped as he watched them walk off with their American families.

A hiss of steam escaped the smokestack, and Leong glanced at the engine. A pang shot through his chest. The train journey had been marvelous, a thrill of freedom. Now it was about to end, and the studying would begin.

He needed to get one last look at that locomotive. While his brother was distracted, helping the Swann ladies identify their trunks, Leong slipped away, running along the length of the train to its front. Splattered with mud, the massive, muscular engine loomed silent now, its chimney towering overhead. This was a shiny, newer one, not the one that had crashed. Leong scanned the wheels, still trying to fathom how steam from burning coal could make them move.

As he reached out to touch a wheel, he felt melancholy. If only he could hop back on the train, he could learn all he needed to know about the modern Iron Horse and the rail tracks that connected distant cities across America.

"Ka-Leong!" This time his name was pronounced the right way, shouted frantically by his brother, who was running toward him. Elder Brother grabbed his arm and dragged him back to the Swanns, scolding him in a steaming hiss of angry Chinese words. "I told you to stay by my side. Now you've embarrassed me! These high-nosed people were frantic with worry!"

Leong's heart sank as he trotted after his brother to the street, where a horse-drawn carriage was waiting. Their trunks were strapped on the back. The two American ladies sat inside, and Mrs. Swann was frowning. He was in trouble.

"Sorry," said Leong. "So sorry, Missus Swann." He struggled to pronounce *sorry* the right way. It was one of the hardest words he had learned and came out as *solly*.

To show he really meant it, he bowed his head. Suddenly, he felt a firm jerk on the single braid that flowed down his back. After less than two weeks in this country, he knew this feeling. Twice before, some rude American boy had pulled at his braid and mocked him. Leong had vowed to smack the next one who did it. So what if he had a braid? All men and boys in China did. It was a symbol of loyalty to the emperor. No one was allowed to cut it off.

He spun around and saw a shabby kid with messy red hair and a mass of freckles, about his age, laughing. Annoyed, Leong swung his arm out wildly. The redheaded boy dodged the blow. His mean face twisted in a dare, and he stuck out his tongue.

"Johnny!" the older lady exclaimed. "For shame!"

Leong leaped after the bully, eager to smack him hard. But his older brother seized his shoulder to hold him back.

A thin man caught the redheaded boy and spoke to him sharply. The boy's lips set in defiance as the man led him behind the carriage. To Leong's dismay, the mean kid stepped onto the back of their carriage, hanging on to their trunks, and the man climbed up to the driver's seat. That boy belonged to the Swanns, somehow.

*Aaiya.* Leong wished he had never left the train. Were there bad-mannered boys like this everywhere in America?

His hands were shaking as he climbed in and sat on the cushioned seat next to the young lady who had introduced herself as Julia. Mrs. Swann's face melted into an apology, and a flood of anxious English poured out of her mouth as she stuffed her hands into a furry muff. Miss Julia quietly took Leong's hand and held it tight, as if that would prevent him from escaping again. When he tried to pull his hand away, she squeezed harder. Her grip felt like a rebuke, but he knew he deserved it. Once again, he hadn't followed the rules.

Leong could feel the boy's glare on the back of his head. He hated that stupid boy. But he also felt embarrassed. Teacher Kwong had made them rehearse this moment many times, how to greet your host family and make a good first impression as a Chinese gentleman. Swinging your fist at an American boy had not been part of the lesson.

As the horses jerked to a trot, he took one last look at the glorious locomotive resting on the firm, straight tracks.

As scary as the robbery had been, Lèong loved the train ride. Now the wonderful journey by ship and rail was over. His last chance for freedom was about to depart the station. American machines were impressive, but American people were unpredictable. How would he ever get used to them?

# Chapter Three

# Suffield Sport

—◇·◇—◁◇▷—◇·◇—

*A* cold wind whipped them inside the open carriage, and Leong shivered. The ladies wore woolen coats and scarves wrapped around their necks, but he and the other Chinese boys had been instructed to wear their silk scholar's jackets over long gowns. Now the freezing wind crept under the skirt of his gown. His feet felt like ice in his cloth shoes, wet from the snow. The tiny skullcap left his ears exposed. Miss Julia tucked her lap blanket around the shoulders of the two boys, who huddled together to get warm. Leong was glad to feel Elder Brother's arm wrap around him under the wool blanket.

They left the city of Springfield by crossing a bridge over a river. After that, Leong noticed that the road was lined on both sides by large trees with bare black branches heavy with snow. He thought they looked like an old lady's gnarled hands, coated with rice flour. After they passed the last houses of the city, the trees ended and snowy fields stretched out on both sides of the road, like vast plains of cooked rice. He was amazed at the way the snow coated everything, as if some giant had splattered the landscape with white paint. It never snowed where his family lived.

The afternoon sun shone in on the right side of the road, so Leong figured out that they were heading south. The street had been partially cleared by the tramping of horses. Still, the carriage ride was much smoother than the mule cart Leong had taken out of his village over bumpy dirt roads.

Although his brother's arm encircled him protectively, Leong could feel tension in Ka-Sun's stiff body. *What an idiot I was,* Leong thought. *Now these Americans probably think Chinese people are all barbarians.*

Still, he hoped his brother would mutter some word like *rascal* to describe the behavior of that bad boy who had pulled his braid. He longed for sympathy.

But as soon as the ladies' attention was diverted, his brother whispered some words of criticism instead. "Remember," Elder Brother said in Chinese. "We are gentleman scholars. Don't act American!"

Leong hung his head. Those three words were a terrible accusation. Back in China, Teacher Kwong had warned them against acting "too American." The thirty boys in their group were the last of one hundred and twenty Chinese boys, between the ages of eleven and sixteen, sent to America by the Imperial Government of China. They were to learn English, complete college degrees, and go back home to help transform China into a strong, modern country. This was the Chinese Educational Mission to the United States.

Some of the first groups of boys had caused trouble, and one had been sent home in shame. High Chinese officials in Peking were now questioning the whole mission. One more naughty boy, making trouble and acting too American, might convince the officials to abort the mission and send them all back home. Teacher Kwong's warnings about this still rang in his ears.

Elder Brother's voice softened, and he continued in Chinese. "These people are not like us. Don't let ignorant Americans get to you. We need to show them we're better than they are."

Leong wished he could lash back at his know-it-all brother, saying "Stop telling me what to do! As if you're so perfect!" But he knew he couldn't. Father had told Elder Brother that it was his responsibility to make sure Leong behaved himself. And Leong knew it was his responsibility to obey his elder brother. That was the Confucian way, keeping harmony by knowing your place. As much as he chafed at the criticism, he knew that Elder Brother was right. He would have to tame his curiosity and control his quick temper.

So he nodded. Then he clasped his hands together, inside his long sleeves, hoping that would keep him from acting badly again.

A pang speared his heart. If he couldn't even follow the Chinese rules, how would he ever learn how to act in America? What was he doing here, in this foreign place? He thought of his home, where he could run freely through the courtyards and rice paddies with his friends, where the air was always warm, where he could be himself. Would he become a different person, here in America, speaking such a strange language?

Elder Brother frowned and grasped his forehead.

"Headache?" Leong stiffened. This was the second time his brother had winced from a bad headache since the bandits. The first time, Elder Brother had thrown up. Would he lose his lunch here in this horse carriage? Now *that* would make a very bad impression.

His brother responded with tense silence. Their bags were in the back, so there was nothing except the blanket to catch the vomit. "Should I ask them to stop?" Leong said.

Elder Brother shook his head. "I'll be all right. I think." He seemed to be focusing on what was happening inside his body. The doctor had only rubbed some lotion on his wound and reassured him that he might have occasional headaches but not for long. Nothing was broken.

The older American lady looked at them in alarm. "Are you all right?"

Ka-Sun smiled weakly. Leong pointed to his own head, trying to remember the English word for headache. The lady seemed to understand. All those months of training, and he couldn't find the right word. He thought of making the gesture for throwing up but decided not to.

After a while, they arrived at a small town. Teacher Kwong had told them their home would be in a town called Suffield, Connecticut. Other boys from their group would be living in different towns, far away.

This place looked nothing like a Chinese rural town. Instead of a solid row of open-fronted shops, its straight streets were lined with stand-alone buildings. A few had signs in front, with English letters, but Leong couldn't tell if they were shops. Houses faced the street over spacious snowy lawns. Some had low wooden fences around a small yard, but all were clearly visible from the street, unguarded and vulnerable to nosy neighbors. How could these people live safely with no brick walls? Wouldn't the bandits get them? He had many questions but didn't know how to ask them.

Mrs. Swann talked as they passed through the village, pointing to different houses as if telling the boys which families lived in each. Leong tried to pay attention since his brother still had his head in his hand. But he could recognize only an occasional English word: *There. Family. Not.* English sounded totally different here than it did in his classroom in China, where Teacher Kwong spoke slowly, teaching them a word at a time. These people ran all their words together in a gushing stream.

Elder Brother lifted his head to stare out at the distant trees. He seemed better.

As they passed through the center of Suffield, Leong saw a small white pavilion with six sides along a square grassy area. Near it stood a large stone building with a white tower that looked like a giant finger pointing to the sky. Mrs. Swann's hand flew out of her muff, and her voice became louder and more animated. Leong heard the word *church*.

He flinched. One of the strict rules the Chinese boys had been taught was that they were not permitted to join a church. Their host families would expect them to attend church every Sunday, and that was all right. But the boys should never, ever "join." Whatever that meant.

Just past the church stood a large stone two-story building, on a slight rise. Mrs. Swann said a word Leong recognized: *school*. Eagerly, he leaned forward to get a better view of it. Perhaps this was the school they would attend, once their English was good enough.

The sound of excited young voices filled the air. Leong strained to see what was going on. Just past the school, a group of boys was playing on a snowy field. Half were gathered on one side, and others were scattered across the field. None of them had queues, of course. One boy held a thick wooden stick, which he swung to hit a small white ball.

The carriage jerked, and Leong realized that the mean boy hanging on to the back had jumped off and was running toward the group of boys.

Leong was glad that the bully had run away. One of the other boys on the field waved, and the redheaded boy joined their game.

"Baseball?" Miss Julia said.

"Baseball," Leong repeated, as he watched the boy with the thick stick drop it and run through the snow.

Miss Julia smiled proudly, as if she had taught him his first word of American English.

*Baseball.* Leong had learned this word back in China. Teacher Kwong had called the game a waste of time, one of many American frivolities to avoid. Now Leong knew what it looked like. Perhaps it was just for low-class boys like that one who had pulled his braid.

How odd it was that so many boys would want to play together in a big group this way, outside. Especially in the snow! Why did they do it? Still, he could see them laughing and shouting, and part of him longed to jump out of the carriage and join them.

Next to him, Ka-Sun clicked his tongue. "When do they study?" he asked in Chinese. "Why do their parents permit them to waste time on this game?" His face wasn't as pale now.

Of course, Julia and her mother did not understand Chinese. Mrs. Swann smiled at Elder Brother as if he had said something clever.

The carriage kept moving, taking them a short distance out of the town to the farm where the Swann family lived. Safe and secure from the forbidden temptation of baseball.

# CHAPTER FOUR

# American Home

—◇·◆—◈—◆·◇—

*T*he Swann house loomed at the end of a long driveway, surrounded by massive trees. Above a solid stone
foundation rose the white wooden planks of its upper stories, adorned with gabled windows, like drawn eyebrows.
The house huddled up against the shade of the woods as if
shunning its neighbors. Only on one side did a field stretch
out, barren and snowy yet hinting of farmland. *Too dry and
hard for a rice paddy*, thought Leong. *What could grow in
such a cold climate?*

The driver pulled the carriage to a stop in front of the
door. He then jumped down and came around to offer his
hand. The ladies held their skirts to one side as they stepped
down to a metal bar before touching the ground. Watching
closely, Leong imitated them, holding aside his long gown to
make sure he didn't trip. Elder Brother stepped down with
no problem.

An extremely tall man emerged from the front door of
the house, greeted Mrs. Swann, and took her hand. He wore
a dark Western-style suit, with a high white collar, vest, and

tie under a jacket that buttoned up the front, tight and confining. His hair was pale brown, wavy over his forehead, and his mouth hid inside a thick beard.

Clearly, he was the master of the household. As instructed, Leong and his brother bowed in unison, side by side, and then offered their right hands for the man to shake. Mr. Swann seemed to understand protocol better than his wife; he shook Elder Brother's hand first, then Leong's. His grip was much firmer than his daughter's.

"Good afternoon, Mister Swann. How do you do," each of the boys said as they shook his hand with solemn dignity. Teacher Kwong had rehearsed this moment with them many times, instructing them on the use of Mister, Miss, and Mrs. It was obvious when to say *Mister*. Leong was afraid he might make an embarrassing mistake by saying *Miss* when he was supposed to say *Mrs*. How was he to know whether a lady was married?

The man's face seemed gentle but worn; he did not smile and held their gaze only an instant before looking away. Then he stepped back and gestured with his hand for them to come inside. Someone had swept the snow from the stone steps, but Leong's homemade cloth shoes still slid on a patch of ice.

Most fathers in China were also stiff and formal, so Leong did not expect a smile or a warm greeting. Still, Mr. Swann seemed distant. Leong wondered if he and his brother were truly welcome in this household. Why hadn't this man come to greet them at the train station? Why had the Swann family decided to host two boys from a foreign land? Since Leong was only eleven, he might be living in this house for six or seven years before going off to college. That was a big commitment; he could not imagine his own family taking in a foreign boy for that many years. The Swanns must be very rich.

The house smelled like wax candles and wood smoke. The boys followed the ladies into a large room to the right of the hallway, a sitting room or parlor. A rug covered much of the wooden floor, and five padded armchairs clustered near the fireplace. The fire's warmth drew them in with welcome relief from the cold outside. Still, the dimly lit room felt stifling.

As they entered, a young voice filled the air with a sweet trill of English words. A girl leaned forward from the shadows of a stuffed chair, her arms reaching toward them, her cheerful gaze fixed on their faces.

Mrs. Swann, who had been moving slowly, strode across the room toward the girl, who hugged her, and Julia's face softened into a smile as she removed her hat.

This girl seemed small, younger than Julia, but her face didn't look childlike. Leong guessed that she was nearly grown-up—perhaps the same age as his brother. She wore a long dress of brilliant blue with an embroidered sash. A gray woolen shawl was draped over her shoulders and upper arms. Part of her hair was held back by a thick blue ribbon, though light brown curls framed her face.

Immediately at ease in her presence, Leong stepped forward and stood in front of her chair. She did not get up or bow, but she greeted him with a delighted smile and held out a soft, thin hand, which he shook. His heart leaped toward her like a deer over a bush.

"Greetings!" she began. Before he could answer, the girl continued in a bubbling stream of words, hanging on to his hand longer than he expected. She seemed to be looking at and commenting on his skullcap, his jacket, his robe, his eyes; everything about him seemed to fascinate and delight her.

When she released his hand, he stepped back and turned to make room for his brother. But Ka-Sun was still standing back by the entrance, looking at Mr. Swann, as if waiting for the man's permission to enter a room occupied by ladies.

Elder Brother's face was blank, but Leong knew why he was uncomfortable. Every good Chinese home had a front section for entertaining men and a back area where women lived, safe from public scrutiny. No decent family in China would bring strange men into their home and introduce them to their wives and daughters. It was one thing to hear Teacher Kwong tell them about American customs, another thing to enter a room that seemed reserved for women.

"My sister, Charlotte," Julia said to the boys.

"Miss Sha-lit," Leong said, adding the polite word he had been taught, *Miss*.

The girl's eyes crinkled, and she clapped her hands. Her eyes flitted to Elder Brother, who was still hovering by the door. "Good afternoon," she said to him in her musical voice. "Welcome to our house!"

Elder Brother bowed his head slightly. Leong wondered about his headache.

Mrs. Swann flopped into a chair next to Charlotte, as if exhausted, and Julia perched on a sofa. Both seemed to relax in the presence of Charlotte. The father gestured for the boys to sit in the other chairs, facing the fire, but he stood behind a chair, at a stiff distance from his family.

Julia answered her sister's questions and nodded toward Leong, who sensed she was telling her sister the story of how he had swung his fist at the boy who pulled his braid. He heard the word Johnny. Charlotte's brows tightened at first, and she looked at Leong with concern. She said something else, shaking her head but smiling. They were probably saying he was a troublemaker. The sisters laughed, but the father did not.

A maidservant brought them a hot drink, served in a porcelain cup with a delicate rounded handle on a small curved plate. The beverage was sweet and brown and milky.

"Tea," Julia said, "from China."

Leong knew this word, *tea,* but this warm drink looked nothing like Chinese tea. On the ship, Teacher Kwong had taught them that Americans poured milk and sugar into their tea, but this didn't have any taste of tea at all. Still, it warmed him up after the wintry air.

"Tea," Leong repeated, eager to please.

Miss Julia nodded at his effort to speak English, and Charlotte clapped her hands again. Clearly, the way to please these people was to try to speak their language.

One glance at Ka-Sun's face and Leong could see that Elder Brother was dismayed by this strange American drink and uncomfortable in this unfamiliar, overheated home.

Charlotte was talkative, like her mother, but in a free, unfettered way that surprised him. She seemed curious and friendly, unlike her serious older sister.

"Ka-Lee-ong." Miss Julia was trying to pronounce his name again.

Charlotte's bright eyes turned toward Leong. "Ka Leon?" she said.

This pronunciation seemed no odder than the way Julia had said his name.

"Can I just call you Leon?"

Again the women laughed. Miss Julia turned toward him and repeated the name as her sister had pronounced it: "Leon."

"Lee-on," Leong repeated, trying to memorize the way they would pronounce his name. His teacher had told him he should not take an American name, like Joe or Pete, but this did not sound like an American man's name—just the closest these people could get to saying his real name. *Leon.* He liked the sound of it. Here in America, that's who he would be.

"And your brother's name is?" Charlotte spoke slowly enough that Leon understood.

Elder Brother looked too unsettled, so Leon responded for him: "Ka-Sun."

"Carson?"

It sounded close enough.

Just then, the maidservant came into the room with an announcement, and Leon heard the word *dinner*. That was a word he knew!

The women stood up and began leaving the room—except Charlotte.

Leon hesitated a moment, then watched as Mr. Swann gently slipped his hands beneath Charlotte and lifted her out of the chair. She put her arms around his neck in a familiar gesture, as if used to this routine, and rested her head against his chest as he carried her.

*Bound feet!* Leon thought in wonder, thinking of his own mother and grandmother, who had to be carried over long distances because their feet had been broken and bound when they were children, to ensure petite, ladylike steps when they grew up. Teacher Kwong had said no American girls had bound feet!

But her dangling feet, in thin slippers, were the size of a boy's, not encased in tiny silk shoes like a Chinese lady's.

Mr. Swann carefully placed Charlotte into a wooden chair Leon had not noticed before. It had two large wheels on the sides, plus two small wheels near the footrests. As she settled into the chair, her curls bounced around her neck. Mr. Swann placed her feet in the footrests and then pushed her wheelchair into the dining room.

Both Leon and Elder Brother stood frozen, their mouths open in identical looks of surprise, as they watched the operation. They had never seen a chair with wheels on it.

Charlotte did not have bound feet. But clearly, she could not walk.

# CHAPTER FIVE

# First Impressions

—◇·◇—◇—◇·◇—

*T*he aroma of cooked meat reminded Leon how hungry he was. A modern kerosene lamp glowed on a sideboard chest, and candles flickered on the table, staving off the early darkness of winter.

The father gestured for Elder Brother to sit in the chair to his right. Leon was glad to see that, since he had been taught that this was the chair for the guest of honor. The mother asked Leon to sit at her right, opposite Charlotte. The table had six chairs, and Leon wondered who usually sat in the two extra seats. This family had only four people, yet the table was big enough for six. At home, meals were lively events, with little children running around and plenty of aunts, uncles, and cousins filling the house.

Suddenly, Leon felt a twinge of sorrow for these Swanns. In China, a family with only daughters was considered unfortunate. Every man needed at least one son— preferably several—to carry on the family name and get an education or do the hard work around the farm.

As Leon wondered why these parents had not tried harder to have a son, he noticed the odd-looking dining table, covered with stiff white linen. In front of each person stood a small white cloth, folded like a tent. On the right side of it lay a silver knife and spoon, on the other side two forks. No chopsticks or rice bowls anywhere.

Elder Brother immediately picked up the small cloth, unfolded it, and laid it on his lap, as they had been taught. But none of the Swanns did so. Instead, they put their hands together and bowed their heads. Leon did the same, keeping his eyes open to make sure he was doing it right. His brother kept his hands under the table.

Mr. Swann spoke a few words, which Leon knew was a prayer to the Christian God.

"When they say 'Amen,' it's over," their teacher had said. Leon listened for that word.

Mr. Swann droned on and on. Leon hoped the food was not getting cold. Finally, he heard "Amen," and they lifted their heads. Charlotte smiled at him and seemed genuinely happy he and his brother were there. Leon's insides warmed up. Maybe American life wouldn't be too bad.

Mr. Swann shook out his napkin as if trying to remove bugs from it. Leon picked up his napkin and shook it out the same way. He noticed that Mrs. Swann dabbed her eyes with it first, before spreading it out on her lap, so he did the same. Charlotte was watching his every move with wide, curious eyes.

The crippled girl began talking to the boys in long sentences, looking first at one, then at the other. Leon guessed that she was asking questions, because her voice would go up at the end of her sentences and she waited for a response. He had no idea what she was saying. He smiled and nodded, hoping to be seen as agreeable.

". . . English words?" Charlotte was looking at Ka-Sun when she asked this question, and Leon caught only the last two words. "Carson?" she added. Elder Brother looked at his plate, so Leon guessed that he had not understood the question. The smell of roasted meat was very strong, and his brother looked squeamish.

"English word," Leon repeated, to show he had understood and to distract the attention away from Elder Brother.

Charlotte beamed at him, and even Miss Julia gave him a quick smile.

At the end of the table, Mr. Swann took up a large, sharp kitchen knife and began carving a big chunk of beef into thick slices. He put one slab on each porcelain plate and passed it down to each person at the table.

Julia repeated Charlotte's question more slowly, and Leon guessed she was asking if he knew many English words. He took a chance and decided to say some of the words he had learned recently.

"Rail," Leon said, parroting a word he had learned from a brakeman. "Railroad. Train." Surely Americans would be happy to hear him say such words in English.

Instead, they all looked at him with blank faces.

Appearing to pay no attention to the conversation, Mr. Swann picked up a bowl full of steaming white mush and used a large spoon to plunk a pile of it on his plate, near the beef but not touching it. He handed the bowl to Ka-Sun, who did the same. Leon was proud to see Elder Brother doing everything just right.

*Carson.* Leon tried to remember the way these Americans said Elder Brother's name. Carson then handed the bowl to Charlotte.

"Rail. Railroad," Leon repeated, with his best pronunciation.

"Lail. Lail-loe," Charlotte parroted. Leon could hear that this was not the way the brakeman had said these words. Charlotte seemed to have no idea what they meant. His cheeks felt hot. That pesky *r* sound. His mouth could just not make it right.

Miss Julia shot a stern look at Charlotte, as if to say, "Stop it. Don't make fun of him."

Charlotte pouted and the conversation stopped. In the silence that followed, it seemed the dark gloom had crept in from outside. The candles flickered and cast shadows on the table.

Mr. Swann also helped himself to green beans, then took a slice of white bread and passed the plate of bread to Carson. The boys took exactly the same portions as they saw others take and put it on their own plates in the same place, including a pat of butter, which they put on top of the bread.

When the butter came to Leon, it slipped off his knife onto the tablecloth near his plate. He quickly scraped it up with his finger and plopped it on the bread, then licked his finger. Carson gave him a withering look. Oops. Leon quickly wiped his fingers on his napkin. How could anyone remember all these rules? "No licking fingers," Teacher Kwong had said.

No one ate until everyone was served. Then Mrs. Swann lifted her knife and fork and cut a small slice off her meat. The slice of beef on Leon's plate was huge—more than enough meat to serve his whole family a dinner at home. All for one person, at one meal! No wonder Americans were taller and fatter than Chinese people.

The meat looked red and undercooked. Still, it smelled great and Leon was famished. His slice had a rim of fat around the edge—considered the best part at home. He cut off a chunk that included a lot of fat and then used his fork to stuff it into his mouth. He was very happy to get the first bite in until he realized it was a much larger piece than Mrs. Swann had cut. It was juicy and tasted good, but it took him a long time to chew.

The silence ended with a burst of chatter from Mrs. Swann, who talked so quickly Leon could not catch a single word. The others just focused on cutting their meat. Charlotte asked her mother a question, and they talked a while, but everyone seemed uneasy. Leon noticed that his brother was eating mostly the white mush and bread.

Charlotte laughed. She was looking at Elder Brother, who had stabbed his slice of bread with his fork and was nibbling it around the edges. What was wrong with that? How annoying that someone was laughing at his elder brother!

Carson quickly put his bread down on his plate, with the fork sticking out the top. Mrs. Swann spoke sharply to Charlotte, who tried to smother her laughter. Miss Julia picked up her bread with her left hand. She used a silver knife to slather butter on it and then ate it without touching her fork. So bread was an exception; you should eat it with your hands.

Elder Brother's cheeks reddened, and Leon felt sympathetic. These Americans didn't know how smart Elder Brother was. Back at home, Ka-Sun had been the best young scholar in their village. Their tutor had said so. By the age of four, Elder Brother had memorized fifty Tang-era poems and six Yuan lyrics. Everyone praised him when he recited what he'd learned.

Ka-Sun was his second elder brother; First Elder Brother, three years older, was not as talented as Ka-Sun. Yet their father, a small-town merchant, could afford to educate only one of his three sons in the traditional Confucian way. Their tutor said Ka-Sun had the best chance of advancing through the national exams and becoming a high official, every family's dream. But Great Uncle insisted that the opportunity go to First Elder Brother, since he was the oldest. So First Elder Brother was sent to the city to study the traditional Confucian curriculum. Ka-Sun was devastated.

Then some colleague of their father's found out about this new program, the Chinese Educational Mission to America. The government would pay all expenses, and they could learn English, a language useful for trade. Ka-Sun didn't want to leave China because he still dreamed of getting a proper Chinese education. But Father insisted he should try.

Of the thirty who were chosen to go to America in their group, Ka-Sun scored the highest on the entrance exam. Leong took the test and barely made it. He just wasn't that good at reading and writing. Leong didn't really want to go to America either, but he changed his mind when he heard about cowboys. Back then he thought cowboys rode around on water buffaloes like "cow boys" in China.

Suddenly, Miss Julia was talking to them again. "More English words?" she asked Carson.

Elder Brother smiled and nodded but said nothing.

Leon hated to see his brother shamed in front of these people. "China," he said.

"China! Yes!" Julia looked at him, pleased.

Leon pointed to his own nose. "China man," he said.

The ladies nodded encouragement.

He looked at Elder Brother, who was busily applying butter to another piece of bread.

"China man," Leon said, pointing to his brother.

"Yes! Right," Miss Julia said.

Leon pointed to Miss Julia. "America man," he said.

Charlotte burst into laughter. This time, Leon could see he had said something wrong but could not think what.

As the meal neared its end, Leon felt exhausted. But he remembered the sentence that Teacher Kwong had instructed them to say after their first meal. Elder Brother should say it, but he had not spoken much in this unfamiliar environment. Leon knew Elder Brother felt more ashamed when he mispronounced English words, worried he would lose face. Besides, Elder Brother's face was looking gray. Good manners required that one of them speak up, so Leon decided he would have to do it.

Leon cleared his throat, and everyone looked at him. "Thank you for inviting us to your home." He pronounced it the best he could, and he faced Mr. Swann when he said it, slightly bowing his head.

His pronunciation was not perfect, but all the Swanns seemed to understand. Leon saw a hint of a smile in the father's eyes.

"Not at all," said Mr. Swann, addressing them at last. "You are most welcome here."

Elder Brother turned to Mr. Swann and spoke in a quiet voice. "Sank-a you, mistah." But the ladies were talking, and Carson's words got lost in the hubbub.

After dessert, Mrs. Swann asked the boys to follow her. She took them up a flight of stairs to the second floor. Her rump looked huge from behind. Leon tried not to look at it.

The large lady showed them the bedroom they were to share. Striped floral paper covered the walls, and a thin rug lay on the floor. The room had a wooden wardrobe and two narrow beds, each with a mattress and quilt. A ceramic bowl, pitcher, and two cups perched on a wooden chest.

Leon shivered as a cold draft rushed past him and out the bedroom door.

Mrs. Swann shivered, too. Standing in the doorway, she pointed to a small metal bowl under the bed and said something. Leon guessed it was for night soil.

Elder Brother rushed in as if eager to get to their private space. Leon glanced back at the lady in the doorway. Her brow was furrowed. "Good night now," she said quickly, as if to brush off some emotion. She closed the door as she left.

Alone, just the two of them, they could be themselves again. Leon breathed in relief, then spouted a stream of Chinese.

"Why can't that girl walk?" he asked as he unbuttoned his formal jacket. "Why is the father so sad? Why do they eat bread with their hands?"

But Elder Brother didn't even try to answer his questions. He sat down on the floor, pulled the metal bowl out from under the bed, and threw up his entire dinner.

The smell made Leon's own stomach queasy. All that meat. Gently, he took off his brother's skullcap and set it aside. Scabs now covered the scrapes, which had not cut too deeply. It didn't look too bad. He poured a cup of water from the pitcher and handed it to his brother.

Elder Brother wiped his mouth, drank, and spit out the water. "I'll be fine," he said.

"I wish we could go home," Leon said.

"Well, keep getting into fights and they'll send you home in shame."

Leon just stood there, holding his silk jacket.

"Hang it up in the wardrobe," his brother said, more gently this time.

Silently, Leon obeyed. As he was hanging it up, he noticed something on the floor, near the back of the wardrobe. He reached in and pulled out a long, thick, rounded stick. Next to it, also on the wardrobe floor, was a white leather ball and a large leather mitt. Someone in this house played baseball. The forbidden game. But who?

The stick shook in his hand, and it clattered on the floor as he dropped it.

"What's that? Don't touch it!" Carson said.

Leon wiped his hands on his jacket. Just touching these things, it seemed, might make him catch the "too American" disease.

The stench made it hard to fall asleep, and Leon's stomach grumbled. Sometime in the night, he kicked off his quilt. Elder Brother quietly came over and covered him.

# CHAPTER SIX

# Object Lessons

—◇·◈·—◁◈▷—·◈·◇—

*T*he next morning, Leon woke up before the first rays of sunlight and lay on the feather-filled mattress, listening to the earliest birdcalls. The edges of the windows were covered with frost, and cold air leaked in. Tree branches cast jagged shadows on the glass. He tried to remember the feel of hot, humid summer air. Home seemed impossibly far away.

After a while, as the sky turned pink, his brother rolled over in the next bed, opened his eyes, and sat up. "Time for lessons!" Elder Brother said, putting his bare feet on the floor. He held Leon's gaze for a moment. "We have to remember why we're here," he said.

Leon nodded. The dawn had washed away all the sickness and worry.

Leon didn't hear any noises from within the house, but he got up anyway. They dressed in everyday Chinese clothing, loose pants and a comfortable shirt that slipped on over the head. These were the clothes they had worn to class in Shanghai and on the train trip.

The brothers waited, but no one came for them. At home, they would know what to do. But here, what was expected of them? The house was so silent Leon wondered if everyone in it was dead.

"Should we go downstairs?" Leon asked his brother.

Carson hesitated. "Yes," he said at last, as if trying to project confidence he didn't feel.

Wearing their cotton slippers, they tiptoed down the creaky wooden stairs.

The parlor stood empty, with only embers in the grate. Likewise, the dining room, cleaned of all the dishes, was quiet, each chair placed under the table, the white cloth still covering it, like a funeral drape. Across the hall from the parlor was a small room lined with bookshelves. Leon popped his head in to look around. So many English books!

In an armchair sat Mr. Swann, quiet and still, holding a book. He looked up at Leon with a startled expression, as if his mind had been far away and he suddenly couldn't remember why a Chinese boy was in his house. Then he frowned, and Leon felt like an intruder.

"Essa-cuse me," Leon said, in his best English, backing out of the room.

He and Carson exchanged worried looks. At home, his father had once beaten him with a rattan stick for interrupting his reading. But Mr. Swann did not come after them.

They retreated to the empty parlor. Suddenly, Leon caught sight of movement outside a window. A freckled face, with messy red hair, slipped out of view. Leon ran to the window and looked out. A figure in a tattered brown coat was running across the lawn toward the back of the house. Leon felt a shiver up his spine. What was that boy doing here? Was he spying on them? He wished the Swanns had sons he could play with.

Mrs. Swann lumbered down the stairs, holding their night-soil bowl. "You were sick?"

Carson looked embarrassed, so Leon answered for him. "Not sick now."

She said something else and herded the two boys into the dining room. Julia wheeled Charlotte in from a bedroom. Charlotte alone smiled at them and wished them "Good morning!"

"Good morning," they both responded. Here was a saying they had practiced.

After they were all seated in the same places as the previous meal, a maid brought in a plate with a steaming stack of what appeared to be thick hotcakes and placed them on the table. They smelled delicious and seemed just right for two queasy stomachs.

After the prayer, Julia turned to the boys. "Let's begin. Pancakes," she said, pointing to the food.

Elder Brother stared at the food but said nothing. Could he eat today?

"Pan cake," Leon said, wishing to please.

Julia smiled and used a fork to place a thick pancake on Leon's plate. Mrs. Swann poured some thick dark syrup over it.

"Pancakes," Julia said, pointedly looking at Carson.

Elder Brother still said nothing.

"I think she wants you to repeat that word," Leon prompted Elder Brother in Chinese.

"I'll wait for the tutor to show up. He'll teach us English," Elder Brother replied.

His plate remained empty. Mr. Swann was staring into space, ignoring them.

"Pan. Cakes." Julia's voice was more insistent. She addressed Carson directly.

Leon shifted uncomfortably. He knew that Carson hated to lose in a battle of wills.

"Carson." Julia launched into a long English sentence, as if explaining what she wanted him to say and why. Her tone was firm but respectful. She ended on the word *pancakes*.

Leon knew that Elder Brother could not possibly have understood that explanation, but he responded to her tone. "Ben kek," Carson said in a quiet, dignified voice.

Julia served him a pancake. But Leon could sense his brother's annoyance. This was no way to learn a foreign language, and the dining table was not the proper place for class.

The taste of the pancakes shocked Leon's tongue. They were very sweet. Too sweet, actually. He longed for a comforting bowl of rice porridge. But at least it wasn't meat.

After breakfast, Mr. Swann rolled Charlotte in her wheelchair out of the room, despite her protests. Then he put on a hat and thick coat and walked out the front door. The maid cleared the table. But Julia told the boys to stay, and she came back with books, paper, chalk, and two slates. So this was where they would study English, and their teacher was Miss Julia.

Carson looked dismayed. At home, most women didn't know how to read and write, let alone teach others. How could this young lady be qualified to teach them?

"Book," she began, holding a book and pointing to it. This was a word Leon knew, but her pronunciation was different from Teacher Kwong's.

"Book," Leon repeated. His brother remained silent, arms crossed, watching. Leon hoped he wouldn't get in trouble with Elder Brother by cooperating with Julia.

"Book," she corrected. "Not boo-kuh."

"Boook," Leon said. He had always been a good mimic, able to imitate even the tone and pitch of other people's voices.

Julia nodded and turned toward Carson. The book slipped out of her hand and landed on the floor with a bang. They all jumped.

As Julia picked it up, she pointed to the floor. "Rug," she said, smiling gamely.

"La-ga," Leon repeated, looking at the odd flowered thing that covered the wooden floor.

"Rug," Julia repeated.

But that was not a sound Leon could say right, no matter how hard he tried. He could hear the difference, but his mouth could not get around the strange sounds.

"Miss Julia?" Leon said, hoping she would let him know if this was the name he should call her.

"Yes?" Her nose was very high between her eyebrows.

"You are Miss Julia?" He didn't know how else to ask the question in English.

"Yes, of course." Leon decided that was answer enough.

Looking nervous, Miss Julia continued her teaching method. She named items around them in the dining room. *Slate. Chalk. Paper. Pencil. Table. Chair. Wall. Ceiling. Floor.*

Leon repeated each word she said, trying to remember it. But Carson refused. She didn't press him to speak.

Each time she said a word, Miss Julia wrote it on a piece of stiff paper. The light from the window was dim, and it was hard to see. Carson didn't relax until she gave him a slate and asked him to copy the English words on her list. Back in Shanghai, the boys had copied many words, spending more time learning to read and write English than to speak it.

Leon was glad to learn how to pronounce the words in the American way. He said them softly to himself as he practiced writing them over and over, while Elder Brother copied them in silence, mouthing the Chinese translation.

Suddenly, though, Elder Brother wiped his slate clean and began writing on it in Chinese characters. He started at the upper right and made each stroke carefully as he wrote in vertical columns. Leon saw that his brother had written one of the famous passages from the *Life and Sayings of Confucius*: "When I was a boy of fifteen, I thought of nothing but studying. At the age of thirty, I stood up."

Julia reached over and took the chalk out of his hand. "English!" she commanded.

For a moment, Leon thought Carson would slap her. No woman had the right to take the chalk out of his hand and interrupt his calligraphy. Carson glared at her.

She backed down and immediately handed the chalk back. "Please. English words only," she said. The confrontation was averted. But the tension continued to shimmer.

Leon saw movement outside the dining room window, behind Julia. The freckled face appeared again, framed by two bare hands and a wool cap.

To see what Leon was looking at, Julia spun around. "Johnny!" she shouted, and the boy disappeared.

"Jah-nee," Leon repeated.

Loud knocking on the kitchen door interrupted their lesson. Julia ran into the kitchen. Leon could hear her and another woman speaking rapid English. On light feet, Julia rushed through the dining room and returned with her mother. The voices in the kitchen grew louder, and Julia came back through the hallway to get her mother's winter coat, hat, and boots. The kitchen door slammed shut.

Julia returned with a worried look. Seeming to forget that they could not understand, she launched into an explanation of what had happened. The only word Leon caught was "sick." He noticed that Carson didn't seem sick at all today. What a relief.

Soon the lesson was over. Julia gave them the list of English words and pointed to their slates while giving them some instruction. Leon and his brother went upstairs to their bedroom. Again, it was a relief to speak freely in Chinese.

"What was that all about?" Leon began. "Was that the same boy at the train station?"

"I can't believe the old bean leaves us at home with all these women," Elder Brother responded. "Why do they have this young female teaching us?"

Leon shook his head. "Maybe they can't afford to hire a tutor."

Shoving aside the English word list, Carson got out their Chinese books. "Now we have time for some real studying," he said. "We can't fall behind."

"Can I write a letter home first?" Leon asked.

"I'll do that tonight. We've got to work on our Chinese every day. Otherwise we'll get back to China and won't be able to read anything."

Elder Brother selected a passage for Leon to read out loud in Chinese, corrected his pronunciation, and told Leon to copy it on his slate until he memorized it. It felt good to get back to real words and real writing. Carson was the best teacher he could have.

As he was copying, though, Leon wondered about the strange boy. What news had he brought to the house? Why had Mrs. Swann left in such a hurry? He also wondered about the baseball mitt and bat in his closet. Whose bedroom were they using?

Outside his window, the sky clouded over and snow started falling in huge flakes. This house was full of mysteries.

# CHAPTER SEVEN

# Sunday Sneers

—◇·◈·◇—◈—◇·◈·◇—

*O*ne morning, the boys woke up at the same hour but discovered a different rhythm. Mr. Swann left even earlier than usual, and the ladies came to breakfast dressed in fine clothing, with hats.

"Today is Sunday," said Miss Julia. "We're going to church."

Leon looked at his brother and could see by the quickly concealed grimace on his face that he understood. "Church," Leon repeated to Carson.

Elder Brother answered in Chinese. "We're not supposed to join a church."

"Remember what Teacher Kwong said? They expect us to attend church once every seven days, but we don't have to join. Don't eat the bread or drink the grape wine."

Carson nodded hesitantly. "Wish we didn't have to."

But it seemed obvious that they did have to. Leon knew that Mr. Swann had a job at the church. He was curious to find out what Mr. Swann did for a living.

As he loaded his plate with bacon and eggs, Leon tried to imagine what the church would look like inside. He thought of a local temple in his home village. Dedicated to Guan Yin, the goddess of mercy, the temple had a huge statue of her, front and center, where people prayed and left offerings. Would there be a big statue of Jesus?

When Miss Julia stood up, Leon could not help noticing that her dress had a huge clump of blue satin fabric that made her rump look three times as big as normal. Her waist appeared pinched and unnaturally small. Did she want people to look at her rear end? She pointed to the big clock in the hallway and said, "Hurry! We have to leave at 9:30."

After eating, the boys ran back upstairs and put on their formal Chinese robes. As they helped each other rebraid their hair neatly, Leon repeated to himself a word that Miss Julia had taught them: *queue*. It sounded like *cue* but meant *braid*. So did *pigtail*, but that was a rude word.

The Swann ladies and the two boys squeezed into the horse carriage, and the driver drove them into town, about twenty minutes away. They stopped at the white wooden church Leon had seen a few days earlier. A light layer of fresh snow covered everything with clean brightness. Leon shivered in his thinly padded blue silk jacket and shoved his hands up his sleeves.

The town was a welcome sight after long days in their isolated farmhouse. Despite the cold, the town square was filled with people, dressed in stiff suits and gowns under thick wool coats, chatting as they climbed up the steps to the church. The men wore black top hats and long frockcoats over white shirts and vests, with polished boots. Many of the young women had bustles on the back of their dresses, like Julia. People greeted each other with warm smiles, and the men shook hands and slapped their friends on the back.

As Leon and Carson looked around at the front of the church, a man reached into their carriage to pick up Charlotte and carry her inside. He seemed accustomed to this. The ladies stepped down, and Leon and his brother followed. Some of the other Americans crowded around and greeted them. Leon braced himself for taunting, but these people were more polite than the ones at the train stations.

"Sunday school," Julia said to Leon and Carson.

Elder Brother tossed Leon an anxious look as they climbed the steps. "School?" he asked Leon in Chinese. He had not brought his slate or any books.

"Christian religion school," Leon responded in Chinese.

Elder Brother looked up at the church as if a monster would come out and bite him.

Julia left Leon in one classroom and took Carson to another. Leon was glad to think that Carson might be with boys his own age. But as he was led away, Elder Brother looked anxious.

The Sunday school teacher had not yet arrived. Looking at the boys and girls in his class, Leon flinched: there was freckle-faced Johnny. Among all the well-scrubbed boys and girls, only he was dressed in dirty, ragged clothing. The room smelled like wet wool.

Several boys gathered around Leon and regarded him with wide eyes—blue and gray and brown. Clearly, these boys had no idea how strange those eyes would look in a classroom in China. Leon braced himself for an onslaught. Most of these boys were bigger than he was.

"Look!" one of the boys said, pointing to Leon's queue. "He's got a pigtail!"

The other boys crowded behind him to gaze at his queue. The girls giggled.

"Is this a boy or a girl?" A tall boy walked around Leon and stared at him as if he were a monkey on a leash.

"Stop it!" said a girl. "Don't be mean!"

Johnny leaned back and burst into laughter. "Must be a girl. He's wearing a skirt!"

Anger began to simmer inside Leon. He wanted to strangle that boy. But he knew he had to control himself. He pulled his fists up inside his sleeves. He would not act like a barbarian again.

"Do you understand English?" asked one boy in a polite tone. He stood apart from the group crowded around Leon.

Leon was just about to answer, "A little," when he felt a tug at the back of his neck. He swung around. It was Johnny, who still had Leon's braid in his hand. With his other hand, Johnny pushed Leon so he turned in a full circle. Leon's hands flew to his neck, his braid wrapped tightly around it. He gagged. *Aaiya!*

"Chinee boy no talkee," Johnny said, in a mocking voice.

Just then the Sunday school teacher walked in, a young man with a handlebar mustache. Johnny let go and sat down so quickly that Leon wasn't sure the teacher saw what had happened.

Leon flicked his queue behind him, wishing the boys would just ignore it.

Several boys talked to the teacher at once, pointing to Leon and Johnny.

"Sit down!" the teacher roared. The children stopped talking and sat in the hard chairs.

Leon sat down, too. He did not want to lose face on his first day of school in America, even if it was Sunday school. But he would not let anyone tug his queue. Not once, not twice. That was an insult to the emperor and to all Chinese people everywhere.

The teacher stared at all of them, one by one, till they stopped fidgeting. Then he walked over to Leon. Leon immediately jumped up and stood by his chair, as he had done many times for teachers in China.

"Welcome," the teacher said, offering his hand for Leon to shake. Then he asked an incomprehensible question in English. Leon nodded.

"What is your name?" the teacher asked next.

"Woo Ka-Leong," Leon answered. Then he remembered what Charlotte had called him. "Leon," he added.

"Leon?" The teacher seemed relieved that this Chinese boy had a name he could remember. He turned to the class and instructed them to say something.

All together they recited, "Wel-come, Le-on."

"Sit down, Leon," the teacher said.

The teacher asked the children some questions. Then he spoke sternly to Johnny, who set his lips in defiance but said, "Yes, sir."

In China, the teacher would have whipped any boy who misbehaved in class.

Leon tried to listen as the teacher explained the lesson of the day. He had no idea what the teacher was talking about, but he recognized the leather book in the man's hand—a Bible. Teacher Kwong had shown them one. What terrible things did it contain that made the government of China disapprove of it?

After a long explanation, the teacher said a sentence, and the class repeated it. He said it again and pointed to Johnny. The boy stood up and repeated the sentence, still looking annoyed. Then the teacher called on one of the girls, who stood up and recited the verse.

Leon relaxed. This sounded like the way things were taught in China. He tried to remember the sound of the words.

"Blessed are the meek, for they shall inherit the earth." The teacher looked at him.

Leon had no idea what that meant, any of those words. But he was a good mimic. He stood up. "Bassah da-da *mee*," he repeated.

The teacher's eyes widened and he nodded. "Yes! For they shall inherit the earth."

Leon grinned. "Fa *day* sala *ha*-da-da-*da*."

"For they shall inherit the *earth*," the teacher repeated,

raising his voice, perhaps thinking that Leon could understand if he just spoke loudly enough.

"Fa *day* sala *ha* da-da *utt*," Leon said.

The teacher looked pleased with himself. He clapped his hands, and all the children clapped, too. Leon sat down. The teacher began speaking in long sentences, pointing at Leon, explaining something to them.

Leon tried to think of some way he might remember such gibberish. How could he ever make sense of it? As in a Chinese classroom, the key to success was to recite back what the teacher had just said. Understanding the meaning was irrelevant.

When the class ended, Julia came to fetch him. Carson was with her. He had put on his aloof, inscrutable look, acting as if he understood everything and nothing mattered. Leon could see right through it.

Julia led them into a large meeting room with a high, pointed ceiling and rows of hard benches. The inside of the room was stark and spare, not at all like a Chinese temple. No pictures or statues or offerings or incense.

The worship service began. Mr. Swann, dressed in a long, black robe similar to a Chinese *cheongsam*, began to speak. Everyone listened respectfully. They responded to him in unison. They sang songs, looking at a book. The tunes were very different from the familiar chanting in a temple or a classroom in China.

Then Mr. Swann began a long lecture. Carson nodded off. Leon thought of waking him up but decided against it. Since that first day, Carson had not complained of a headache or stomachache at all. But maybe he needed his sleep.

Leon's mind wandered. He wished he could get back at that Johnny and teach him a lesson. But he had promised to stay out of trouble, and things had been going well lately. Why was Johnny so mean to him? Leon wished Johnny would leave him alone.

At one point, Mr. Swann paused, then said the passage Leon had learned: "Blessed are the meek, for they shall inherit the earth." When he said it, he glanced at Leon and Carson.

Leon smiled like an angel and repeated the line inside his head, wondering what it meant. If he asked Julia, he wouldn't understand the answer. He wished someone there spoke Chinese.

# CHAPTER EIGHT

# Chinese Boy in America

After the last song, everyone stood up and began to leave the church. In the aisle, another family bustled up to them. Leon noticed that they had a son, dressed like the other boys, about Elder Brother's height.

"Welcome to America," the boy said in their dialect, Cantonese. Astonished, Leon looked closely at the boy's face: he was Chinese!

"I'm Yew-Fun. I live with the Travis family."

Carson was awake now. "You live here, in this town?" He asked eagerly in Chinese.

"I've lived here for two and a half years. I was in the second group of the Chinese Educational Mission. You just arrived, in the fourth group?"

Leon could not believe his ears. He looked for the boy's queue and realized it was tucked inside his shirt. Hearing his Chinese words was like refreshing a dry mouth with cool water.

Yew-Fun came from a village not far from their hometown. He had a round, smiling face, broad shoulders, and a sturdy build. He seemed totally relaxed in this strange setting.

"My American family is inviting yours to dinner. Come on over, and we'll get to know each other better," he said, sweeping his hand in a broad gesture of welcome.

Yew-Fun's American mother and father spoke to Leon and Carson and shook their hands, as if repeating the invitation in English.

"The father in my host family is a medical doctor," he explained to them as they began to walk toward the door. "You've only been here a few days, right? I remember how strange that feels! Glad you're here."

Someone knew how he felt. It was like magic.

Leon was curious. "Are you here alone? Or is there another boy living with you?"

Yew-Fun looked away. "There was. He got very sick and was sent back to China."

"He got to go home? After how long?"

"About a year. That was unusual. They send you back only if you're very sick or if you do something very bad. But you'll see. After a few months, you get used to it here and start picking up the language. I have a lot of American friends."

As if on cue, several boys crowded up to Yew-Fun as they walked out the door into the wintry air. Yew-Fun spoke to them in fluent English, switching back and forth between languages as easily as Leon went from walking to running. Leon was jealous. He wished he could have friends like that and speak to them so easily. Leon suspected, though, that Yew-Fun was glad to have Chinese friends, too.

The whole Swann family walked through the slippery streets to the Travis home. Suffield was a small town, and everyone seemed to know each other. Most belonged to the same church, so they all knew Mr. Swann. Yew-Fun called him "Reverend Swann."

Leon looked around for Johnny, that devil of Suffield, but he was nowhere to be seen.

It was only after they entered the Travis home that

Leon figured out which of the many people he'd seen at the church belonged to the Travis household. To him, these Americans all looked alike.

"Thomas! Meet my new friends from China!" Yew-Fun said as they took off their coats in the vestibule. "This is the older brother in my American family," he explained in Chinese.

Leon looked straight up at a tall, young American man, who grabbed Leon's hand and shook it vigorously. "Hello there, old boy. Delighted to meet you." Leon liked the way Thomas looked him straight in the eyes and addressed him as if he were an equal.

"My name is Leon," he responded, carefully pronouncing each word.

"Well, there, Leon. I'm Thomas. Hope we'll be seeing more of you." The young man had a shock of blond hair, a high nose, and a set of the straightest teeth Leon had ever seen.

"Thomas is in college," Yew-Fun explained. "He just got home for vacation."

Leon wanted to know more, but Thomas was helping Miss Julia take off her coat. Then Thomas led the ladies into the sitting room, talking in a spirited, confident tone that made Julia smile. The lights were bright in this home, and everyone was talking at once.

Yew-Fun took them up the stairs and into his bedroom, which was similar to theirs but cluttered with books, papers, clothing, and knickknacks. He chatted with them in Chinese about life with an American family.

"I haven't spoken Chinese in months. Not since last summer," he said.

That seemed impossible to imagine.

To Leon's delight, Yew-Fun pulled out some old American clothing he had outgrown and offered it to Leon. Relieved at this chance to look like other boys, Leon accepted a pair of cotton trousers, a pair of woolen trousers, and three shirts with buttons made of shell. Yew-Fun offered clothing to Carson, too, but Elder Brother refused. Leon took one large shirt he thought would fit Carson, just in case.

When Leon tried on the large shirt, Yew-Fun laughed merrily. "You'll grow into it."

Leon buttoned the top button and realized his queue was inside the shirt. He asked his new friend, "Do you always hide your queue?"

Yew-Fun's face grew serious. "Yes, it's easier that way. Americans just don't get it. But see? If you trim the hair around your face like an American, they won't notice the queue."

Leon looked closely. The hair around Yew-Fun's face was not shaved but combed to the side in the American style. That's why Yew-Fun didn't seem Chinese to him at first. Leon was about to ask how he got his hair to look like that when Elder Brother broke in, asking, "Why do you want to look like an American?"

Yew-Fun hesitated, looking at Elder Brother as if he might be a spy. "It's just easier. Everybody does it."

Leon felt relieved. Maybe there was a way to fit in, without cutting his queue.

Later, at the dinner table, Leon noticed that Thomas and his parents seemed outgoing and energetic, and Yew-Fun laughed and joked with them. Sometimes several of them talked at the same time, making it even harder to follow the conversation. But the atmosphere put Leon at ease—and made him realize how tense and formal the Swanns were. Only Charlotte acted warm and carefree like these people. He envied his new friend.

After dinner, Yew-Fun took the boys out to show them around the town. Outside the door, Yew-Fun immediately began to run, and Leon chased after him through the snowy streets. He welcomed the cold air on his cheeks and the feel of his legs in motion.

"Do you play this game, this baseball?" Leon asked Yew-Fun as they slowed down and waited for Carson to catch up.

"Of course, every boy does. In America you can't just be good at studying. You have to be strong and fit, too," Yew-Fun said, picking up a stone and tossing it. His sturdy build made Carson seem scrawny by comparison. At home, scholars like his brother were expected to sit still for hours, not encouraged to play or exercise outdoors.

Carson followed them at a more dignified pace. Leon wished his brother were more like Yew-Fun.

"This is the baseball field. They call it a diamond. Can you see why?"

Leon looked at the white field, which had tracks where the local boys had been running. He didn't see anything that looked like a shiny gem.

Yew-Fun walked them around the bases, showing them home plate, where the batter stood, and where he had to run in order to score. The snow quickly made Leon's cloth shoes wet and uncomfortable.

"You'll need to get leather shoes," said Yew-Fun.

"Is baseball hard to learn?" Leon asked.

Yew-Fun laughed. "It's easy to *learn*," he said, standing at home plate and pretending to hold a bat and hit an incoming ball. He swung hard. "But it's hard to play well. You have to practice a lot. But that's what all the boys do, especially in the spring and summer. The neighboring towns all have a tournament in August, to determine the best team in the area. Last summer, Suffield came in second. We should have won!"

Yew-Fun talked to them nonstop in Chinese, often tossing in English words Leon didn't know. He walked with long strides and talked in a free and easy way, just like an American.

Carson didn't seem interested in baseball talk. "Can we look at the school?" he asked, pointing to a nearby building.

"Yes! I'll show you!"

They followed as he loped across the lawn of the grammar school to the front door. Yew-Fun turned the knob, but the door was locked. "Ah, phooey," he said.

"Do you go to classes here?" asked Carson.

Yew-Fun beamed. "Yes! I just passed the test last summer. You have to study at home until you can pass it."

"How long did it take you?"

"Two years," said Yew-Fun, peeking in a window and pointing to a classroom. "That's how long it usually takes. I just started school in September. Some boys can get in after one year, though, if they're really smart."

Leon stood on his toes and looked in the window at a roomful of wooden desks. He envied Yew-Fun, living in town, so close to school and friends.

"Was it hard, this test?" Carson asked. He was always good at tests.

"Pretty hard," Yew-Fun admitted. "It will be harder for you, though, because the high school entrance test is tougher."

"Elder Brother is really smart," Leon piped in. "It won't be hard for him." *But it will be for me,* he thought. He hated taking tests.

As they turned around and headed back toward Yew-Fun's house, Leon peppered him with questions. Why do Americans go to church? What was Mr. Swann talking about in his lecture? Why do we have a lady teaching us? Isn't that an insult?

"I had a lady tutor, too," said Yew-Fun. "Americans have special schools to educate young ladies. Miss Julia went to one of those. I hear she graduated with honors."

Carson shook his head in disapproval. "But why isn't she married? Why is she teaching us instead of finding a husband?"

Yew-Fun laughed. "The ladies in my household talk about her a lot. Miss Julia Swann."

"Is she betrothed, at least?" Carson wanted to know.

Yew-Fun grew serious. "Not yet. Thomas thinks she is very pretty. But she won't talk about marriage. She insists on staying home and taking care of her parents, since the accident."

"Accident?"

Yew-Fun stopped still and his face darkened. "You don't know about that?"

And so they heard the story.

Yew-Fun had many friends in town, and one of them had been Owen Swann, the only son of Reverend Swann. Owen was a popular boy, a promising pitcher, and one of the best hitters on the team.

The previous winter, snow fell more than four feet deep, higher than the head of a three-year-old child. Many of the town's children went sledding, using a plank of wood to slide down a hill, on top of the snow. Yew-Fun went, too. After sliding down the hill just one time, though, Yew-Fun stopped. His fingers and toes were just too cold.

He was pulling his sled away from the hill, heading back toward the warmth of his American home, when he heard screaming. He ran back.

Owen Swann and his sister Charlotte, sharing a sled, had slid down the hill and crashed into a tree. Owen's head had slammed into the tree, and his neck had snapped. Just like that. Gone. Charlotte nearly died, too. She recovered, but her back was broken. She would never walk again.

Carson and Leon stared at Yew-Fun in shock. In an instant, the Swann family had been damaged beyond repair. Owen, a boy the same age as Leon, once vibrant and playing, now dead. Charlotte, laughing, loving Charlotte, confined to a wheelchair forever.

Owen. This must be the boy who once owned that baseball bat in their closet, the boy who had lived in their room, less than a year ago. Why had the family agreed to host two Chinese boys, almost the same age as their own son, so soon after such a tragic accident?

"His only son," Carson said. In China, no father could get over such a blow.

This explained a lot: Reverend Swann's coolness, his distance. Why Julia stayed at home with her parents instead of getting married. Why Mrs. Swann seemed so jittery.

A tear leaked out of Leon's eye and rolled down his cold cheek. He felt so sad for them.

"That's all right, old boy," Yew-Fun said to him in English. "Take it easy."

But this changed everything. Leon and his brother were living in a house with a ghost. Probably an angry ghost. And Leon knew that angry ghosts can latch on to you and make you sick. That explained why his brother got so sick that first night.

# CHAPTER NINE

# Sickness and Ghosts

—◇·◇——◈——◇·◇—

*T*hat night, Leon could not sleep. Long after he heard his brother's breath grow soft and even, he lay awake, staring at the ceiling. He had shut tight the door to Owen's wardrobe, but he sensed Owen's ghost in there, trying to get out.

*Scritch. Scratch.* At first soft, then louder. Could ghosts scratch on a door? Did they have fingernails?

Under the quilt, his body went stiff. The sounds got louder. Finally, he sat up. A dark shape brushed against the windowpane, and he nearly jumped out of his skin. *Scra-a-a-tch*. It was a tree branch. That's all. No ghost.

He lay back down and tried to think of something other than the ghost. He thought of home: the sun glinting on the light-green rice paddies after spring planting. His family's round table covered with many bowls of delicious food, including a whole fish with head and fins, and the laughter and smiles as all his relatives reached in with their chopsticks.

The scratching got louder, and branches swayed outside his window. The wind was picking up. It was a storm.

That's all. Still, the scratching seemed to be coming from the closet. Was Owen's ghost angry with him for sleeping in his bed? His hands felt clammy.

*Thunk!*

Leon jumped. What was that?

*Thunk!* Something dark hit the window. It wasn't a branch.

Leon slipped out of bed and padded across the room in his bare feet. The windowpane was edged with frost, so it was hard to see out. Snow was blowing sideways. But Leon could see something dark lying on the windowsill, just outside. It looked menacing.

He went back to bed and lay still for a long time. What was that dark shape? The wind whistled, and he thought he heard a boy's angry voice in it. He shut his eyes and tried to sleep.

The next morning, the sun was shining but the field outside their window was covered with a quilt of pure white. Several tree branches had fallen. Leon rubbed the glass to see better. He lifted the window slightly and bent over to look out. On the sill was a dead bird, a brown wren. Frozen.

"Close the window!" his brother shouted. "What are you doing?"

Leon slammed it shut and shivered. Had Owen's ghost thrown the dead bird at their window?

☀ ☀ ☀

At breakfast, Leon looked hard at Charlotte, who was cheerful as ever. How could she laugh like that? The rest of the family, though, seemed morose. Now he knew why.

On this day, Miss Julia told them to follow her into the parlor. She pointed out objects in the room and said their names in English. *Hearth. Grate. Poker. Mantle.* Leon had to force himself to concentrate and repeat after her.

Then they returned to the dining room table, and she wrote the words in English, making them pronounce the words after her. She made them practice writing these words—once in their copybooks and many times on their slates.

Sitting still for so long made Leon antsy. His legs jumped with energy. Outside the window, the snow had piled in drifts along the side of the house. He wished he could go out and run in the snow. Just run and run.

"Leon!" Miss Julia's voice was stern. "What is this word?"

Leon stared at the word she had written. S-N-O-W. He sounded it out in his head.

"Sah-no-wuh?"

Miss Julia smiled her approval and pointed out the window. "Good! Snow."

"Snow," he said again, looking sadly out the window. It reminded him of the Chinese word for *dead bird*.

Mrs. Swann came into the room, dressed in her winter coat with a scarf and hat, and spoke to Julia. She was holding a heavy basket with two hands.

One of her hands slipped, and she fumbled. Leon jumped up and ran over, grabbing the basket from the bottom so it wouldn't fall to the floor.

Mrs. Swann smiled and asked him a question that ended with the words "come with me?"

Leon glanced at Miss Julia, with hope. Carson was frowning. Miss Julia hesitated, then nodded. "Go ahead. Mother needs help."

Hurrah! Leon felt like he was escaping from jail. Mrs. Swann took him to a hall closet and got out a thick, green coat and leather boots for him. Had they belonged to Owen? The boots and coat were both a little big, but he put them on anyway. The side of one boot caught on his toe, and Leon thought it might be Owen's ghost. But in the daylight, that didn't seem so scary.

He picked up the heavy basket and followed Mrs. Swann out the kitchen door.

*Snow!* He thought in English. *I get to go out in the snow.*

Before him spread a magnificent expanse of white, much deeper than he had seen before. Mrs. Swann stepped into it without hesitation, so Leon followed. The snow came up to the tops of his boots. It made a crunchy sound when he stepped in it, and it smelled like pine needles. The cold air burned his cheeks. He wished his hands were free, so he could pick up snow. He wished he could roll in it.

They trudged across the field. The basket felt warm in his hands, and Leon could smell sausage and eggs. Where were they taking it?

He tilted his head back and opened his mouth. Snowflakes fell on his cheeks and nose. One fell on his tongue. Soft and cold. His spirits lifted. The flakes that fell on the basket melted, but he could see patterns in the snowflakes on the arm of his coat.

They entered the woods and walked along a path that had one set of footprints on it already. Someone with big feet had walked out of these woods, this morning.

Mrs. Swann jabbered at him as they walked. Leon wished he understood.

The path wound downhill through the trees. After a while, Leon could smell smoke, and then he saw a small house. It was a ramshackle hut, really, with a low doorway and no windows. It looked as though it had been built in a few days with leftover building materials.

Leon was shocked. This hut could not have been more different from the grand two-story house where he was living. In southern China, wealthy landowners often hired farm laborers in the village, and they lived in similar huts. But Leon had never been inside one.

Mrs. Swann did not hesitate before stooping her head to enter the hut. Leon followed.

The moment they entered, two little kids ran up to them. They had long, scruffy hair and high voices; Leon could not tell if they were boys or girls.

Mrs. Swann took the basket from him and set it on a rough wooden table. The children crowded around her as she pulled out dishes of warm food. They each grabbed some bread and began eating it with their dirty hands.

The shack was dark, but Leon could see it had only one room. There was only one large bed, made of wooden planks with a thin mattress. Leon's nose flinched from the stench and the smoke.

Mrs. Swann went over to the bed and spoke to someone lying there. Leon heard a woman's weak voice responding. She barely raised her head.

Leon wanted to run. This woman was sick. She could not clean the house or take care of the children. Leon, who had grown up in a sprawling house with servants and many aunts, had never imagined a home with only one woman, who was seriously ill.

His stomach flipped over. Why had Mrs. Swann brought him here to this disease-ridden place? She should have stayed at home where she belonged.

The dark interior smelled like a latrine. Leon turned on his heel and left. Outside, he breathed deeply of the crisp air. He cleared some snow from a tree stump and sat on it. His mother would never have entered such a house. Didn't Mrs. Swann know she might be bringing back bad luck?

When she finally came out of the house, Leon refused to touch the basket. Mrs. Swann carried it home. This time, she was silent.

Back at the Swanns' house, he ran to his room and lathered his hands with soap.

Carson didn't want to hear about the sick woman. He had news of his own. "We got a letter from home!" Leon stood behind him as Carson read it out loud. Father had hired a local scribe to write it for him.

"We are all well," Father wrote, "except for First Elder

Brother, Ka-Shing. He has a fever. Your mother has gone into the city to care for him. Do not worry. He will be better soon."

Leon sank onto the bed. "A fever?"

Carson's mouth twisted. "It's probably worse than he says. Otherwise, they wouldn't mention it. This letter took a month to get here."

They sat in silence. Their father had put all his hopes on First Elder Brother, investing his savings to educate Ka-Shing to be a high official. He had to get better. Someday the whole family would rely on him. Mother would not have gone to the city unless he was very sick.

Carson pounded his fist into the wooden doorjamb. Leon knew that Carson would have given anything to have the opportunities First Elder Brother had been given. Now it was too late.

Leon wondered if he would ever see First Elder Brother again. He felt he was in the wrong place, too far from home. And he worried that this troubled American family could be part of the problem.

Could an angry ghost cause sickness on the other side of the world?

# CHAPTER TEN

# Oh, Christmas Tree

—◇·❖—◈—❖·◇—

*O*wen's ghost disappeared and reappeared. It didn't make Carson get sick again, as Leon feared. But one afternoon, Leon was reciting his Chinese lesson to Carson, saying the lines, "Filial piety is the foundation of virtue. The body, the hair, and the skin have all been received from our parents, so we don't dare damage them in any way."

Suddenly, the baseball bat fell over and clattered to the bottom of the wardrobe. Both boys froze. A bat had fallen, that was all. But Leon could see in Carson's eyes that he was thinking the same thought: that dead boy was in the house.

One night they came back to the room after dinner, and Leon's slate was gone. Just gone. He had left it on the table in their room. For sure. He knew that the ghost had taken it. Later, Carson found it, under a book. Still, Leon knew he had not left it there.

The worst, though, was one morning, early, when a noise woke Leon up. He lay still, listening. The noise came again. It sounded like a stone hitting the window. He sat up in bed, shivering. He checked to make sure the wardrobe door was closed.

*Thunk!*

He tiptoed over to the window. Outside on the sill was something dark and furry. In case he needed to defend himself, Leon got his slate and thrust open the window. A dead mouse lay on the sill. Ugly and disgusting. Definitely a sign of bad luck. He shivered. Using the wooden frame of his slate, he pushed it off. Down in the snow, he saw a set of human footprints, leading up to his window. But he couldn't see any person. This was too much of a coincidence. Would Owen Swann leave footprints?

☀ ☀ ☀

Just as Leon's worries about the ghost grew more troubling, grasping the English language proved to be ever more difficult. Carson and Leon often talked about it at night, alone in their room.

"This language is ridiculous!" Carson said.

Leon had to agree. "Much too hard."

"The writing is all about the way a word sounds. There's no way to figure out if the word is a type of grass, a tree, a mineral, or a bug."

This was true. Chinese characters gave hints about a word's meaning. For example, the character for *female* was hidden inside the characters for *mother* and *sister* and *aunt*.

Still, Leon was beginning to like English. One day, Miss Julia saw him drawing a picture of a train on his slate and taught him some more words: *locomotive* and *caboose*. He could almost pronounce *railroad* now, but still had trouble with the *r* sound.

That night, after dinner, Mr. Swann asked the boys to come into his study. One whole wall was covered in bookshelves, and it smelled like leather and tobacco smoke. Leon wondered if he had said something wrong and was going to get into trouble again.

"Come here. Look at this," Mr. Swann said. On his desk

lay a large leather-bound volume, open to a page with an illustration. Leon recognized it immediately: a drawing of a locomotive, showing English names for all the parts. Mr. Swann pointed to various parts and pronounced the names for him: "Johnson bar, stoker, throttle lever, water gauge, piston, cylinder, grate."

Leon nearly peed in his pants. "What's this?" He pointed to a big empty space in the middle of the locomotive.

"Firebox."

"And this?" He pointed to stripes in front of the firebox.

"Boiler tubes."

Mr. Swann tried to explain how it worked. Leon didn't get it, but it was enough to know the names. And to know that Mr. Swann knew. A minister who knew about engines! Mr. Swann didn't tire of talking about trains for a long time, and then he said, "I will leave this here. You can look at it any time." Leon couldn't believe his good fortune.

By the time they finished, Carson had disappeared. When Leon got to their room, Carson was writing a long letter to Father. Every few sentences, he put down his brush and pounded his fist on the top of the desk. Leon tried to be as quiet as a dead mouse.

❅  ❅  ❅

The next day, Miss Julia taught them a new word, *Christmas*. Leon was puzzled about what it meant. "A big day for us," was the only explanation Miss Julia gave that Leon understood. He figured out that it was coming soon and decided it must be a big holiday. Carson reminded him that they had learned about this holiday, back in Shanghai, but Leon had not been paying attention then.

Mrs. Swann spent less time out of the house visiting needy people and more time in the kitchen, baking batches of cookies and hams and sweet potatoes and bread. A local seamstress came with fabrics and began making new dresses for Mrs. Swann, Miss Julia, and Miss Charlotte. Mrs. Swann ordered leather boots, shoes, and belts for the boys and had them fitted for new winter coats.

The bustle reminded Leon of the excitement before the Lunar New Year celebrations back home, when every member of the family got new clothes. His mother and sisters spent days cleaning the house and preparing lots of cold meats because no one was supposed to cook on New Year's Day. So far, they hadn't heard any more about First Elder Brother. Alone in bed, Leon clasped his hands the way he saw the Swanns do and silently said, "Gah-bless First Elder Brother. Make him not sick."

One afternoon, Julia came up to their room to get them. Her cheeks were flushed, and she talked faster than usual. Leon understood only three words, *tree* and *come now*.

He and his brother followed her downstairs and saw Mr. Swann standing in the hallway. He had come home from work earlier than usual. Mrs. Swann got out their new leather boots and some old heavy coats, hats, and mittens, since their new ones hadn't arrived yet. Leon was thrilled. He had not been outside in days, and he longed to escape into the fresh air. Even Carson greeted the interruption with eager eyes.

They followed Mr. Swann out into the wintry air to a woodshed behind the house. Outside it stood a man and a boy, bundled up in coats, like dark blotches on the white snow.

Leon slowed down. The man, he recognized, was the horse carriage driver, Patrick. He had a sickening feeling about the boy. As he got closer, he could see it was, indeed, the freckled redhead who hated him, Johnny. The boy had a blank expression and was kicking at some ice on the ground. Leon had seen him only once since the Sunday school episode—at Sunday school the following week. But Johnny had ignored him, as he was doing now.

In front of Mr. Swann, surely Johnny would behave.

The driver opened the woodshed door and got out an axe, and the men exchanged a few words. Snow started falling as they tromped into the woods behind the house. The two men were leading, followed by Johnny. Leon and Carson trailed behind.

At one point, a large bush was close to the pathway. Johnny pushed some branches of the bush out of his way, then let them fling back as he passed. The bush tossed snow into Carson's face. Surprised, he stopped to wipe his cheeks. Leon immediately assumed Johnny had done it on purpose.

"Don't hit him," Carson warned.

A little farther along, a low tree branch crossed the path. The men ducked under it. Johnny jumped up and grabbed it with both hands. He pulled it down, then let go and ran as the branch bounced back up. When it came down again, it rained heavy snow on Leon and Carson. This time, Leon was sure he saw Johnny look back with a grin.

"Ignore him," grumbled Carson.

Finally, they came to the edge of a pond. The driver pointed to an evergreen tree not far away, and Mr. Swann nodded. It was taller than either man, though not by much, and shaped like a perfect cone. Mr. Swann held up the lower branches, and the driver began to chop the tree down. The boys stood and watched, mystified. This tree seemed too small for firewood.

Suddenly, Johnny snatched Carson's red wool hat right off his head and took off toward the pond. When he got to the edge, he jumped onto the ice and slid a long way. Then he turned around and waved Elder Brother's hat in triumph.

Carson froze in surprise, and the men just laughed. But Leon had had it. He needed to teach that boy a lesson. So he chased after him, also sliding along the ice on the pond. He slid right into Johnny's bony body and grabbed for the red hat. Johnny leaned to the side and held the hat above his head with his long arm.

Leon jumped up and grabbed the hat. He landed so hard that the ice started to crack. After trying to push him, Johnny tipped back on his rear end and slid away. The ice began to crack under Johnny, too, who looked startled. Leon didn't realize what that sound meant; his mind was set on revenge. He kicked, hard, and got the rascal in the knee. Just then the ice gave way. With a shout, Johnny fell into the freezing water.

Leon was overjoyed to see Johnny flailing in the shallow pond. Finally, this mean boy had gotten what he deserved. But Leon's joy didn't last long. As he scrambled back toward shore, his feet broke through the ice. His arms swung wildly as he regained his balance and climbed out. Only his new boots had touched the icy water. Still, the bitter cold sent a shock through his system.

But Johnny was thoroughly soaked. His father dropped the axe and waded in after him, pulling him to shore, shouting words in an accent Leon didn't understand. Johnny acted like he was wounded and limped away under the man's protective arm.

Carson smacked Leon across the face. "I told you to behave! Now you're in trouble again. What will Father say when he hears?"

But Mr. Swann just laughed. He grabbed the red hat and swatted the dirt off Leon's bottom. "Feet all wet are they? You all right?"

Leon wanted to explain that it had all been Johnny's fault. But he didn't need to.

At dinner, Mr. Swann told the story as if it was a big joke. Charlotte smiled at Leon, who felt confused. At home, Father would have punished him for such high jinks. Here, they didn't even frown. Only Carson still seemed upset.

"Such a naughty boy," said Charlotte, looking at Leon. But she smiled when she said it. It was almost as if they *approved* of naughtiness.

"Johnny's a good boy. He doesn't mean any harm," said Mrs. Swann. "Maybe the two of you could play together."

As if that would ever happen! Johnny was *not* a good boy. Leon was sure of that. Then again, Leon wasn't good, either. Elder Brother's face grew harder and sterner.

After dinner, in the parlor, Charlotte played the piano. Mr. Swann erected the tree in a corner of the parlor and decorated it with wax candles. Then the ladies added glass balls, carved wooden ornaments, and red-striped candy canes.

Miss Julia handed each of the boys a glass ball to hang on the tree. Carson hung his just right. But Leon's fell on the floor and broke. At the sound of breaking glass, the whole family stopped and stared. Leon wondered if it brought bad luck. Or if that glass ball had been a favorite of Owen's.

"Don't worry," Charlotte said. "Julia will let you hang another one."

And she did, this time showing him more carefully how to hook it firmly onto a branch.

When they were finished, the tree glowed like magic, but Mrs. Swann was crying. Miss Julia gave them each a candy cane to suck on. It tasted like pure sugar. The whole evening felt bittersweet.

"Owen's spirit is here with us," said Mr. Swann. "I'm sure he wants us to be happy."

That was a new way to think of ghosts. Could they be happy instead of angry? If anybody knew about spirits, it would be Mr. Swann. Leon hoped he was right.

❖ ❖ ❖

Leon dragged his feet going up the stairs to bed. He knew he had it coming. As soon as the door closed, Carson turned on him. "What were you thinking, chasing after that boy? Can't you control yourself?"

"He took your hat!" Leon said. "He's a bad one, that boy."

"Don't you remember what Father says at the end of every letter?" Carson had a cold look in his eyes.

Leon looked away. "It doesn't matter how I behave. These people don't care."

"It does matter. I care. We're better than these people. Lean over." Carson picked up a branch he had brought in from outside.

Leon froze. "Don't. Please don't."

"I was thinking of using that baseball bat, but Father always used a branch. Put your hands on the bed and lean over. And don't cry out. I don't want them to hear."

Father often beat him, but Carson never had. Carson hit him with that branch, right on the rear again and again, probably ten times. It wasn't the worst beating Leon had ever experienced. And he swallowed all his cries. But it soured his heart in a way no other beating had. Of course, Carson had the right to punish him, but he didn't have to hit that hard. Leon knew he deserved it, but the beating hurt his pride.

# CHAPTER ELEVEN

# Christmas Eve Surprise

—◇·◇—◇—◇·◇—

On the day before Christmas, Leon slipped into the kitchen to watch the women cook. Miss Julia was too busy for classes. The kitchen maid pulled out a large ham, pink and shiny and steaming hot, from the oven. Leon's mouth watered. He loved pork of all kinds. Another whole ham was cooling on the countertop.

"Leon!" Mrs. Swann walked over. "You can help me." She was wrapping hot bread rolls in a linen napkin. Eager to be part of the action, he went to her side. Sure enough, she handed him a fresh roll to eat. He couldn't believe how delicious it tasted. Light and fluffy as a *bao*, but there was no meat inside.

She wrapped the cooling ham in an old cloth and placed it inside the basket. Then she tucked some baked potatoes and bread rolls around it.

"Can you carry this?" Mrs. Swann was learning to speak in shorter sentences.

Leon hesitated. He hoped they were not going to the sick woman's house again. But Mrs. Swann assumed he would help, and he didn't know how to say no.

He put on the new winter coat that the seamstress had made for him, as well as his own boots, hat, scarf, and mittens. Then he picked up the basket.

Mrs. Swann, also dressed warmly, picked up the old, green coat Leon had worn before, as well as a smaller basket. She pursed her lips in a firm line as they left the house.

Once again, they headed across the field and into the woods, along the same path. Leon wished he had thought of some excuse. He dragged his feet.

This time, a man came out of the ramshackle hut to greet them. It was the driver, Patrick. He took the heavy basket from Leon and thanked Mrs. Swann again and again.

*Aaiya*, thought Leon. *Is this hut where Johnny lives?* His heart froze over.

That moment Johnny came out of the house. Both boys stopped still, their eyes locked on one another. "Leon," said Mrs. Swann, "say hello to Johnny."

The freckles on Johnny's face looked like a disease, and his wild hair made him look like an ogre guarding a temple. Leon choked out the words, "Hello, Johnny."

"Johnny?" Mrs. Swann said.

The redhead kicked at the snow. "Hallo," he mumbled.

"Johnny, I want you to have this." Mrs. Swann showed him the old, green coat. "Merry Christmas."

Johnny looked at the coat with alarm. He seemed to recognize it and refused to touch it.

"Take it," Mrs. Swann said. "Owen would want you to have it."

Tears sprang into Johnny's eyes. He backed away. "Thanks," he said, but he turned and ran into the woods.

Leon stared after him. Tears? From this bad boy? Because of a coat?

Mrs. Swann took the coat into the hut, but Leon refused to enter this time, fearing germs and bad luck. He waited outside, but Johnny did not return. When Mrs. Swann emerged through the low doorway, he took the empty basket, and they began walking back.

"Johnny mama," Leon began, "very sick?"

This time, Mrs. Swann's eyes watered. "Yes, very, very sick."

"What kind of sick?"

"She lost a baby last fall, and she is very weak."

So not a sickness Leon could catch. But Johnny's mother was very, very sick. The ice in Leon's heart started melting at the edges.

&#9728; &#9728; &#9728;

Christmas was supposed to be a joyful holiday, but it didn't make Leon happy. It wasn't very much like Chinese New Year at all—mostly going to church services and singing unfamiliar tunes. Mr. Swann seemed pressured by extra work, and Mrs. Swann was busier than ever caring for other people. The ham and sweet potatoes they ate tasted wonderful, but the family dinner on Christmas Day was the saddest yet. There were no empty chairs at the table, but Owen's ghost was there. Leon could feel it. It didn't seem angry, but it sure wasn't happy either.

After dinner, they all went to the Travis home, and things were livelier. Leon was glad to see Yew-Fun, who told them about Christmas traditions. Leon wished they lived closer to town so they could see Yew-Fun more often. Mrs. Travis gave Mrs. Swann an extralong hug, and Leon thought he saw tears in their eyes.

But then Thomas insisted that Charlotte play the piano, and people gathered around and sang songs. Julia's face glowed when she looked at Thomas. Once, Julia and Thomas stood side by side and sang a duet. After they finished, everyone clapped. Thomas offered his arm and escorted Julia back to her seat.

"They must be betrothed by now," Leon said to Yew-Fun, later, in Chinese.

The older boy laughed. "You don't know? In America, young men and women talk about love and decide on their own whom to marry."

"Did you see that?" Carson muttered. "I can't believe her parents let that man touch her."

Yew-Fun shook his head, giving Carson a "you'll learn" look. "It's all right to do that, here in America."

"What's wrong is wrong, no matter where you are," answered Carson.

But seeing their joy just made Leon's heart hurt. All the people he cared about most were back in his village—or scattered all over New England. He wondered what Tik-Chang was doing. Did he get along well with his host family? And First Elder Brother—was he still tossing with fever? It was terrible to have to wait so long for the next letter from home.

The only really good thing about Christmas was the gift Mr. Swann gave him: a big book, full of illustrations, about American railroads. The words were too difficult to read, but Leon pored over the pictures of locomotives, Pullman cars, and cabooses. Mr. Swann sat down with him and traced the route of the First Transcontinental Railroad on a map, pronouncing the names of the states it passed through: Nebraska, Wyoming, Utah, Nevada, California.

"Chinese workers built this part," Mr. Swann said, showing him the western tracks. "And Irish immigrants built this part." He pointed to the eastern tracks. "You know Johnny's father? He's Irish." So that explained why Leon could never understand him.

Another map showed all the railroads in America. So many! And China had none.

"Do you know about Jesse James?" Mr. Swann asked. "He and his friends were bad men who robbed many trains.

You know, guns. Gold." Mr. Swann made a hand gesture like he was shooting a gun.

"Guns! On train!" Leon wished he could say longer sentences so he could tell Mr. Swann about what happened.

"Jesse James," Mr. Swann said. "Here." He turned to another page with a drawing of men on horseback with guns, inside a railway carriage.

Leon grabbed the book and examined the picture. Robbers did not ride their horses inside train cars. Didn't this illustrator know anything about train robberies? But some day Leon could read all about it, when his English got better.

He grinned at Mr. Swann. "Thank you!" This book was the perfect gift.

☀ ☀ ☀

Leon enjoyed having a few days off from lessons over Christmas, but soon he grew restless. Carson took advantage of the extra time to work on his Chinese studies. But Leon couldn't stand the long hours of sitting still. One morning, the snow piled up so high that it was almost impossible to open the door. Even Mr. Swann didn't go to work, although he closed himself in his study. Leon wanted to run in the snow, but he was afraid Elder Brother would beat him again. He spent hours looking at his train book, but still he hated being cooped up in the house. How would he get through the long winter?

He even daydreamed about cutting off his queue, just so he would get sent home. Teacher Kwong had told them that was the penalty, since the emperor would not support any boy who was so obviously disloyal. Of course, Leon would never do that.

A few days after Christmas, though, came a ray of hope. One evening, at the dinner table, Miss Julia made an announcement. "Today I received a letter from Mr. Yung Wing of the Chinese Educational Commission," she said.

"Carson and Leon are instructed to go to Hartford for three weeks, starting January 10."

Leon's English must have gotten better, because he understood immediately, and he let out a whoop of joy. It sounded too good to be true!

"What did she say?" asked Carson. Leon translated for him.

"Three weeks, that's more than twenty days!" explained Leon. "We get to see our friends!"

Carson grinned, too. After just a month of living with their American host family, they would get a taste of home.

It took longer for Julia to explain the details. She had to speak slowly and repeat the information many times. Along with twenty-eight other boys, they would have daily instruction in Chinese. That made Carson even happier. They would stay at the large house in Hartford, owned by the Chinese government, that the commission used as its headquarters. Then they would stay to celebrate the Lunar New Year holiday, which fell on January 26 in the American calendar. A big party was planned.

As he drank in the details, Leon grabbed the edge of the table to keep from flying to the ceiling. In Hartford, he could spend time with Tik-Chang and the other friends he had come to know during training in Shanghai. He could celebrate the best holiday of the year with firecrackers and familiar food. It would be almost as good as going back to China.

Leon could barely eat his dinner that night. What a relief that would be, to speak Chinese all day long! It would be as wonderful as splashing in the rain after a drought.

Carson smiled, too. Leon knew that the one thing Elder Brother cared about the most was his Chinese scholarship. He took pride in it and feared he was falling behind without an instructor. In Hartford, Leon was sure, Carson would shine again, like a fine piece of jade taken from a farmer's hut to the emperor's palace. His quality would be appreciated.

The next Sunday, Leon shared the news with Yew-Fun.

"Oh, poor you. We all hate going to Hartford!" Yew-Fun made a face. "Don't you remember how strict Chinese teachers are? All day long, every day, study, study, study. No exercise, no fun."

Leon shook his head. It had sounded like fun to him.

"My brother and I are looking forward to it," Carson insisted.

Yew-Fun laughed. "You'll see." He lowered his voice to a whisper. "We call it 'Hell House.'"

# CHAPTER TWELVE

# Hell House

—◇·◇— —◆◇◆— —◇·◇—

*T*he night before they left for Hartford, Leon could barely sleep. He kicked off the quilt, then pulled it back. His eyes were watery and his nose so stuffed up that he had to breathe through his mouth. Miss Julia had told him this sickness was "the rheum."

But mostly he was thinking about the upcoming trip. Hartford, a big city. Would he get lost? The Chinese Educational Mission building, where he would take classes, why did they call it Hell House? Mr. Yung Wing. How strict would he be? A new idea crept into his mind. Maybe he would inquire about being sent home to China. He could say the winter weather made him sick and American boys were mean to him. Would those be good enough reasons? It might help if he got even sicker. He wanted to go home and see his parents and First Elder Brother.

Carson didn't sleep much either. He stayed up late, writing a composition in Chinese by candlelight. The subject was something about loyalty. Every month, they had heard, the Chinese teachers in Hartford honored one student for excellent composition and another for calligraphy. Carson hoped to attract attention by winning a prize.

For the journey, they dressed in their official scholar's robes and skullcaps. They would need them for the ceremonies.

After they said their good-byes and got on the train for Hartford, Elder Brother turned to Leon and looked him in the eyes. "Watch what you do. Behave yourself."

Leon nodded and looked out the window as the four-car local train pulled out of Suffield's tiny station. He had no doubt Elder Brother would beat him again if he did or said anything bad.

The train ride to Hartford was short—only sixteen miles. Leon itched to jump up and explore the train, as he had on the transcontinental trip. But he sat quietly next to his brother and tried to behave. Mrs. Swann had given him a stack of clean, pressed handkerchiefs, and he clutched one the whole way, using it to wipe his nose. Carson said he had a headache again, so they hardly spoke a word. But it didn't matter. Leon would see Tik-Chang soon!

Hartford seemed like another world. It was a city, as different from Suffield as Shanghai was from their home village in the Guangdong countryside. But it didn't look like Shanghai at all. Instead, it had broad, straight streets lined with trees and separate homes lined up, one after the other, for miles and miles. Each home had a walkway from the front door to the street, and Leon noticed many men and boys shoveling snow off their front walks.

A driver took them by horse carriage to the headquarters building, a large, three-story house, surrounded by trees and an expansive snow-covered yard. Leon was proud to see that this house was much larger than the Swanns' house.

At the front door, the famous Mr. Yung Wing himself greeted them. Although he was only the associate commissioner, he was the man who had proposed the idea of a Chinese Educational Mission to America. Everyone knew that.

He welcomed them in their home dialect of Cantonese and asked each of them their name and the name of their host family. He was the one who had found all the American families to host them.

Mr. Yung looked like a dapper American gentleman, dressed entirely in Western clothing, wearing a dark frock coat, full vest, and high white collar with a black bow tie. He had a lot of thick hair around his face and a long, thin queue down his back—a compromise of sorts. Yew-Fun had told Leon that Mr. Yung was planning to marry an American lady, the very next month. Leon could not imagine a Chinese man married to an American. What kind of life would they lead? What kind of strange-looking children would they have?

Mr. Yung escorted the boys into the sitting room of the big house, where several other boys were waiting. Leon immediately found Tik-Chang's face in the crowd and wanted to run up and greet him, but he followed Elder Brother's example and sat down quietly. Mr. Yung started speaking to the boys in English. But apparently observing their blank faces, he then switched to Chinese. Leon was in awe of him. Here was a man who could be thoroughly American yet also Chinese. Mr. Yung was, Leon knew, very patriotic. Educated in America, he could have stayed in America to live, but he had gone back because he wanted to find a way to serve his fatherland.

"The primary reason we brought you to Hartford is to study Chinese. You must study very hard," Mr. Yung told them, looking serious. "When I went back to China, after years in America, I could hardly speak my mother tongue. Someday in the future, you may take up high positions in the government, so you must be able to read and write in Chinese as well as English.

"But," he continued, "don't be afraid of becoming 'too American.' You need to succeed here in the United States.

To do that you need to win the respect of your teachers and classmates. You need to show them you can be just as American as they are."

Leon was confused. Teacher Kwong had warned them against becoming too American. Now Mr. Yung said not to worry about it.

After his talk, Mr. Yung led the boys out to the hallway. He stopped in front of a portrait of the emperor. "Now, line up in three rows by height. It's time to show our respect and loyalty."

Leon and Tik-Chang stepped to the front with the younger boys, and Elder Brother lined up with the taller boys in the back.

"Three kneelings and nine kowtows!" said Mr. Yung. "One!" In unison, they fell to their knees, dropped their hands to the floor, and tapped their foreheads on the floor three times—a gesture they had all practiced many times together in Shanghai. Then they all stood up. "Two!" They kneeled and tapped their foreheads three more times. "Three!" The emperor in the painting was a little boy, only five years old, dressed in a stiff yellow robe with dragons embroidered on it. He didn't look very happy.

Next, the boys were led into another formal room, to greet the emperor's representative in America, the head of the Chinese Educational Mission, Commissioner Ngeu. He didn't look anything like the frightened man calling out to the Chinese goddess of mercy during the train holdup. Now he sat in a throne-like chair, wearing an official scholar's gown, and the boys lined up and bowed to him, too. This time it was just one kneeling and three kowtows.

At last, the boys were led to the second floor to a dormitory-style bedroom, lined with small wood-frame beds. The minute the door closed, they all relaxed. Joy flooded Leon's heart as he greeted each of his friends: the tall, narrow-faced brothers Tak-Fay and Tak-Yaw, the laughing eyes of Yew-

Yong, pockmarked Wing-Ho, the daring grin of the jokester Luen-Fai, thick-necked Luen-Shing, and his personal favorite, tiny Tik-Chang. Luen-Shing seemed even fatter now; apparently American food agreed with him! During their training in Shanghai and long weeks of travel, Leon had come to know these boys like brothers. He had missed them.

The boys could not stop talking, comparing their American families and their experiences learning English. Many of them had lady teachers, like Miss Julia, although some took lessons with the father of the family. Some of them had American brothers; Leon envied them. Most of them were staying with kind people, but a few had rough times.

Tik-Chang pulled Leon aside to tell his story in confidence. "The father in my family is too strict. He gives me a test on English words every morning," he said. "If I miss more than one, he beats me. Then I have to spend the afternoon mucking out the horses' stalls."

Leon was shocked. Tik-Chang showed him his hands, which were calloused and bruised. Tik-Chang's father was a wealthy merchant in Macau, who never made him do manual labor. He couldn't imagine Mr. Swann beating him and punishing him like that.

Tik-Chang lived in an isolated, rural farmhouse. Others lived in city neighborhoods. Some of the boys lived together in groups of three or four and had little opportunity to practice speaking English. One boy complained of nonstop digestive troubles, unable to adapt to American food. Another had gotten in four fistfights in just six weeks, including one at church. Yet another had learned a lot of curse words and insults in English, which he gladly taught to his fellows.

Leon jumped in to tell how an American boy had tried to strangle him with his queue—and his revenge, pushing him into icy water. Elder Brother frowned.

"Did you hear about Lum Yun-Fat?" one boy said. "He's being sent back to China."

Everyone stopped talking. "What happened?" asked Leon in a hushed voice.

"He ran off with an American girl."

This was news. Bad news. Leon could not even imagine doing that. "Why?"

"Who knows? They found him with the girl, alone, in a barn. He was sent home within a week, in shame. He has no future now."

No future. Leon wasn't sure what that meant, but it sounded terrible. Maybe he didn't want to be sent home after all.

❋ ❋ ❋

The next morning, their wake-up call came at five thirty. They had to be in the classroom at six o'clock, where they studied for three hours until breakfast. Then they had classes again from ten to one. They had a short rest break after lunch, but they had to return to the classroom again from two thirty to six o'clock. Even after dinner, they had to sit quietly and practice writing until ten o'clock at night.

Leon hated it. This was the same schedule they had followed in Shanghai, but now, after living a less regimented life with an American family, it seemed impossibly grueling. Sitting still was hard for him. Once he jumped up and walked around the classroom, and the teacher punished him by beating his hand with a bamboo switch.

The Chinese classes were held in the largest room in the house, the attic. In one corner was a large wooden table, the teacher's desk. The students sat at long tables. They worked at four main tasks: studying books, writing characters, explaining the meaning of the passages they read, and composing commentaries. They had to copy passages again and again, forming each Chinese character just right. What a contrast with Miss Julia's way of teaching!

The teachers used the traditional Chinese instruction

methods. All thirty of the students would read out loud at the same time, each reciting a different passage, making a huge din. Fortunately, Leon was sitting with other boys his age who were studying the same lesson, from the *Classic of Filial Piety*. Whenever he forgot how to say a character, he listened to Tik-Chang, who usually pronounced it right. Then Leon tried to remember. But the Chinese characters slipped out of his mind like water out of a cracked bowl.

Each boy had to go, one by one, up to the teacher at his desk to recite the lesson. Leon watched as Tik-Chang went up to the front. He could not hear his friend's words because of the tumult of voices reading aloud. When he was finished, Tik-Chang returned to his seat and shrugged. Apparently, his recitation had gone okay.

"Woo Ka-Leong!" Leon dreaded hearing his name. He walked slowly up to the podium, where Teacher Chiu looked at him sternly and whacked his switch against his own left palm. Leon knew the teacher would not hesitate to hit him on the head if he made too many mistakes.

"People with virtue must speak out," Leon began. "But people who speak out are not all virtuous." He recited the first few lines perfectly, in the singsong way he had been taught. This was an easy passage, one he had first learned two years ago, with his tutor in southern China.

But the racket of students reciting out loud rattled Leon, and he stumbled on his words. Suddenly, he could not remember the next word. The teacher said it for him. Leon repeated it, but the following words, too, had evaporated like late-summer rain.

*Whack!* The teacher rapped him on the head. "Go back to your seat. Study harder."

In China, teachers often hit their students to help them learn better. This blow wasn't even very hard. Still, it stung, and Leon resented it.

As Leon returned to his seat, Carson glared at him.

Elder Brother always recited his passages perfectly. With a twist of his heart, Leon wished he were back at the Swanns' house, with Miss Julia. There, each new English word seemed immediately useful. These Chinese sayings he was memorizing, written many centuries ago, seemed irrelevant.

Each day that passed, Leon felt more irritated with his Chinese lessons. His mind couldn't think that way anymore. Ten hours of studying every day was just too much. Besides, his head was stuffed up, and the Chinese words wouldn't come out right. He felt sick and inferior and lost. He stopped trying hard, and the teacher rapped him more and more frequently.

What was that term Yew-Fun had used? *Hell House.*

# CHAPTER THIRTEEN

# New Year Celebration

—◇·◇——◆◇——◇·◇—

*A*fter dark, on the eve of the Lunar New Year, the boys gathered for the celebration Leon loved best. After dinner, dressed in heavy coats, they all went outside in the cold air.

Just inside the door, Elder Brother took Leon aside. "You know how important this holiday is," he said quietly.

Carson's eyebrows drew into a thick line, and Leon thought he looked just like Father. In fact, his voice sounded like Father's, too, deeper than before. Carson was behaving just as Father expected, but he seemed more menacing than Father ever had.

"I promise," Leon said, "I will behave."

"If you don't, you'll be sorry."

Leon gave him a confident smile. "You'll be proud of me." He meant it. Ever since the ice-cracking incident, Leon had done everything he'd been told. It was easier to do the right thing when no one was harassing him. Besides, nothing could spoil the happiness of the holiday.

Elder Brother smiled, too, as if relieved. "Good!"

On the front porch of the house, two long strings with

rows of red cylinders tied to them were hanging from the rafters. Commissioner Ngeu lit the first one, from the bottom.

The bottom firecracker went off with an ear-piercing boom, then—*bang-bang-bang*—the fire climbed up the string and each cylinder exploded in fast progression.

Leon's heart pounded. He stood close to the other boys and covered his ears, but in truth he loved the loud noises. When the first string of firecrackers had finished exploding, he and the boys erupted in cheers and shouts. Then Associate Commissioner Yung lit the second string.

The noise made tears pop into Leon's eyes. A year earlier, he had celebrated the holiday with his family. Less than ten days later he and Carson had left for Shanghai. Leon remembered how naive he had been, leaving behind everything that was familiar, full of excitement. A year ago, he had no idea how badly he would miss home.

The next morning, the sky was clear blue. The ground was covered in a fresh layer of pure white, like someone had scattered rice flour everywhere. Fortunately, Leon's nose was no longer stuffy. It did feel like a new year was starting, full of promise.

This day, the first day of the first month of the Year of the Rat, was also everyone's birthday. In China, every baby was considered one year old at birth. Then, everyone turned one year older the next Lunar New Year.

As of today, he was twelve years old, even though many of the other twelve-year-olds were much taller. Born in the Year of the Rat, he had lived one full cycle of the zodiac, through all twelve animals. This meant that childhood was over. Leon decided he would act more grown-up this year. No getting into trouble. And as of today, Carson was fifteen. That sounded so old.

On this special day, the boys didn't have to come down until breakfast at nine o'clock. Even the cook had a day off, so breakfast consisted of cold meats and dried tofu. The cook had managed to buy oranges—very expensive—one for each boy. They came all the way from a warm place called Florida, a two-day train ride to the south. Imagine eating tropical fruit in the middle of a snowy winter! That's what trains could do. Every year, the Chinese Educational Commission hosted an annual reception. Before the guests arrived, the boys had to perform their kowtows and prostrations to the emperor. Then they were herded into the formal reception room. There, Commissioner Ngeu sat in a stiff wooden chair, and Mr. Yung Wing sat at his side. They received the students as the emperor would receive his officials, with a nod of acknowledgement. The boys held their hands together in the traditional celebratory greeting, saying "Kung-hei, Kung-hei"—meaning "best wishes."

Then the students stood in neat rows, arranged according to height. An American photographer set up a black box on a three-legged stand and took their photo. They had to stand perfectly still, with a solemn look on their faces. Some of the boys had gone to photography studios in San Francisco, but Leon and his brother could not afford it. This would be the first photo taken of him. Leon wondered what it would look like.

"Everyone go into the parlor now," Mr. Yung instructed. "The commissioner has an announcement to make."

In the parlor, the commissioner had a rare smile on his face. Leon could not imagine what would make this stern official look so pleased.

"You may have heard that this new year, 1876, is the one hundredth anniversary of the founding of this young country, the United States of America," he said. "To celebrate, the United States is holding a world's fair in Philadelphia, called the Centennial Exhibition."

Leon had heard other Chinese boys talk about this world's fair, too, saying it would be full of amazing delights. His heart began to beat faster.

"The Imperial Government of China has decreed that all one hundred twenty boys of the Chinese Educational Mission are to attend this Centennial Exhibition, in August—together."

The boys shouted in glee. For Leon, this was a dream come true. Mr. Yung told them there would be exhibits from countries all over the world! A delegation from China would set up a display of precious objects made of jade and silk. Machinery Hall would house all the latest American inventions. A train would connect some exhibits. A huge engine, the largest in the world, would power all the machines.

The rest of the day, the boys could talk of nothing else. Leon wasn't sure what he wanted to see more, the train or the massive steam engine. Just thinking about it made the holiday even happier.

At dinner that evening, the boys were particularly loud and lively. All the visitors had left, and even Commissioners Ngeu and Yung were out eating dinner with some Americans. After dinner, the teachers went back to their rooms to rest, so the thirty boys who were living at the mission were free to do as they pleased. This was their last night together until the big trip to Philadelphia in August. With full bellies and good news and cheerful conversation, anything seemed possible.

"Let's go outside and play in the snow," suggested Tik-Chang.

"Good idea!" shouted a few of the younger boys. Leon badly wanted to go but wasn't sure Elder Brother would allow it.

Carson was sitting by the fire with some of the older boys, talking like grown-up gentlemen. Leon asked him for permission to go outside with his friends, and Carson smiled his assent. Surrounded by friends who admired him, Elder Brother was much nicer here.

Outside, the boys ran around, making tracks in the big

snowy yard. They made snowballs and threw them as hard as they could against the house. Some splattered into bits; others stuck against the wooden walls in a big clump.

That gave Leon an idea. "Let's have a contest! Who can throw a snowball the farthest!"

"Good! Good" The other boys began making snowballs and testing how far they could throw them. Bigger snowballs were not necessarily faster than small ones. Leon discovered that what really made a difference was how hard the snow was packed.

"Look," said another boy. "If you do this, it flies farther."

Leon watched as the boy built his snowball around a small rock. It did fly farther! So Leon tried that, too. This must be the right way.

"Let's have two teams!" one of the bigger boys shouted. He lined them up in two groups and pitted them against each other. Taking turns, they each aimed a snowball at the back wall of the carriage house. Each team got one point for every hit.

The last contest was between Leon and his best friend. Although small, Tik-Chang was remarkably strong. The teams were tied, so whoever won this last throw would win for the team.

Tik-Chang went first. Instead of throwing his snowball at the side of the carriage house, he threw it up and over. It landed on the roof, near the ridgeline, and rolled back down toward them. His team clapped. One boy thought they should get an extra point for this good shot.

Leon was next. He had packed his snowball hard, with a small rock in the middle. Mustering all his strength, he threw the snowball as high as he could. If he could make it past the ridgeline, he would impress everyone.

The snowball sailed higher and higher—up and over the ridge of the carriage house roof! Leon began to clap in delight, and the other boys laughed and clapped, too.

Suddenly, from the other side of the carriage house came a loud, startled yell.

The boys ran around the small building and skidded to a stop when they saw a horse carriage in front of the open door. Commissioner Ngeu was running from one side of the carriage to the other. Mr. Yung had stepped out of the carriage and was holding his ear as if something very hard had hit him: Leon's snowball.

Leon's stomach twisted. *Aaiya!* Of all people, Mr. Yung, who had made it possible for him to study in America.

Commissioner Ngeu ran over to Mr. Yung and steadied his arm. "Are you all right?"

"Sorry!" shouted one boy.

"Sorry! Sorry!" Leon and the others shouted.

Mr. Yung held his ear. A trickle of blood lined his cheek. Commissioner Ngeu's face contorted with fury.

"Who threw that missile?" he demanded.

The boys all looked at each other. Leon felt sick.

"We were all throwing snowballs. We didn't expect to hit anyone. Deep apologies," Tik-Chang said. They all hung their heads.

Leon knew they would all be punished for his mistake. He stepped forward. "I was the one," he admitted.

"It was me," said another boy, also stepping forward.

"I threw it," said Tik-Chang.

Leon could not believe they were all taking responsibility for his mistake. He should have known Tik-Chang would be a loyal friend.

"All of you! Back to the house!" Commissioner Ngeu's voice shook with anger.

Teacher Chiu carried out the punishment. All the younger boys stood in line, and he hit their palms ten times each with the rattan stick. The older boys, who should have been watching them, were each hit five times, for failing to stop the game.

Forced to stand with his hand out to be smacked, Elder Brother's face was red with rage and humiliation. He had been chatting by the warm fire with old friends. Yet, of course, he had been neglecting his duty. In front of Teacher Chiu, none of the younger boys squealed about who had thrown that snowball. But later, when they had all gone to bed, Leon confessed to his elder brother.

Carson slapped Leon and beat him with his fists as hard as he could. Leon moaned in pain, but, once again, he knew he deserved it.

# CHAPTER FOURTEEN

# Consequences

—◇·◇—◆—◇·◇—

*T*he next morning, at their last breakfast together, the other boys pretended they did not notice that Leon had a swollen black eye and bruises on his face.

Teacher Chiu looked him straight in the face and said, "How do you feel today, Woo Ka-Leong?"

Leon hung his head. He felt terrible, and his head ached, but some part of him was glad he had received worse punishment than his friends.

Still, a deeper dread filled his gut: Would he be sent back to China in shame? This thought had kept him up all night. Just two weeks earlier, Leon had been eager to find a way to go back to China. But now he knew better.

The idea of being sent home in shame terrified him. He imagined showing up at his father's house, just a few months after leaving China. He would be sent back like a prisoner. He would have to say good-bye to Julia, Charlotte, and the Swanns, to Thomas and Yew-Fun. And he would miss seeing the big machines at the Centennial Exhibition. He had not been in the United States even two months, and he had failed. He had brought shame on his family and on all the boys of the educational mission. There was no way he could undo what he had done.

After breakfast, the cook called him into the kitchen. A thickset man with greasy hands, the cook mixed some white powder with water, then applied it to Leon's black eye. Leon was surprised at the gentleness of his touch. Then the cook dabbed a bit on each of the scratches on his face and arms.

"Thank you, see-foo," said Leon, using the term of respect for skilled workers.

Leon slowly packed his bag and brought it to the front hallway, hoping he could get away without a lecture. Then Mr. Yung called Leon and his brother into his office.

"Here it comes," said Carson. Elder Brother looked almost hopeful. Did he want to be sent back to China?

The two boys stood before Mr. Yung with their heads bowed.

"Do you see my ear?" Mr. Yung turned his head, and they looked closer. Mr. Yung's ear was a little swollen and red, but in truth it didn't look too bad. "I am getting married next month. What will my new wife say?"

"Sorry, sorry," they both said, hanging their heads again.

"Woo Ka-Leong, did you hit me with a snowball yesterday?"

"Yes, I was the one. I apologize deeply." Leon never intended to hit any person with that snowball, but he knew better than to give excuses. Instead, he fell to his knees and put his forehead to the floor, a sign of prostration and complete obedience. Elder Brother did the same.

They stayed in that position a few moments.

"Stand up," Mr. Yung barked.

The two boys stood, hanging their heads. Leon knew he deserved to be sent back to China in shame. Because of his bad behavior, Elder Brother was in shame, too.

Mr. Yung addressed Elder Brother first. "Woo Ka-Sun."

Leon could see Elder Brother's hands shaking.

"Woo Ka-Sun, is it true? I heard that during the train robbery you kept your calm and protected all the gold your leaders were bringing to America."

Elder Brother brightened as he nodded humbly.

"You showed maturity beyond your years, and our commission owes you our gratitude."

This was going better than Leon expected. But when Mr. Yung turned to him, he trembled.

"Woo Ka-Leong, you threw that snowball all the way over the carriage house," he stated in a tone of disbelief.

"I did. I'm so sorry," said Leon. "Please accept my deepest apologies."

Mr. Yung hesitated. Then he said, "Have you considered playing baseball?"

"Huh?" Leon thought he had misheard.

The old man smiled. "You have quite an arm!"

Leon stared in disbelief. Had he heard correctly?

"I'm sure you did not mean to hit me," Mr. Yung said. "You have been punished enough. No one is to speak of this again."

"Thank you, sir, thank you." Elder Brother found his voice before Leon could. "We do not deserve your kindness."

Leon felt dazed. Is this how Americans thought, that it was okay for a boy to hurt someone if he didn't mean to? Was this a sign that Mr. Yung, who had been in America long enough to find a wife, was becoming Americanized?

Later, Elder Brother took credit for the pardon. "If it weren't for me, you would be dead meat," he muttered on the train ride back to Suffield. Then he added, darkly, "I'll have to do more to keep you in line."

❂  ❂  ❂

This time, Mr. Swann met their train.

"Got in a tussle, did you?" he asked Leon. "Looks like you copped a mouse." Leon didn't want to ask what that meant.

Julia did not dismiss Leon's black eye so easily. "Oh, no!" she said when she saw his face. "Who hit you?"

She seemed indignant that anyone would dare to hit Leon, and he wasn't about to tell her that his brother had beat him up. He didn't have enough English vocabulary yet to explain what had happened. Even if he did, he would never tell her.

"How terrible!" Charlotte exclaimed later, as Julia lathered some American cream on the scrapes and cuts. "Who would hit a small boy?"

Small boy. Who *wouldn't* hit a small boy, if he misbehaved?

&#10040; &#10040; &#10040;

The next day, their English lessons began again and continued all morning. Carson was even stricter about doing their Chinese studies after lunch. "I didn't realize how much your Chinese had slipped. You'll have to work extra hard to catch up," he said to Leon. "When we see our mother again, you don't want to forget how to greet her!"

Leon thought that was extreme. After all, he had just spent three weeks speaking nothing but Chinese. Still, in Hartford Leon realized he had forgotten how to read and write a lot of Chinese words he'd once known. Elder Brother was right. He needed more practice. Writing characters again and again felt like punishment, but it kept him out of trouble.

After their return from Hartford, Carson became even more distant and stern. Perhaps, at fifteen, he realized more than ever that he needed to be responsible now. Or perhaps Teacher Chiu's punishment had made him see his younger brother's behavior as it would be viewed back home. Or maybe he was just feeling rotten, far away from his own friends.

Somehow, Elder Brother had acquired a rattan stick like the ones Chinese teachers used to beat students. He used it to hit Leon on the head or on the hands if he didn't study long hours or if he didn't concentrate. Leon hated this, but he knew it was a time-honored way of making students work harder. Father would approve.

One afternoon, he forgot one word—just one word!—in a long poem. Elder Brother slapped him on the cheek. Then he punched Leon in the stomach—one sharp punch. Leon doubled over and yowled.

Suddenly their door opened, and Julia rushed into their room. Leon tried to straighten up but couldn't.

"What have you done!" she screamed at Carson. "This is your younger brother!"

"He was bad," Carson managed to say.

"I don't care how bad he was. He's a little boy. Don't you ever hit him again!"

Carson stared at her sullenly and made no promises. When she left, he switched back to Chinese. "She has no right to interfere. Who is she to give me orders?"

But after that, he only beat Leon when Julia was not around, but sometimes his eyes gleamed as if he enjoyed the power it gave him. And Leon was not allowed to make any noise no matter how much it hurt.

❋ ❋ ❋

Two days later, they received a letter from their father, only the second they had received. They had written more than ten. When Miss Julia called them, they rushed down the steps to the front hall.

With his longer arms, Carson grabbed the letter first, but Leon crowded in next to him as he tore it open with his one long fingernail. In the dim light of the hall, the words were hard to read. Carson sucked in his breath. Leon caught up to that part of the letter.

"We are all in mourning. First Elder Brother has died. His fever lasted twelve days. Your mother cannot stop crying. But I am sure you will be strong because . . ."

Leon fell to his knees, unable to read on. Ka-Shing was the future of their family. Now Father had no sons at home, only daughters, just like the Swanns.

"We should go back," Carson said in Chinese.

"What is it?" Miss Julia asked. Neither boy could answer. They just shook their heads. Then they trudged blindly up to their room and did not go down to dinner that night. Instead, they both wrote letters to their father. Leon's was short. He didn't know what to say. But Carson's was long. And when he was finished, he wrote another letter to Commissioner Ngeu at the Chinese Educational Mission office in Hartford.

"I asked them to send us home," he told Leon.

"But we just got here. And it took more than a month to get here. Do you think they would do that?"

"Father needs us. If we went home, I could take First Elder Brother's place and study for the national exams. I would get a proper education. In the future, the whole family will rely on me."

That night in bed, Leon hugged his pillow tightly. It was terrible being so far away from his family. He had never been close to First Elder Brother, who teased him for being small. But he wondered about his mother and his father and his little sisters and his many cousins. Who else might die while they were in America? He wondered about the ghost of Owen Swann. Could it have caused this awful thing to happen? Was it trying to kick them out?

They did not have any mourning clothes to wear. But the next day they told the Swanns their sad news. Mrs. Swann made each of them a black armband of mourning. She didn't know that the Chinese color for mourning is white.

Within a week, they got an answer from the commissioner: No. "Your father agreed to your participation in this program," the letter stated. "We invested almost a year training you and bringing you to this country. Your duty is to stay here and continue your education. You must remain strong and remember your duty to the emperor and the Imperial Government."

After that news, some dark fury seemed to bubble up inside Elder Brother. If Leon made the tiniest mistake in writing some Chinese character, Carson would beat him with the wooden stick. Sometimes Carson punched him in the stomach for no reason at all. When he ground his ink on his inkstone, he seemed to be punishing it. He slammed his books on the table.

One day, Leon went outside and found Elder Brother behind the house, crashing a stick against a stump, muttering curse words. Another day, Leon found a piece of paper where Carson had written a list of all the things he hated about America. "These Americans are cruel to us," it said. "They feed us their worst food and lock us in our rooms." Leon knew that wasn't true, but he wasn't about to contradict Elder Brother. He figured it was just Carson's way of being sad.

Still, Leon sensed that something was changing inside his brother's head. Sometimes Carson talked to himself, in Chinese, saying things Leon couldn't quite catch the meaning of. He said things like "Americans are uncivilized" and "American women are loose." Leon wondered if Elder Brother had been talking about American women with his older Chinese friends back in Hartford. When Leon asked what he meant, Carson smirked. "You'll understand when you're older."

Miss Julia noticed the change in Carson, too. "Is something wrong with your brother? Is he feeling unwell?" she asked Leon.

"Oh, no, he's fine," Leon reassured her. What else could he say?

But the elder brother he had known in China was slipping away, replaced by a stranger. Maybe the ghost of First Elder Brother was mixing things up inside Carson's head.

# CHAPTER FIFTEEN

# A Ray of Hope

*W*inter in New England was far longer and bleaker than Leon could ever have imagined. After a few days of warmer temperatures, some of the snow would melt; then another storm would drop two or three more inches of snow. He had heard that northern China had a lot of snow, too, but he could not imagine any place with as much snow as Suffield, Connecticut.

Their English lessons got harder, too. Miss Julia had received a long letter from Mr. Yung, with specific instructions on how much the boys were expected to learn by August. She didn't use a wooden stick, but it still hurt Leon to see her frown when he misspelled a word.

Leon felt more alone than ever. He missed the sunshine and warm air. He missed his mother, who always smiled at him, even if he did poorly on his lessons. He even missed the way Elder Brother used to talk constantly about how much better life was in China. Now Carson barely spoke to him at all.

The only thing that got Leon through the barren New England winter was the anticipation of summer, especially of August. Miss Julia found a newspaper article about the upcoming Centennial Exhibition in Philadelphia and helped him read it. He practiced writing the words *centennial, exhibits, machinery, display, agriculture,* and *industry.*

One evening, Mr. Swann showed him an article in the newspaper about something called the Corliss steam engine, which would be displayed in Philadelphia. It produced something called electric energy. It would be so big it would run dozens of other machines. There was a sketch of the Corliss in the paper, and Leon traced its outline, wondering how big and noisy the steam engine would be. How could one machine run other machines? Electric energy was a mystery to him. Was it science or magic?

Elder Brother did not care about engines. For weeks, he didn't seem to care about anything. But then he started talking about the school entrance exam, which was to be held on August 15. Although that date was only eight months after their arrival in the United States, Carson was convinced he had to pass the exam this year.

"I have to get out of this house. It's terrible to be locked up with these women," Carson said. "All the other boys my age are already in school."

Leon was glad to see his brother trying hard at English again. But he couldn't see how Elder Brother could possibly pass. Carson focused on reading and writing English, rather than speaking. But Leon could read and understand even more than his brother could. Each time this became obvious—especially when Miss Julia gave them a test and handed back the results—Carson would take out his anger on his brother. In their room, after English lessons, Elder Brother would hit his palm with the stick. Sometimes Leon's hand hurt so much afterward he could barely keep writing, but Carson would not let him slow down.

Leon also daydreamed about going to school. When he heard Yew-Fun talk about the boys at school, he wished he had a group of friends like that. He did not relish the idea of another winter cooped up with his brother and Miss Julia. So he studied hard for the test, too.

One day, in the late afternoon, when he finished his required time of studying Chinese, Leon went downstairs to the parlor. Charlotte greeted him with a smile. She was alone and seemed eager to talk to someone.

"Show me what a house looks like in China," Charlotte said. She shoved a piece of paper at Leon.

Leon wasn't used to the idea that paper could be wasted like this, drawing pictures that would be thrown away. "Wait," he said, and he ran upstairs to get his slate.

First he drew a plan that showed the various courtyards of his house, with smaller rectangles that showed where each person slept.

"There's a separate section for ladies?" Charlotte asked. "Can't ladies go out?"

"Ladies," said Leon, carefully pronouncing the plural, "go out, but not often."

"Tell me about their feet," Charlotte whispered. "The ladies have bound feet, right?"

"Bound feet." This was a new term in English for Leon. "Small feet. Very small feet." Leon showed her, with his fingers, the ideal size of a lady's foot, about three inches long.

"Ohh." Charlotte sounded horrified. "Why do they do that?"

"Why?" Leon had never thought about why. "All girl do this. All lady. Very pretty."

"Can they walk?" Charlotte asked.

"Yes, but very slowly."

"They are lucky then. I wish I could walk."

Leon wasn't sure what to say. "Welcome you to come to China."

Charlotte's eyes clouded over. "I can't travel. I'll never go anywhere."

"Yes. You come to China, to my father house. I show you my family."

A tiny ray of hope glistened in her eyes. "I appreciate the invitation."

After that, Leon came to see Charlotte most afternoons, while his brother continued the endless writing of Chinese characters. Often she started with the same words. "If I go to China, to visit your family, I need to learn about Chinese people. Tell me more."

At first, Leon did not know what to tell her. But gradually he thought of things. Using his slate, he drew pictures of Chinese clothing, for men and women, for poor farmers and officials. He talked about holidays, Chinese New Year, Dragon Boat Festival, Mooncake Festival. He would draw a picture, and she would write the English words he didn't know. He talked about firecrackers and kite flying and a game that Chinese boys played, kicking a shuttlecock with feathers on top.

Without realizing it, Charlotte taught him more English than Julia did. Instead of slowing down and pronouncing each word carefully, as her sister did in their formal lessons, Charlotte just spoke at her normal fast pace. At first, Leon was lost, but he picked out a word here and there. When he repeated that word, Charlotte would say the sentence again, just as fast. Gradually, Leon got used to the pace and cadence of conversational English.

Usually, no one else listened to their conversations. One day, though, he looked up and saw Carson standing in the doorway. "Ka-Leong!" he commanded. "Come upstairs now."

*Aaiya.* He was in trouble again. Up in their room, Elder Brother let him have it.

"You know better," Carson began. "Remember that boy who got sent back in shame?"

"We were just talking," said Leon.

"She's a beautiful young lady. Don't you see that?"

Frankly, Leon didn't. He loved Charlotte's radiant smile, but he never thought of her in *that way*. Did Carson?

"From now on, you are not allowed to talk to the young lady alone."

Leon's heart ached. Charlotte was the one ray of light in this otherwise gloomy house in the dead of winter. She was his sister now. How cruel of Carson!

# CHAPTER SIXTEEN

# Spring Training

—◇·◇—◈◇—◇·◇—

*O*ne morning in March, Leon woke up and realized it had been raining all night long. Looking out the window, he could see that the field next to the Swanns' house was mostly bare, brown and muddy, with a few snowdrifts near the driveway where the snow had been shoveled into high piles. Even those drifts were no longer white but dingy gray. In one corner of the sky, the dark clouds had parted and fresh sunlight leaked through. At last, the snow was beginning to melt.

It was Sunday, so Leon dressed for church. He carefully tucked his queue inside his starched white shirt, so it would not be visible. Although Carson didn't do this, Leon made a habit of hiding his queue whenever they left the Swanns' house.

After church, they went to the Travis home for Sunday dinner. This was now a habit, every other week. Sometimes the Travises came to their house, but not as often, since the Swanns lived outside the town. Leon looked forward to it, because he and his brother could talk to Yew-Fun in Chinese and find out what was going on in town. Yew-Fun was their ally and friend. Leon wished Carson felt closer to Yew-Fun; they were the same age. But Carson kept his distance from people, more and more. He just wanted to pump information out of Yew-Fun.

"Tell us about the entrance exam," Carson asked.

Yew-Fun grimaced. "Just another test, you know? But baseball practice will start soon!" That's what Yew-Fun wanted to talk about, and Leon listened eagerly. The baseball games that counted were played in the summer, against teams from nearby towns. The last few years, Suffield's team had been fairly good, but their star pitcher had graduated from high school and had gone on to college.

"This season, Johnny will be our pitcher," Yew-Fun said. "I wanted to do it, but Johnny is better. He's also a good hitter. Lots of home runs."

"What does it mean, a pitcher?" Leon asked. Yew-Fun had used the English word, since there was no such word in Chinese.

"He's the one who throws the ball. It's important to get it right over home plate, so the batter can hit it." Yew-Fun threw a lot of English words into his Chinese sentences. The words *pitcher, batter, home plate, home run*—all had no good translations. Even the word *baseball*. If there was a word for it in Chinese, Yew-Fun did not know it.

"After dinner, we'll go out and hit some balls, okay?" Yew-Fun said.

Leon looked at Elder Brother, who had been examining some of Yew-Fun's schoolbooks during all the baseball talk.

Carson scowled. "No," he said to Leon. "It's a waste of time. Besides, it's muddy out."

Ever since Carson had given him that black eye, Leon had been extra careful around his brother. He could get away with some things, but playing baseball in the mud in his new clothes was not one of them.

But after Sunday dinner, Yew-Fun changed into old

clothes, and Leon followed him outside anyway. He just couldn't stand the thought of sitting in the Travis parlor when Yew-Fun was outside with other kids. A neighbor boy, Frank, came over, and Leon watched as he threw balls to Yew-Fun, who hit them with his bat. Then the boys switched places, so that Yew-Fun pitched at Frank. Frank was tall and skinny with an enormous crop of yellow hair, like wheat.

Leon knew better than to touch the ball or the bat, but he was fascinated. Even Leon could see that Yew-Fun and Frank were covered in mud by the time they stopped playing. But they were laughing and joking in English, clearly happy after the exercise and fresh air. Leon was tired of being closed up in the house all day like a chicken in a coop, pecking at his English and Chinese homework.

"Next Sunday, I'll bring some old clothes," Leon whispered to Yew-Fun. But he didn't have any old clothes that could get muddy. The clothes Yew-Fun had given him were for everyday wear, too nice to ruin.

That week, Leon could think of nothing but baseball. During English lessons, he drew a baseball bat and mitt on his slate and asked Miss Julia how to say them in English. She gave him a vocabulary list to learn: *mitt, bat, batter, ball, pitcher, catcher, first base, home plate.* Carson had to learn them, too.

On Tuesday it snowed again, and Leon fell into despair, sure that winter would never end. But by Friday the sun had come out and melted the new snow. Leon forced himself to spend extra hours that week doing Chinese homework, and he worked extra hard doing an English writing exercise Miss Julia had given him. So by Friday, he felt he deserved to stop early.

On Friday afternoon, after just one hour of Chinese calligraphy, Leon stood up. "May I have your permission to stop now? Please?" Leon asked his brother.

Carson sighed. He looked at the string of Chinese characters Leon had written. "Write these three more times," he said. "Then you can go."

When he had finished, Leon ran down the steps two by two, as if escaping from jail.

"Leon?" Charlotte called to him, and he bounced into the sitting room.

Leon put his finger over his lips. He didn't want Elder Brother to hear them talking. The night before, when Elder Brother was bathing, Leon had taken Owen's bat, ball, and mitt out of the closet and had hidden them downstairs, in the sitting room behind a sofa. Now he dove behind the sofa and retrieved them.

"Is okay?" he whispered to Charlotte. "I can use these?"

A shadow crossed Charlotte's face. "My father doesn't want anyone to touch them."

Leon's chin dropped, and he laid the items on the coffee table.

"But I think it would be all right," she said. "What's the harm? No one else is using them."

Leon dared to hope. Could he take this girl's word?

"You can't play outside in those clothes," she continued. "There is a wooden chest in my room that contains some old shirts and pants. Wheel me over there, and I'll show you."

Leon felt nervous as he wheeled Charlotte over to her room, which he had never entered before. The bed was neatly made with a chenille bedspread, and the curtains, a bright-blue cotton print, were pulled aside so that sunlight could stream in. Like Charlotte herself, the room was cheerful and bright. This was dangerous territory. If Elder Brother found out he was here, he'd be in big trouble again. But he had to do this.

"Open that." Charlotte pointed to a wooden chest in the corner. When Leon lifted the lid, a musty smell of mothballs poured out. Inside, folded and stacked neatly, were boy's clothes. A lot of them. It seemed to Leon that not one thing had been thrown away. There were more clothes here than Leon had ever owned. On top was a set of go-to-meeting clothes, a wool jacket and vest. He thought he could smell tears.

Leon slammed the chest shut. The dead boy's ghost. This was where he lived.

"What's wrong?" Charlotte seemed startled by his reaction.

Leon wasn't sure what Americans believed about ghosts, but he knew that a Chinese ghost could cause all kinds of mischief if disturbed. "It is not right."

Charlotte's face took on a soft, sad, gentle look. "It is right." She reached over and opened the chest again. "Find something very old and worn. Mother refused to throw out even the most tattered clothing." She did not say her brother's name: Owen.

To Leon, it seemed like extreme bad luck to touch the clothes of a dead boy—especially one who had haunted him. But Charlotte urged him on, and he pushed aside the fancy clothes to see what was underneath. Sure enough, there were older, everyday clothes, some of them spattered with ground-in mud stains.

Leon pulled out a pair of blue pants with a drawstring waistband and a faded red long-sleeved shirt with a mended tear in the arm. These had once hung on the dead boy's body.

"Perfect," said Charlotte. "Try them on."

He pushed her wheelchair back into the parlor and then hid behind a chair to change into the old clothes. They were a little large and loose but comfortable and—yes—perfect for playing outdoors. He pulled the shirt over his queue, so that it was out of the way. He stood still for a moment, waiting for the dead boy's ghost to pinch him or kick him. Nothing happened. In fact, he felt a warmth from the clothing—which was impossible. Maybe Owen approved.

When he emerged, Charlotte clapped her hands in delight. "Just right!" she said.

"I ask Mother first?" Leon asked. "Or Father?"

"I say it's all right," Charlotte declared. "Take the bat and ball and go outside." Leon closed the door tightly and went to the back of the house, where Elder Brother could not see him out the window.

First, he swung the bat several times, the way he had seen Yew-Fun and Frank do it. He started with the bat resting on his right shoulder, then tried to swing it in a straight line, as if meeting a ball. The wooden bat was heavier than he had expected, and at first it kept dropping down at the end of his swing. It took strength to try to keep the swing even.

He wished he had looked more closely at the way Yew-Fun held the bat. Which hand was supposed to be on top? And how high up the bat should he grip it? He tried different grips. None of them felt quite right. He wasn't used to the weight and size of the bat.

He quickly realized that one boy can't practice baseball alone. A few times he tried tossing the ball up with his left hand and hitting it with the bat, but he missed every time. So he decided to try pitching the ball. Even Mr. Yung had said he could throw well.

The baseball was heavier than he had expected. The outside was made of white leather with stitching; he wasn't sure what was inside. He threw it as far as he could. Then he ran to get it. The backyard was still muddy, and he was wearing his Chinese cotton shoes, which soaked through quickly. Why hadn't he looked for shoes in the chest of clothes? His shoes had no grip, so he slipped in the mud and fell. At first, he was dismayed and hesitated, but then he decided he didn't care. Yew-Fun and Frank had fallen and gotten muddy. That's what old clothes were for.

He picked up the ball and threw it back toward the house. It came dangerously close to hitting a kitchen window but bounced off the back steps instead. Leon decided he should not throw directly at the house. He couldn't risk hitting someone again!

Leon ran and picked up the ball, tossing it up and down to get used to the weight and feel of it. Was he supposed to throw it overhand or underhand? What was the best way to aim? There was no one to give him answers. He decided to try aiming at a large tree in the backyard. He threw the ball again and again at the tree. When he was close to the tree, he could hit it. But the farther away he got, the harder it was. Still, it seemed like a good way to practice.

Leon had no idea how much time went by. His feet were wet and cold, but he was so absorbed he barely noticed. After pitching the ball more times than he could count, he decided to practice with the bat again. He had left it on the back steps.

When he turned to get it, he saw Mr. Swann standing there, in his suit and tie, holding the bat.

Leon froze. Mr. Swann had not given him permission to wear Owen's clothing or play with Owen's bat and ball. Would Mr. Swann beat him for disobedience? He had every right to.

Leon trudged toward Mr. Swann, hanging his head in shame but also peeking up to try to read the expression on the man's face. He looked grave but not angry. Leon couldn't tell if he was in trouble.

"Sorry," Leon began, "I . . ."

Mr. Swann handed him the bat. "Here," he said. "Take this. Give me that ball."

Leon handed him the muddy ball and took the bat.

Mr. Swann took a few steps into the yard. "Watch," he said. He held the ball in a particular way, with his thumb and two fingers. Then he pulled his arm back and snapped his wrist as he threw the ball. It whistled as it flew, and it hit the tree square in the middle of the trunk.

"Waaah!" Leon could not help admiring the throw. It was perfect. His eyes shone as he looked up at Mr. Swann in admiration. "How you do that?"

Mr. Swann, who was so full of words in the pulpit, said nothing but gestured for Leon to run through the mud to retrieve the ball.

Again, Mr. Swann showed him the proper grip. He went through the pitching motion slowly, without releasing the ball. Then he handed the ball to Leon.

Leon took the ball and tried to imitate the grip. Mr. Swann adjusted Leon's fingers and then nodded. Leon pitched the ball, trying to mimic the older man's movements.

Mr. Swann laughed. Laughed! This was the first time Leon had heard him laugh.

"Not quite right," he said. "Watch again."

After watching Mr. Swann throw the ball once more, Leon picked it up near the tree. "Stay there," Mr. Swann said, grabbing the mitt from the steps. "Throw it to me."

Standing under the tree, Leon held the ball carefully in his right hand. Then he imitated the pitching motions as well as he could, tossing the ball straight at Mr. Swann.

It was a perfect pitch. Mr. Swann caught it in the mitt.

So Leon didn't understand what happened next.

After catching the ball, Mr. Swann pulled the mitt to his face. His hands fell to his sides, and he pulled off the mitt. Mr. Swann wiped his sleeve across his eyes. He tossed the mitt and the ball down onto the steps, turned on his heels, and went in the back door.

Perhaps it was the smell of that leather mitt. Perhaps it was the sight of Leon, wearing his son's old clothing. Perhaps it was the *thwack* sound of the catch.

Mr. Swann was weeping.

CHAPTER SEVENTEEN

# The Redheaded Rascal

—◇·◈—◈—◈·◇—

*L*eon knew he was in trouble again.

He ran up to his bedroom, slammed the door shut, and panted. Overflowing with remorse, he confessed to Elder Brother what had happened. He deserved whatever punishment would come. The color drained out of Carson's face, and he was too shocked to speak at first. Then Elder Brother began yelling at him in Chinese and slapped him on the face. "Take off those clothes! They're not yours! What were you thinking?"

Mr. Swann came to their door, knocked, and then barged in. Elder Brother stopped yelling. The two boys looked at him, guilt in their eyes. Would Leon be in trouble for playing baseball, or would Carson be yelled at for hitting his brother?

Mr. Swann said nothing at first. The expression on his face was intense and frightening. It seemed he was trying to control his emotions so that he could speak steadily. Mr. Swann had never beaten either of the boys, but Leon knew that today was the day he would get his first beating by an American. He deserved it.

Leon began taking off Owen's shirt.

"Stop." The storm in Mr. Swann's eyes calmed. "Leon. It's all right. I'm sad because . . ." His eyes glistened. Seeing tears made Leon squirm. Mr. Swann looked around the room, as if remembering how it used to look.

"I had a son. Owen. He would have . . ." This man who had so many smooth words on Sunday mornings could barely finish his thoughts. Carson, for once, had sorrow and compassion written all over his face. Losing an only son would be too much for any father to bear. "He would have loved to have two brothers from China. He would have played baseball with you."

For a few heartbeats, Mr. Swann stood with his hand on the doorknob, looking at Leon and Carson as if trying to find Owen's face in theirs. "I'm glad you're . . . both here."

Then he turned and left. No beating for either of them.

Stunned, Leon stood motionless, Owen's shirt still hanging on his body.

Elder Brother stared at the door. It seemed his heart had gone out with the old man. Then he turned to Leon. "You need a bath," he said with a gruff tone that wasn't convincing. "Go wash."

At dinner, no one said anything about the incident. The girls were quiet, looking at their father, perhaps uncertain about what to say in front of him. Leon wondered how they knew, but he was sure they did. Mrs. Swann filled the awkward silence with chatter. Something about taking soup to yet another sick woman. She worried about whether she had time for so many needy people. The cook was starting to complain about making so many extra meals. Leon noticed that Charlotte looked away when her mother spoke this way. He was beginning to see under the surface of this family.

After dinner, alone in their room, Carson sat at the desk and wrote a long, long letter, probably to their father. Leon went straight to bed and hugged the pillow. How could anyone explain baseball to someone in China?

✦ ✦ ✦

The next day, during their lessons, Miss Julia tried to explain about her father.

"I had a brother, named Owen," she said to both of them. "He died last year, when he was only ten years old. This is why my father is sad. We all miss him."

Leon knew all this, but it was the first time Julia had mentioned Owen.

"Your brother," Leon said, "he play baseball?"

Miss Julia smiled sadly. "Yes, he loved baseball. My father taught him everything he knew. Father was an excellent pitcher when he was at Yale. He hoped Owen would be good at baseball, too."

"I should not play this game," Leon said, glancing at his brother, who nodded approval.

"No. I talked to Father last night. He says you may go ahead. He wants you to have a good American experience."

A tiny flame of hope lit up inside Leon. He didn't dare look at his brother.

"But my father can't help you," continued Julia. "It brings back too many sad memories. He has asked Johnny to help you practice."

"Johnny?" Leon flinched. Didn't she remember how nasty Johnny had been to him?

"Johnny O'Malley is that boy who lives near here," Julia said. "His father does the farming on our land. My father is busy at his church, so he pays Johnny's father."

*Ah,* thought Leon. *This explains it.* Johnny's father was not just a driver. Leon's own father, back in China, hired many men to work his fields. So Mr. Swann did that, too.

"Johnny has no money," said Leon.

Miss Julia smiled at his wording. "Something like that. He and his family are poor. They work hard. But Johnny is a good baseball player. He will help you. Carson, you can play, too."

"No, no," said Carson. "I study. My brother study, too. No baseball."

"Spring is coming," said Julia. "It's good to play outdoors."

But Leon had a bad feeling. When Carson said "no baseball," he meant *no baseball.* And Elder Brother would not hesitate to enforce his will.

❉ ❉ ❉

Halfway through that night, Carson began moaning. Leon woke with a start. Moonlight was streaming in through the window. Was it a headache again? A stomachache?

"What's wrong?" Leon asked in Chinese, jumping out of bed and going to Elder Brother.

"It's my tooth," said Carson. "It hurts. I can't sleep."

"When did it start?"

"After dinner last night. I thought it was nothing. But it's getting worse."

They waited till morning, but by then, Carson could barely stand the pain. He was gritting his teeth and holding his jaw. Leon tried to appear sympathetic, but inside he was thinking, *Good. Maybe the American god is punishing Carson for hitting me. No, I shouldn't think that way.*

At the first morning light, Leon went to Julia's room and knocked softly. But it was Mrs. Swann who emerged from the room next door. Her eyes were round with worry. "What's wrong?"

"My brother," said Leon. "His tooth is—ouch."

Mrs. Swann rushed into their room and put her hand on Carson's forehead, as if by instinct. Carson pointed to the tooth that hurt. "Very bad?" she asked him.

He nodded and moaned.

Mr. Swann and Julia both dressed quickly, and Mr. Swann went out to harness the horse and roll out the carriage. Leon helped his brother get ready. Carson was shaking from the pain.

When it came time to take Elder Brother into town to see the doctor, Mr. Swann insisted that Leon stay home. Leon wasn't sure why, but Carson didn't object. The sun had already risen by the time Leon waved as Carson rode off with Mr. Swann and Julia. He assumed the doctor would pull Elder Brother's tooth; he wondered how badly it would hurt.

Leon felt lighter and freer with his brother out of the house, if only for an hour or so. It was a Saturday, and Leon ate breakfast with only Mrs. Swann and Charlotte. Mrs. Swann talked about every toothache she or anyone else she knew had ever experienced, including one man, who got an infection and died.

"Mama!" Charlotte cried out. "Think of how Leon feels when he hears that."

"Well, it's possible," Mrs. Swann said.

Leon concentrated on buttering his toast.

After breakfast, the horse carriage returned, and Carson's mouth was wrapped shut with a cloth around his head. He looked miserable and went to bed immediately.

*It's a bad-luck day for Elder Brother*, thought Leon. *But maybe not for me.*

After Carson was settled in bed, Julia asked Leon to follow her downstairs. On the hall table sat a neat pile of old clothes, with Owen's baseball mitt on top. Nearby, on the floor, were his bat and an old pair of soft leather shoes. Julia picked all this up and handed it to Leon.

"Johnny is waiting outside," she said.

Leon's heart leaped. He wanted, badly, to practice baseball. But he hated Johnny. Plus, he knew Elder Brother would disapprove. But Julia had told him to go out. So he obeyed.

He quickly changed into the old clothes, hiding his queue again. On the bottom of each shoe, two triangles of metal had been attached, one on the heel and one on the sole, with spikes at each of the corners. These, Leon guessed, were to ensure he didn't slip in the mud. *How ingenious*, he thought.

To avoid putting the spiked shoes on inside the house, he walked out the door in his socks, carrying the shoes. The redheaded rascal was waiting there, sitting on the edge of the porch, and swinging his feet. He wore raggedy clothing, too big for him, and had brought a worn mitt.

"Hi," said Leon. If Johnny so much as gave him a mean look, Leon decided, he would slam the door and leave him dangling on the porch. But when he turned to look at Leon, he just seemed embarrassed.

"Hi," the freckled boy replied, looking away. "Ready?"

Leon hesitated. He hated this kid. Hated his guts. So many times, he had dreamed about kicking him or slapping him. Unlike Elder Brother, who was trying to help him succeed, Johnny just wanted to taunt him and tear him down. Johnny had come only because he had been ordered to. But it was a beautiful blue-sky morning, perfect for baseball. Carson was in bed. And Leon wanted to learn how to play. Besides, he had once seen tears in Johnny's eyes.

Leon sat down on the edge of the porch to put on the spiked shoes. When Johnny saw them, he looked away again. Johnny wore ordinary shoes, worn and scuffed.

Suddenly, a thought struck Leon. Johnny and Owen had probably been good friends. Johnny's best friend had died. Could that explain why Johnny was always so mean to him?

Johnny bit his lip. He didn't seem like such a bully anymore.

Johnny and Leon spent the whole morning in the backyard, practicing baseball. After just a few minutes, Leon forgot that this poorly dressed, low-class boy was the son of a common farm laborer. He forgot that Johnny's mother was sick and lived in a smelly, filthy hut. Johnny had a strong arm and a steady throw, skills Leon admired. He could see it was going to take a lot longer to learn how to play baseball than he thought.

At first, they just threw the ball back and forth; Leon practiced catching it in his mitt and tossing it back. Johnny didn't talk much. "No. Like this. Watch. Good."

After about an hour of throwing the ball, Johnny pointed to Leon's bat. "Batting practice now. You stand there." Leon held the bat the way he thought was right. Johnny came over and showed him a better technique for gripping and swinging the bat. They practiced without the ball at first. Then Johnny stood near him and tossed easy pitches his way, trying to help Leon learn to hit the ball.

When they started pitching and hitting, Johnny's eyes began to sparkle. Every time Leon missed, Johnny ran to get the ball. His energy was contagious; before long Leon was running, too. The fresh air felt great.

By lunchtime, Leon was exhausted and sweating, despite the cool spring air, but he felt exhilarated. Every time he hit the ball well, Johnny broke into a grin. They laughed at mistakes together. Within a few hours, Johnny was no longer someone he hated. Not exactly a friend, but certainly not an enemy.

# CHAPTER EIGHTEEN

# Playing for Real

—◇·◈·◇—◈·◇—

When Leon tiptoed into his bedroom to change, he hoped his brother was asleep. But Carson was sitting up in bed, his head still wrapped; his face burned with anger. Leon's good feelings collapsed.

"How do you feel?" Leon asked. "Does it still hurt?"

Carson could not open his mouth completely, but he had no trouble making himself understood. "I said no baseball. It's a waste of time. It's too American. It will take you away from your studies."

"But Mr. Yung said it was fine. I've heard that he even played football at Yale."

Carson glared at him. "Well, I say baseball is not fine. I forbid it."

His words hit Leon like a bat to the head. "Miss Julia told me to go out," Leon said. "Mr. Swann wanted me to play. It will make me strong and healthy. I'll put in extra hours of studying Chinese. Elder Brother, please don't forbid it." He felt like getting on his knees and begging.

"Four hours of study this afternoon," Carson said. It was a Saturday, and normally he let Leon get away with only two hours on Saturday.

If Leon weren't twelve years old, and too big to cry, he would have wept. After the whole winter of study, study, study, he wished he could stay outside and play baseball all day.

Why did Carson have to be so strict? Leon hoped he would relent a little once his pain went away. Four hours! It wasn't his fault Carson had a toothache.

The next day, Carson asked to stay home from church. His mouth still hurt. He wanted Leon to stay with him, but Mr. Swann insisted Leon had to attend Sunday school, and for once Leon was glad. He dressed in his fine go-to-meeting suit, which felt too heavy and thick now that the air was warmer. On the hall table, again, he saw a neat pile of old clothes, with the mitt, bat, and cleated shoes.

Julia pointed to the items. "The boys in town will be playing a game this afternoon."

"No baseball," Leon said mournfully. "Brother says no."

Julia seemed surprised. "You always do what brother says?"

Leon nodded. "I must." Forbidden meant forbidden.

She regarded him for a long moment. Then she picked up the baseball items anyway and carried them to the horse carriage.

Excitement filled Leon as they neared the town. It was wrong. He knew that. Elder Brother would find out, somehow, and he would be furious. But this was a chance to play a whole game! With the other boys in town! Besides, it was Julia who took the bat and mitt.

Overnight, it seemed, the trees had grown light-green buds. A few smaller trees were covered in tiny pink buds, promising full blossoms soon. Tall, yellow flowers grew in some gardens, as well as shorter, purple ones. The air felt fresh and cool but not cold, and the sun made dappled patterns on the road.

Spring had arrived at last.

❁   ❁   ❁

After church, dinner at the Travis home seemed to take forever. Yew-Fun knew that Leon had brought his clothes and bat. Leon had decided not to tell him what Carson had said. Both boys could barely sit still. Finally Mrs. Travis said, "You may be excused."

They quickly changed and ran up the street to the baseball diamond. Other boys were already there, including Johnny, who greeted Leon with a curt nod.

The sunshine had partly dried out the diamond so it was less muddy than the last time Leon had been there. He could still see drifts of snow along the edges of the field, but the sun was warm on his arms.

Yew-Fun introduced Leon to the boys he hadn't met, who seemed friendly enough. They were used to Yew-Fun, so they didn't make fun of Leon's queue. Mainly they wanted to get started. They divided into two teams, with Leon on the same team as Yew-Fun, in case he had to ask questions.

Yew-Fun quickly reminded Leon of the rules, speaking half in Chinese, half in English, showing him first base, second base, third base, and home plate, which were really just marks in the dirt. Then he told Leon to stand far out in what he called left field and catch the ball if it came to him.

Johnny was the pitcher, and Leon could see that he was pretty good. Mostly the batters did not hit the ball far enough for Leon to reach it. But one batter, Frank, hit it hard in his direction. Leon went running after it. When he picked it up, he wasn't sure where to throw it.

"Over here!" shouted the boy at third base. Leon threw it toward him, but he was so nervous it wasn't a good throw, and the boy had to run to get it. By then, another boy had rounded third base and crossed home plate.

Leon could tell he had made a mistake. It was his fault the other team got a run. But no one blamed him. They just kept playing.

Later, his team got a chance to hit the ball. Two boys reached base on hits that barely bounced past the gloves of the infielders. Then it was Yew-Fun's turn, with his teammates standing on first and second base. He hit the ball so hard it went flying over all the opposing players. Two of them ran after it, but by the time one boy threw it back, Yew-Fun had run around all the bases. Their team had three runs!

"Home run!" everyone was shouting. Clearly, Yew-Fun was a star. Leon felt proud of him, a Chinese boy who could play this American sport.

Leon was the last on his team to bat. Four times he swung at the ball and missed, but Yew-Fun shouted words like "ball one" and "ball two." The boys on the other team called back "strike one" and "strike two." The two captains argued, and eventually Leon got to walk to first base anyway—for reasons he didn't quite understand. When the next batter hit the ball, Leon ran for second base but was tagged out.

The rules were confusing, but the game was fun. He loved the running, the shouting, the throwing, the excitement, the competition. Some girls and parents were watching and cheering.

Partway through the game, Leon noticed that Miss Julia had come to the field with her father. They stood in the crowd and watched. Mr. Swann did not shout or cheer. But Leon thought he saw the minister smiling. That made him want to play better, to make his American father proud. Perhaps Mr. Swann could learn to enjoy baseball again, without weeping.

In the carriage, on the way home, Leon turned to him. "Rebban Swann," he began, using Mr. Swann's title, as he had heard others do. "Play baseball—is it a sin?" That was a word the minister used a lot in his lectures at church.

Surprise lifted the man's eyebrows. "A sin? No, of course not."

"His brother says he shouldn't play," explained Miss Julia.

Leon's lip was trembling, but he met Mr. Swann's gaze.

Mr. Swann searched his face for a few moments. "Your brother disapproves?"

Leon looked at Julia, who explained. "Carson thinks Leon should spend his afternoons studying Chinese. He says baseball is a waste of time."

Leon nodded.

The minister looked out of the carriage, as if contemplating the new leaves on the trees. For a moment, Leon wondered if he had forgotten the question.

"Do you study Chinese every day?"

Leon nodded. "Two hours."

The minister shifted his somber eyes back toward Leon. "Good. As long as you finish your lessons, then playing baseball is no sin. I say you should."

# CHAPTER NINETEEN

# A Good Scrubbing

—◇·◇—◆—◇·◇—

*T*he master of the house had spoken. That was as good as their father giving an order. Even Carson could not claim a higher authority over Leon. Elder Brother's eyes narrowed when he heard Leon tell him about this.

"Well, I don't like it," he mumbled, his words still garbled inside the bandage. "It's a stupid game. I hope you grow tired of it."

That night, in bed, Leon's muscles ached, but joy coursed through him. He reviewed every play of the game—and the minister's words. *I say you should.* Oh, yes.

But as the week wore on, Leon could feel the deepening crack in his relationship with Carson. His brother withdrew into himself and broke their pattern of casual chatter after dinner, while washing up and getting ready for bed. He often had a sour look, with his mouth shut in a firm line. He slammed doors. This angry person didn't seem like the same boy who had faced down a robber to save his little brother.

Each afternoon, Leon did two hours of Chinese study with his brother in their room. Carson grew even stricter, often rapping Leon on the knuckles with the rattan stick when he mispronounced a word. Once when Leon made a mistake, Carson picked up the baseball bat with his right hand and hit his own left hand a few times, as if to test the weight of it. Leon froze. Carson looked him directly in the eye but put the bat down. After that, Leon decided to store the bat in the front hallway.

Each day, the minute the grandfather clock struck four, Leon closed his book and stood up. Elder Brother glared, but Leon changed his clothes anyway. Then he ran outside to meet Johnny.

All the boys on the team went to school together— some to grammar school and some to high school. Hearing them talk about teachers, classes, and girls made Leon eager to join them. He paid closer attention to Miss Julia's lessons so he could learn English more quickly.

Oddly, the fresh air and exercise every day gave Leon added energy for his studies, and he seemed to learn twice as fast. Before, English words had seemed like jagged rocks in his mouth, but they now slipped out like fish through seaweed. Leon found he could easily change the word order for a question, saying "Is it true?" Rather than "It is true?" He still mixed up *he, she, him,* and *her*—there was only one word in Chinese for these four words. And he often left off the letter *s* at the end of words. But verb tenses, which had seemed impossibly complex at first, became more natural: We are playing. Did you play? When can you play? Carson's English remained stilted with a heavy accent.

Miss Julia often complimented Leon for the English words he had picked up from his baseball buddies: not just sports terms but also sayings like "Take it easy, old boy," "Dinna fret about it," and "Bully for our team!"

During one of their lessons in the dining room, Miss Julia said to Leon, "It looks like baseball is good for you." Carson stiffened, but he said nothing.

Carson was eager to go to school as soon as possible, so he spent more time on his English, too. Although pronunciation was still harder for him than for Leon, Elder Brother had always had a better memory. But oddly, Carson's memory seemed to be getting worse. While he could remember Chinese poems and passages he had learned before they came to America, he had trouble committing new ones to memory. He wrote out his English vocabulary words twice as many times as Leon yet he still missed a lot on spelling quizzes. Whenever Leon got a 100 percent, he tried to cover it up so Carson wouldn't see.

One evening, at dinner, Julia mentioned that the boys had begun memorizing a very long poem called "The Raven" by Edgar Allan Poe. "You wouldn't believe the way they can memorize! No American schoolboy has a memory like they do."

Mr. Swann's eyebrows rose. "Really?" He turned to Carson, who was helping himself to extra mashed potatoes. "How does that poem go? 'Once upon a midnight dreary, while I pondered, weak and weary . . .'"

Carson put down the spoon and took up the challenge. He stood up and began reciting. Pride surged through Leon. Now they would know how smart his brother was. But he also worried. They had only learned the first four stanzas, and it was a hard poem. Carson prided himself on reciting poetry, and even one slip might make him mad.

"Once upon a midnight dreary, while I pondered, weak and weary / Over many a quaint and curious volume of forgotten lore . . ."

Carson's pronunciation was atrocious, but the words came out smoothly.

Mr. Swann smiled with pride and nodded. Charlotte lightly clapped her hands a few times. Carson should have stopped after the first two stanzas. It was dinnertime after all. But from his very earliest years, he had been lauded for his memorization of poems. So he continued through stanza three, stumbling only once on *entreating*.

The fourth stanza started out well, but halfway through, he faltered on what should have been an easy part.

"But the fact is I was napping, and so gently you came rapping, / And so faintly you came tapping, tapping at my chamber door, / That I . . . That I . . ."

Julia jumped in. "That I scarce was . . ."

Carson continued. "That I scarce was . . ." The flood of words stopped completely. It was as if a stopper had been put in the sink.

Leon tried to help. "Sure I heard you . . ."

Carson glared at Leon. "That I scarce was sure I heard you . . ." He was flustered.

Mr. Swann started to applaud him. He had done very well, after all. But Carson stopped midsentence and couldn't seem to think of another word. Everyone shifted awkwardly.

"It's amazing. Such a difficult poem," Mr. Swann said, filling the uncomfortable silence. "And to think that just a few months ago—"

Carson threw down the napkin he had been clutching. "Stupid poem. No good." And he turned and stomped upstairs.

"No, really, Julia, it's incredible how much you have taught them."

After dinner, Leon was afraid to go up to their room, sure his brother would beat him again. But Carson was in bed with his eyes closed. Later, Leon thought he heard his brother grinding his teeth.

☀ ☀ ☀

Every day, at four, rain or shine, Leon changed into Owen's old clothes and shoes, and escaped with his bat and mitt. Most days, Johnny met him in the field, after getting home from school. They established a routine, throwing the ball and catching it, then pitching to each other, taking turns at bat.

One afternoon, Johnny insisted on pitching until Leon got a good solid hit. The ground was so muddy his shoes were soaked through, and a drizzle made it hard for Leon to see the ball coming at him. He swung that bat every time but couldn't control it.

"Here, try this." Johnny came over and showed him, yet again, how to hold the bat, this time a little higher. Leon wiped his eyes with his sleeve and adjusted his hands. Maybe Elder Brother was right. Maybe it was a dumb game.

Johnny waited till Leon stood in just the right posture before he pitched the ball again, this time more slowly. Leon focused on the ball and swung the bat straight and hard, angling it up a bit. The bat smacked against the white ball, which whizzed straight past Johnny, far out into the field. Leon's arms throbbed with a satisfying ache.

"Hey! What's that?" Johnny's father was out there with his plough, breaking up the mud in the field.

The two boys ran out. "Sorry, da'! I didn't think he could hit it so far!"

"Sorry! Sorry!" Leon said, looking up into the bearded face of the tall man, whose reddish hair was so wet it looked brown.

The man's dark eyes looked kind. "Na worries, lads. It were a good hit!"

Johnny slapped Leon on the back as they returned to the house. "Ya, good hit!" he said.

Leon felt very American.

*Even if I never get very good at baseball*, Leon thought, *I love being out here hitting the ball.* That feeling was one of the things that attracted him to baseball.

On Sundays at first, then on Saturdays and Sundays, Johnny and Leon went into town to play with the team. The Suffield team chose Yew-Fun to be captain, a big honor for a Chinese boy who had been in America less than three years. Anybody could play on the team. That included a girl for a few months. She found it too hard to run in skirts and refused to wear boy's clothing to play. So she quit.

❋ ❋ ❋

One afternoon, on the first sunny, warm day of spring, Johnny showed up late, breathless. "I've been helping my da' in the fields. Two weeks after the frost. Time to plant corn," he said. "Had to skip school today. Let's go get my bat."

Leon ran with Johnny across the field and into the woods. "Did your da' let you go early?" he asked.

"It's okay. We're done for the day."

As they approached Johnny's home, Leon braced himself for the sight of the slovenly hut. He wondered if Johnny's mother was feeling better now.

Just as the house came into sight, two small, dirty children came running up to them. Leon had seen them just once and had forgotten about them. But they knew who he was.

"Yay! He brought Leon!" one of the urchins said. "I'm Paul."

Leon squinted at him, trying to make out a boy's face in the mass of dirty-blond curls.

"And I'm Polly!" said the smaller of the two, who had a similar tangled nest of hair.

"Can we play, too?" Paul asked.

"No. I'm busy." Johnny pushed them aside as he approached the front door.

"Johnny," said the weak voice from inside. "You need to take care of them today. I'm too tired."

Johnny stomped his foot. "Drat! Not again." He turned to Leon with an apology on his face. "Sorry. Can't practice today."

The two little ones were jumping around like eager puppies that had been roped up all day.

"It's all right. Today we play with the kids," Leon said.

Johnny looked surprised but relieved. The children cheered.

Johnny led them all to a small clearing, up the hill, not far away. Clearly, he had played ball with his brother and sister here many times, for they immediately took up positions and crouched, waiting for him to throw them the baseball.

Johnny threw it to his sister, who caught it and threw it to Paul, who fumbled and dropped it. Little Paul chased after the ball and threw it to Leon, who tossed it back to Johnny. The game went on, changing order, so that they all had to be ready to catch. Then Leon lined up with Paul and Polly, and they each got a turn at bat. The little ones, who could not have been more than four or five, often missed, even though their big brother stood very close when he pitched to them. Still, they laughed in their high voices and kept trying. Just being outdoors and playing with their big brother seemed to make them happy.

"I feel bad, taking you away from them in the afternoons," Leon said to Johnny.

Johnny rolled his eyes. "I'd much rather be with you!" he said, as if the little ones were a burden. He tossed the ball at Polly, who caught it and did a little happy dance that reminded Leon of his own sister. But his sister had never been this dirty.

Polly threw wildly and the ball rolled into the nearby stream. Paul ran after it.

"Let's all take a bath," said Leon. He took off his shoes and socks and ran into the water after Paul. The shock of cold water made him shiver, but it felt good in the warm sunshine. Johnny sent Polly back to the cabin for soap and joined them in the water, stripping off his shoes, socks, and shirt. Leon stripped off his shirt, too, though he felt self-conscious about his queue.

When Polly reappeared with a small bar of soap, she commented on it. "Oooh, lookee! Leon has a braid!"

Leon reached for his queue, which was wet, and gently swatted her arm with it. She squealed and said nothing more.

Leon and Johnny both scrubbed themselves with the soap before washing down the two little ones. Johnny even gave their hair a good scrub. Paul and Polly giggled and splashed each other. Paul seemed shy, but Polly talked in such a fast, high-pitched voice Leon couldn't really understand her. Johnny washed the children's clothes, too, squeezing them out and draping them over a bush to dry.

When the washing was done, the two older boys, still wearing their cotton pants, lay back against a rock and let the stream splash over them. The little kids, both naked, played in the water, jumping in and out.

Johnny smiled at Leon. "Good idea. They needed a good scrubbing!"

*I'll say,* thought Leon. But he just smiled.

If Johnny was embarrassed, he didn't show it. Instead, they made a game of cooling off on a warm day and also caring for children whose mother was ill.

"Usually, my mom washes them up once a week, for church," Johnny explained. "With Mom sick, we haven't been going lately."

Leon watched some fresh green leaves in the stream flow over a rock. He wondered if Elder Brother sometimes resented his responsibilities, too. But something else bothered him. "You didn't go to school today?" Leon asked, trying not to sound accusing.

Johnny sighed. "I can't. But it's okay. Lots of other students have to work during corn planting, too. Got to get the seeds in the ground. The teachers all know that."

Leon stayed quiet, trying to imagine skipping school to help plant crops. He was lucky.

"Anyway, it's my last year," said Johnny. "I'm not too good at book learning. If I don't finish sixth grade, it don't make no difference. After that, I go work the fields anyway."

In China, the sons of landless farmers couldn't go to school at all, let alone attend through sixth grade. Why should he have assumed that would be any different in America? Of course, many American boys could not afford to go to school. Families like Johnny's could not host boys from China; the family Leon lived with was not typical. They were well-off.

He remembered something Mr. Yung had told them: only two out of every one hundred American boys had the opportunity to go to college. Here he was, Woo Ka-Leong, worried about passing a test to get into seventh grade and assuming he would go to college, when American boys like Johnny had no hope of even attending high school.

Little Paul scooped up some water and splashed his sister. Both Leon and Johnny laughed, and whatever tension Leon had felt about this family washed away downstream.

# CHAPTER TWENTY

# Clouds and Rain

—◇·◇—◇◇◇—◇·◇—

*A* few days later, a heavy spring rainstorm interrupted batting practice, and Leon had to come in early. As he rushed up the stairs to change into dry clothes, he heard voices in the parlor: Charlotte's musical laugh and a man with a deep voice who was talking to her.

Leon was stunned. *Does she have a suitor?*

But when Leon came downstairs in his clean clothes, dressed for dinner, he was surprised to see who was chatting with Charlotte: Carson. When had his voice gotten so deep?

Leon paused by the entrance to the parlor, listening to their conversation. Carson was sitting in the chair Leon usually sat in.

"Once upon a midnight dreary, while I pondered, weak and weary . . ."

Carson's pronunciation of the Edgar Allan Poe poem was terrible, Leon realized, but Charlotte did not laugh at him or correct him. Instead, she clapped and said, "Wonderful!"

It wasn't wonderful at all, thought Leon.

"This is famous poem? What it mean?" Carson asked.

"It's about love," Charlotte said. "The man has lost his love and he is very sad."

"His wife died?" Carson asked.

"Not his wife. Well, maybe his wife. He doesn't say. . . ."

Leon couldn't believe it. His brother was alone with a pretty American woman, discussing love.

"You have no love stories in China?" she asked.

"Have. Cow boy and king's daughter. Girl's mother take her away. Cow boy fly to sky."

"Ooooh. That sounds like a nice story! Do you have any Chinese poems I could read?"

Carson laughed lightly—a sound Leon didn't even recognize. What was going on in there? "Velly hard, reading Chinese word."

At first, Leon had missed his afternoon talks with Charlotte. But in recent weeks, he had been playing baseball. He hadn't thought twice about whether Charlotte was lonely.

Leon walked back a few steps, silently, in his cloth Chinese shoes. Then he jumped, as if he had just come down the steps, and ran across the hallway into the sitting room.

"Oh, there you are!" Leon said, interrupting the conversation. He plopped down in another chair, opposite Charlotte. "It's raining!"

Charlotte smiled at Leon the way she always did, delight in her expression. "Water, water everywhere . . ."

Leon finished the line from "The Rime of the Ancient Mariner" for her, with his best pronunciation: "Nor any drop to drink."

Surely Charlotte would see that Leon's English was much better than Carson's.

Elder Brother seemed annoyed at the interruption, but he didn't stop staring at Charlotte.

"We have first game of season this Sunday," Leon said. "You want to coming?"

Charlotte tilted her head to the side, as if surprised by this invitation. "Can I?"

"Ask your da'," Leon said, consciously imitating Johnny's American speech. "Why not?"

☀ ☀ ☀

On the following Sunday afternoon, Julia wore a newly made dress of lightweight silk and seemed extra animated. Charlotte was lively, too. After Sunday dinner, Thomas offered to carry Charlotte to the baseball diamond, a few blocks away. As Leon ran ahead with his teammates, he noticed that Julia followed, carrying a porch chair for Charlotte to sit on. The air was warm despite clouds, a good omen for the first game of the season against an out-of-town team.

A team of boys from a town across the Connecticut River arrived in several horse carriages, driven by their fathers, mothers, and older brothers. There were only six on the visiting team, versus ten on the Suffield team, but they adjusted the rules to make do.

One of the out-of-town boys pointed at Yew-Fun's queue. "Is that a braid inside your shirt?" he asked. "Are you a girl?"

Leon was glad the kid had asked Yew-Fun, who was much taller and thicker than Leon.

Yew-Fun turned to the kid and stood up as tall as he could, holding his hands up like a bear's paws. "No! I'm a heathen Chineeee," he said, and he began charging toward the boy, who yelped and dodged out of the way. The other boys laughed, and no one else dared say anything about their queues. Leon admired Yew-Fun for responding that way. It worked much better than swinging your fists.

Leon had been promoted from outfield to third base, and he guarded it like a watchdog. In the very first inning, one of his teammates threw him the ball, and he caught it and tagged out the player who was hurtling toward third base. "Good play!" Yew-Fun shouted, and Leon beamed.

The other team's pitcher was very good. He put a spin on some of his pitches, and he often was able to strike out the players from Suffield. Johnny was getting better at pitching, but he was not as consistent—or as tricky.

When Leon was waiting for his turn to bat, he noticed that Carson had come to watch the game, too. That surprised him. Carson stood next to Charlotte's chair during the whole game, talking to her. She kept glancing up at Elder Brother and seemed to be listening carefully.

This made Leon uneasy. It was a good sign that Carson had come to watch baseball, but something seemed wrong about the way Elder Brother leaned over Charlotte. Carson was standing a little too close, and Leon didn't trust him.

By the time Leon got up to bat, he was flustered and distracted. He swung at every pitch and missed them all. A shout of "strike three!" struck his heart, and he slumped back to the bench.

Other Suffield players were off their game that day, too. The other team beat the Suffield team, ten to two. With only six players! In the first game against outsiders. All his friends seemed disheartened, and Leon was, too.

Later that night, when Leon confronted his brother in their bedroom, he was in a very bad mood. "What are you doing with Charlotte?"

"She's very pretty."

Elder Brother's smirk confirmed Leon's suspicions. "She's like our sister," Leon said. "It's best to leave her alone."

"Are you giving orders to your elder brother?" Carson was oddly calm.

But Leon wouldn't give up. The boys had been strictly instructed not to get involved with American girls. It was just as much against the rules as cutting off your queue. "What's wrong is wrong, no matter where you are. That's what you said."

Carson laughed at him. "Is it wrong to leave your studies and play games in the mud?"

"In China, people don't play baseball, but it's not wrong. Touching a girl is wrong."

"I didn't touch her. Not once."

"Why do you spend time with her?"

Carson looked away with a quiet smile. "Same reason you play baseball. I enjoy it."

"She doesn't like you." Leon wasn't sure why he was so testy. Why should he care? He wanted to protect Charlotte from Carson. She didn't know his true character.

"She doesn't seem to mind talking to me," Carson said.

"She's just lonely. She doesn't want what you want!"

"What do you think I want? Clouds and rain?"

Leon recognized this as an idiom representing forbidden behavior, and it brought up an ugly image in his head, with the hint of a scream from Charlotte. He hated the smug grin on Elder Brother's face. Somewhere along the line, his brother had become menacing and unpredictable. How had this happened? Before, Carson had always followed the rules and enforced them. And now he was dangerously close to breaking them. Leon was furious. But there was nothing he could do. Or was there?

# CHAPTER TWENTY-ONE

# Howling

Suffield's team won the next two games. They were only practice games, but that made Leon feel much better. The games that counted would start in June, against these same teams. There were only six teams close enough for them to play, so if they won five out of six games, they might be in the "play-off," a new word in Leon's growing English vocabulary. It meant a big, important game at the end of the season. The winner of the play-off would be "the champions." That meant number one. All the boys wanted to be the champions.

Johnny played in every game, but he no longer practiced with Leon in the afternoons. The reason Johnny gave was "planting season." But even after planting season ended, Johnny didn't come over to practice. Leon felt annoyed.

Meanwhile, Mrs. Swann spent more and more time at Johnny's house, tending to his mother. Miss Julia said Johnny's mother now had a high fever and was very weak. Leon was astonished that a lady from a prosperous family would risk her own health to help a poor, sick woman. His own mother always told him to stay away from people who were sick.

"Why your mother do that?" Leon asked Miss Julia one day, after Mrs. Swann had rushed off. They were sitting with their books open, getting ready to start the day's lesson.

Julia looked glum and worried. "I wish she wouldn't. She thinks it's her duty."

This made no sense to Leon. "But why?"

She looked directly at Leon, and then at Carson. "You want to know the real reason?"

A distant look clouded her eyes. "I think it's because of my brother. After he died, she started spending a lot of time with sick people. She thought . . ." Julia hesitated, looking at the two Chinese boys, perhaps wondering how much to confide in them. "I guess she thought she had sinned somehow. That God took her son to punish her because she was not a good enough person. She needs to help other people to prove to God she is a good Christian."

Carson looked at his younger brother, confusion on his face. Leon understood the words, but not the meaning. "God took her son?" Surely he misunderstood.

Julia nodded, and her eyes filled with tears. "God took Owen from us. We don't know why. But I don't think it's my mother's fault." Her voice quavered. "I think it's my fault."

"Your fault?" Leon knew these words. It was his fault that the snowball had hit Mr. Yung Wing. He had thrown it. But how was it Miss Julia's fault that her brother died in a sledding accident? Why would God punish her?

Julia's eyes were overflowing now. "I was thinking only of myself. That day, when they went sledding, I should have been watching them. Instead I was at home, fixing my hair. I wanted to look pretty for Thomas. I should have been taking care of my brother, and all I could think of was finding a good husband."

Finding a good husband. This was something Chinese girls wanted, too, but it was the job of their parents and the matchmakers. Still, it didn't seem like a sin. Leon frowned, trying to understand. Carson shifted in his chair and looked out the window.

Julia sniffled and wiped her nose with a handkerchief. "I need to serve others. To love others as I love myself. That's what we are called to do. That's what my mother is doing."

Suddenly a lot became clear to Leon. This was why Miss Julia was still unmarried. She had stopped looking for a husband after her brother died because she thought it was her fault. Maybe this was even the reason the Swanns had agreed to host two Chinese boys. Julia spent so much of her time with them because she thought God wanted her to help other people. Because she thought God wanted to punish her. It struck Leon as a strange way to think.

"What about Thomas?" Leon asked Julia.

Julia cast her eyes down. "I don't know what I should do. Thomas is too good for me."

Leon shook his head in disbelief. In China, no one sat around thinking they weren't good enough, thinking they needed to help other people to prove they were good enough to enjoy life. It was a totally foreign notion.

Carson was still confused. "What is she saying?" he asked Leon in Chinese.

By now, Leon's eyes were filled with tears, too. He couldn't explain, in English or Chinese. It made no sense. But he knew that Miss Julia believed, deeply, in what she had said.

"Miss Julia," Leon said, "your father say Owen's spirit wants you to be happy."

Julia smiled sadly at him. "You really think so?"

"That's why I play baseball."

❂  ❂  ❂

Late that afternoon, Mrs. Swann came home exhausted. Leon wanted to ask her about Johnny's mother, but he didn't dare. He had not seen Johnny for several days. It seemed obvious that his mother was worse. Just after dinner, Mrs. Swann went straight to bed.

Up in their room, Carson picked up a Chinese book and began reading.

But Leon had a bad feeling. He looked out the window, across the field, toward Johnny's house. All this talk of serving others, and Johnny was in need. What had Leon done to help his friend? Or anybody at all?

"I left something downstairs," Leon lied. Then he slipped out of their bedroom.

He walked down the stairs in his stockinged feet and picked up his shoes in the hallway. Charlotte was in the sitting room, with Julia, whose back was to the door. Charlotte looked up and saw Leon, but he put his finger to his lips, in the American sign for silence. Her eyes widened. To cover his noise, she began singing a hymn, and Julia joined her.

Leon opened the door as quietly as he could. On the porch, Leon tied on his baseball shoes. They helped him run quickly across the field.

As Leon approached Johnny's house, the summer evening was pierced by a howl. It sounded like a wolf, but Leon knew it was human.

Just as the hut came into view, Leon caught sight of the reddish hair and beard of Johnny's father, who ran out of the door and blindly crashed through the underbrush.

Leon rushed to the door but stopped. Should he go in? He had a sinking feeling that the spirit of Johnny's mother had just left her body.

"Daddy!" The two little ones rushed out of the hut and straight into Leon. They grabbed Leon's legs and clung to him, wailing "Daddy!" as if they didn't realize this wasn't their father.

Johnny came out last, dragging his feet. His face didn't even register surprise to see Leon standing outside the door, one child clinging to each of his legs. Leon said nothing. He just reached out his hands, and Johnny grasped them. Then Johnny collapsed, sobbing. His little siblings grabbed him, and they all wept in a heap. Leon felt useless. All they wanted was for their mother to come back, and he couldn't bring her back. At least Mrs. Swann had tried, all these weeks and months, to keep their mother from dying. That was more than anyone else had done.

Leon knelt next to Johnny and put his arms around all three of them. Soon, he was sobbing, too, even though he didn't really know Johnny's mother. Too many people died. It wasn't fair.

CHAPTER TWENTY-TWO

# Doing Good

—◇·❖·◈·❖·◇—

"**C**ome back to the house with me," Leon said.

"I can't." Johnny could barely get the words out.

"I'll go get Mrs. Swann." Leon pulled away and stood up.

"No," said Johnny, "get Reverend Swann."

So Leon hurried back home. The lights in the two-story Swann house looked warm and content and prosperous. Is this how Johnny had seen it, all these months?

When he burst in, Charlotte saw his face. "Julia," she said, nodding toward him.

Julia jumped up and turned around. "Johnny's mother? Is she gone?"

Leon nodded, relieved he didn't have to say the first sentence he was practicing in his head. Instead, he said the second sentence: "Your father. Can he go there now?"

Julia ran to her father's study. When Reverend Swann came out, Leon was still standing in the hallway, feeling forlorn.

"Blessings be upon you, Leon," the minister said. "Did you touch them?"

Leon nodded.

"Go out back and take a bath now."

Leon thought he should go back to Johnny's house with Mr. Swann, but he didn't have the courage. It was too awful there. So he went into the kitchen and asked the maid to heat up some water for a bath in the backyard. That's where the men bathed in the summertime. He used lots of soap, and scrubbed and scrubbed, to get the smell of death off of him.

❋ ❋ ❋

All night, Leon could not sleep. He didn't even try. Carson ordered him to come to bed, but instead, Leon sat downstairs in the parlor, in the dark, even after Mr. Swann came home. Thinking. Feeling. Grieving for his dead brother. Grieving for his friend. Yes, Johnny was his friend now.

Back in China, when his aunt had died, his cousins had continued to live in the family compound, and his grandmother and mother had cared for them. But who would care for Johnny, Paul, and Polly?

What would happen to Johnny now? Johnny's father worked hard all day, six days a week, every day, and could barely earn enough to support the family. Leon had never heard Johnny mention a grandmother or aunts or uncles. In fact, Johnny's parents had come to America from Ireland, so all the rest of their family was back in the old country.

In just three weeks, Johnny would be finishing sixth grade—if he was allowed to stay in school. It seemed wrong for him to drop out. Even a farmer might find it useful to have a primary school certificate someday. But clearly, Johnny couldn't finish school. He would have to stay home to care for Paul and Polly. They were too young to be left alone—although apparently they had been left with only a bedridden mother for months.

Life was so unfair. Johnny was just as smart as he was

and a much better ballplayer. Why should he have to drop out of school? Leon wished he could do something to help. But what?

Long past the middle of the night, Leon came up with an idea. He wasn't sure it would work. But he wanted to try.

☀ ☀ ☀

The next morning was a Friday. A school day. Of course, Johnny would not go to school the morning after his mother died.

Early that morning, Leon went to Johnny's house. The mother's body was wrapped in a sheet, lying on the ground outside the door. Leon shivered. This ghost had reason to be angry.

Leon waited in the trees until he saw Johnny's father stumble out of the house to relieve himself and wipe his face and hands in the stream. Then he knelt for a long time by the mother's body, as if in prayer.

Leon felt he shouldn't be there, observing that private farewell.

Soon Johnny came out, followed by the two sleepy children. His father said a few words to Johnny about driving into town with Mr. Swann, then headed toward the big house. Were they going to get a coffin? Leon shivered. Death was awful. No wonder people refused to talk about it.

When they were gone, Leon approached Johnny. "You must finish school," Leon said. "I will take care of the children."

Johnny looked at him as if he were crazy. "What?"

☀ ☀ ☀

Over the next few days, before and after the burial service in the town cemetery, Leon could think of nothing else. He would care for Paul and Polly. After all, didn't the Swanns believe in helping others? He could do that. He had months and years to study English and Chinese. These next three weeks were crucial for Johnny. He needed to finish sixth grade.

"They can sleep with Carson and me," he said to Charlotte.

"No. They probably have lice," she said.

"I will shave their heads, to get rid of the lice," he said to Julia.

"Impossible. Their mother had a fever before she died. The children probably have germs. It might kill us all."

But Leon could not stand the idea of those small children living in that shack, or Johnny having to leave school. He didn't believe in germs. Besides, Johnny's mother died because she lost a baby, not because of germs. But he did believe in bad luck, and Paul and Polly had to get out of that place.

The day after the burial service, he took a metal tub from the Swanns' stables to Johnny's house, with some strong soap and a sharp knife. With Johnny's help, he bathed the two small children, and Johnny washed himself, too. When he discovered the children did have lice, he shaved off all their hair and washed their heads with soap. Paul and Polly cried with pain and grief. Leon helped Johnny shave his head, too.

Leon was tempted to shave his own head, in solidarity. That would be one way to get rid of his queue! But he didn't dare.

Charlotte had helped him find some of Owen's old clothes for each of them. The children laughed when they saw how silly they looked in the big clothing. But at least the clothes were clean and mended. Leon worried that their mother's ghost might interfere with his plans. Or Owen's ghost. He kept his eyes open for signs.

Johnny refused to leave his home, but he agreed to let Leon take the two small ones to the Swanns' house. His da' was too weary and grief-stricken to object.

When Leon arrived, flanked by the two bald children, Mrs. Swann was sitting in the parlor with Charlotte, Julia, and Carson. Mrs. Swann was waving a sandalwood fan the boys had presented to her after their arrival, a gift from China.

At the entrance to the parlor, the children balked. They had never been inside the Swanns' house.

For one long moment, Mrs. Swann and her daughters stared at them. Carson's face registered total disapproval.

Then Mrs. Swann opened her arms, and the two children rushed into her embrace. They climbed onto her lap, and she snuggled with them.

"You smell so good. Did you take a bath?" she asked them.

Polly burrowed her head in Mrs. Swann's armpit, as if to hide her baldness.

"Leon says we can live here with you, and he'll take care of us," said Paul.

A wave of shock passed over Mrs. Swann's face for a minute, and she looked up at Leon, still standing in the doorway. "I never said that!"

"I will take care of them until Johnny finishes school," said Leon. "Just three weeks. Can they stay here three weeks?"

Leon trembled at the size of this risk. Either his plan would work, or he would be in trouble again. Big trouble. Maybe the biggest yet. He had wanted to do the right thing. But this wasn't his house. This wasn't his mother or his sisters. He had overextended his generosity. But it was a Christian pastor's house, right?

Mrs. Swann looked skeptically at the wriggling pile of children in her lap.

"God took their mother," said Leon. He was on thin ice. What did he know about God?

Mrs. Swann's face softened. Clearly Leon had chosen the right words. "Only if I can make you new clothes. All right?" she said to Paul and Polly.

From that moment, Leon knew his plan would work. This time, he wouldn't get in trouble, at least with the Swanns. He wasn't sure about Elder Brother.

CHAPTER TWENTY-THREE

# Changes Underfoot

—◇·◇— ◈ —◇·◇—

"**I** want to sleep with Charlotte!" said Polly. She ran to Charlotte's chair and cuddled with her.

Paul looked around. "Leon! I sleep with Leon!" He snatched Leon's hand and danced around, making Leon twirl.

Carson's face darkened. "Not possible," he said in Chinese.

"Please! Please!" Paul hugged Leon around the waist.

"We'll see," said Leon.

At dinner, the children could not sit still. Mrs. Swann and Julia put them each in a chair and put their napkins on their laps, but Paul's napkin slid off when he jumped up and grabbed a piece of bread before the blessing. Mrs. Swann took the bread from him and held his hands together for the prayer. Mr. Swann wisely made it short.

"This may not be a good idea," Mr. Swann said when Polly started eating a chicken thigh with her hands. Leon felt guilty.

"It's just for a short time," said Mrs. Swann.

Carson barely touched his food and he frowned as he watched Paul and Polly gulp down their milk and eat raven-

☀ 149

ously. They squirmed out of their seats as soon as they were finished, not waiting for the others.

"Where are Johnny and Patrick?" Mr. Swann asked.

"I ask them, but they say no," Leon said. "They wanna eat at home."

Something crashed in the parlor. "I'll go," said Julia. "May I be excused?"

After dinner, Mr. Swann closed the door of his study, but Paul opened it and ran in anyway. Mr. Swann took him by the hand and escorted him out, saying, "This is my room. You are not allowed to come in here."

Paul ran to Leon. "Show me your room," he said. "Does everybody have a room?"

Leon took him upstairs. "This is my bed. That one belongs to my brother." Paul tried to climb on Carson's bed. "No—don't. He will get mad."

Then Paul clambered onto Leon's bed instead. He pulled down the blanket and crawled in. "Oooh, this is nice. So comfy."

By the time Carson came up, Paul was asleep in Leon's bed. "I don't want him in here," said Elder Brother. But it was too late.

Later, Leon edged into his bed and curled around the little boy. He hadn't slept with anyone since leaving home. It reminded him of his own childhood, when he and Carson used to huddle together at night.

But Paul wiggled and kicked so much that Leon could not get any sleep. The next day, Carson complained about the noise, so Julia insisted that the little boy sleep with her. She had a big bed, with more room.

The whole atmosphere changed at the Swanns' house. Mr. Swann spent even more time in his study, and Carson refused to enter the parlor when the kids were there, even to talk to Charlotte. The chaos and noise were too much for them.

But Mrs. Swann seemed to be in heaven. Before Paul

and Polly were living with them, she had spent all day visiting needy people. Now she seemed to believe that the neediest people were Paul and Polly, so she stayed at home instead. Leon wasn't sure what happened to all those other sick people Mrs. Swann used to visit. But it was great to watch the way she smiled. Instead of being drawn and weary, Mrs. Swann seemed energized by the presence of small children. She talked nonstop about Paul and Polly, their needs, the household, the Chinese boys, and the family. She was a woman who overflowed with words and caring, and finally she was redirecting that energy toward her own house.

"This is what Mother was like when Owen was alive," Miss Julia told Leon.

Mrs. Swann measured the two children and bought some bright-blue fabric to make two outfits for them: one for play and one for church. She and Charlotte sat for long hours in the parlor, sewing the little shirts, pants, and dresses. Polly often snuggled with Charlotte and decided it was her job to fetch whatever Charlotte needed. Polly even learned how to push Charlotte's wheelchair to the piano and back, and Charlotte taught her hymns and simple songs.

Leon noticed that Owen's ghost didn't toss any more dead birds or mice at him. Instead, Leon sensed it was smiling. He suspected that Owen's ghost had put the idea to care for Johnny's siblings in his head in the first place. Where else could it have come from?

During the morning lessons, Julia had to close the dining room door to keep the little ones out. Leon found their noise distracting at first. But when he thought of Johnny, who was finishing sixth grade but wouldn't get to go on to high school, Leon studied extra hard.

Carson recoiled when the children made noise or came close to him, and he seldom hit Leon anymore. Just as the rest of the household was coming to life with the warmer spring air, Carson retreated inside himself. At dinner, he ate very little, said almost nothing, and went to bed early. He slept long hours, grinding his teeth. Sometimes, in the afternoon, Carson would lie on his bed and stare at the ceiling. He stopped writing letters home.

During English lessons, he seemed listless and showed no interest in memorizing new poems. During their afternoon Chinese lessons, Carson didn't even correct Leon when he made mistakes.

"It doesn't matter," Carson said. "By the time we get home, we'll be old men."

For days, he would ignore Leon completely. When Leon asked him what was wrong, he grunted. But mainly, Leon was glad that his brother left him alone to do what he wanted.

One day, another letter arrived from Father, and Leon rushed upstairs to show it to Carson, who showed a little spark when he saw it. "Keep on studying hard," Father wrote. "I have started selling fireworks to some Englishmen. I don't understand how they think. When you come home you can help me negotiate with them."

"That's good!" said Leon. "He wants us to help him." He didn't really want to go back to the village to work with Father, but he wanted to cheer Carson up.

But Carson didn't take the bait. "He has plenty of help. We won't go home for ten years at least." His eyes seemed empty.

Leon decided he didn't care that Carson was sad. He welcomed the chance to get out of that stuffy room and play baseball. Sometimes he got a ride into town and spent the afternoon tossing the ball to Yew-Fun and his neighbor Frank. Johnny still had to work in the fields after school, but on Saturdays he came over for batting and pitching practice with Leon. Sometimes they tossed the ball to little Paul. When Johnny was playing baseball, he seemed to forget his sorrow about losing his mother.

One Sunday, at church, Mr. Swann announced to the congregation that he was donating money and time to build a new house for Johnny's family, and he encouraged others to pitch in. Within days, lumber began showing up, support beams and siding. One man in town designed a simple four-room house and directed a group of volunteers to erect it. Johnny and his father finished the planting in time to participate. Leon was surprised at how quickly the men built the structure. He helped whitewash both the outside and inside walls. The ruddy face of Johnny's father beamed with pride the day the house was finished.

Of course, Paul and Polly stayed with the Swanns while the house was being built and Johnny finished school. But even after the children moved into their new home, where they had their own beds for the first time, Mrs. Swann insisted that they visit her every morning.

Mr. Swann had a long talk with Johnny and encouraged him to take the test for entrance into seventh grade. If Johnny passed, Mrs. Swann promised she would care for the little ones while he was at school. She insisted it would be a pleasure. Johnny resisted, saying he wasn't good at book learning, but he agreed to try. That gladdened Leon's heart.

Finally, summer vacation arrived. Baseball season entered full swing, and every weekend the team played a game that counted. Johnny's father was too busy in the fields to drive them to town, but Johnny and Leon didn't mind walking in the good weather. Some days Johnny couldn't go, but Leon rushed to the baseball diamond every afternoon and practiced with the team for hours. After each game, the boys walked the long way home together, arriving hungry for dinner. Leon could hit the ball more often now, but he was nowhere near as good a player as Johnny or Yew-Fun.

❁ ❁ ❁

One morning, Leon woke up and saw Carson pacing their room. He seemed like a different person, bursting with energy. He was talking to himself in Chinese, so fast that Leon could not understand. It seemed like someone had pressed the Johnson bar, and the train was now running at full speed.

Leon watched him with growing alarm. Then he sat up. "What are you talking about?"

"It could work. Yes, it could work," said his brother, still pacing. "I'm sure she will say yes. Why wouldn't she? She knows how smart I am. And she can't walk. So I'd be in charge."

"What?" Leon stood up and blocked his brother's pacing. "Are you talking about Charlotte?"

Carson laughed, and his eyes looked wild. "Of course. I'm sure Father and Mother will like her. She is obedient and doesn't run around like typical American ladies. She doesn't bat her eyes at men like that older girl."

Leon's heart twisted. "Elder Brother," he said. "What are you saying?"

"I plan to take Charlotte as my wife."

The words passed through Leon like a lightning bolt. "Your wife?"

"She likes me." Carson was staring out the window, at the leafy trees.

"Elder Brother! I thought you disapproved of free-love marriages."

"It's different here in America. Even Mr. Yung Wing has an American wife."

"He's a grown man. You're only fifteen!" Could his brother be serious?

"In China, many people are betrothed at fifteen. Father is not here to arrange it, so I will talk to her father. He will be pleased."

"But we are here to study," Leon argued. He sat on the edge of Elder Brother's bed. "Someday we have to go back and modernize China."

"I won't marry her yet. I'll just get her father's approval. We can wait until I finish college." His eyes glowed strangely.

"You won't finish college for at least eight years! What if you change your mind?"

"I won't. I want her to be my wife. I can see she will be a good mother."

Leon could not believe his ears. *There's no way she will have you*, he thought. But instead he said, "She can't walk."

"In China, that won't matter. Our mother can't walk very well, either, on her bound feet. It means she will not run away like some American women."

"Elder Brother, this is wrong." Leon thought he knew Charlotte well enough to know she would not be happy to hear a proposal of marriage from Carson. Elder Brother never could read people's faces very well. Just because Charlotte smiled at him didn't mean she would want to marry him. Or would she? Leon wondered. What did he know of such things?

"No," Carson said in his firmest know-it-all voice. "This is right. I plan to speak to her father soon, to ask his permission."

"Are you crazy? Please, please don't do that!"

"Don't tell me what to do. I'm your elder brother."

Everyone in the Swann family would be appalled. At least Leon thought so. If Elder Brother actually went through with this terrible plan, he would ruin everything, just as their lives at the Swann house were starting to improve. Leon had to stop him. But how?

# CHAPTER TWENTY-FOUR

# Proposals

—◇·◆—◈—◆·◇—

Summer gushed out in a torrent. Bushes in front of the Swanns' house burst into blooms of red, white, and blue, as if mimicking the American flag. Corn in the nearby field, planted by Johnny and his father, grew taller daily. Fireflies brought magic to the evenings. Sweet-smelling grasses by the sides of the road swayed in gentle breezes. Leon could feel a surge of his semitropical childhood flowing into his veins.

In the warm weather, he didn't mind walking all the way to town, even on days when Johnny could not go with him. Every day, after lessons and lunch, he nearly ran to town to spend all afternoon playing baseball. Some days he barely made it home in time for dinner.

During his long walks alone, he worried about Elder Brother. One day, Leon left practice early and arrived home an hour before dinner. Mrs. Swann was in the rose garden with the children. Carson was in the parlor with Charlotte. He was wearing his best Chinese gown, pacing in front of her, nose in the air, reciting a Chinese poem she could not possibly understand. Leon stood by the door and watched.

Maybe Charlotte liked Carson. Maybe she would want to marry him. He couldn't see her face.

"You want to hear 'The Raven' again?" Carson asked her.

"No. But you did it perfectly last time."

"Yes. Perfectly. 'Rare and radiant maiden.'" It sounded like "lair and laden maiden." To Leon, Carson looked ridiculous, strutting around like that.

"Like you," Elder Brother continued. He put Charlotte's hand on his cheek. She swatted him away.

"Stop it, Carson. I told you I don't like that."

Leon dropped his cleated shoes in the hallway and strode into the parlor. "Hello," he said. "What's for dinner tonight?"

Carson scowled at him, but Charlotte smiled. "Oh, Leon! I'm glad you're home. Tell me about the baseball team. Is Johnny able to practice most days?"

Leon wondered if he should tell the Swanns about the way Carson was acting. But he decided it was up to Charlotte. Instead, later that evening after dinner, he talked to Carson.

"She doesn't like you," Leon said. "You should leave her alone."

"Of course she likes me. She always talks about visiting China."

"Elder Brother, it's a bad idea. Leave her alone."

Carson laughed. "I know what I'm doing." Leon hoped he did. Carson seemed full of grand ideas about himself.

❋ ❋ ❋

The next morning, Miss Julia had an announcement. "I found out more about the school entrance exams. They'll be on August 15, and you need to know a lot about American history and geography, as well as famous authors. So I'll be teaching you more about that."

"Good," said Carson, acting as if he were in charge. "You do that."

From then on, the lessons were full of even more unpronounceable names—of states, of presidents, of battles.

"There's not enough time to memorize all this!" Leon said to his brother. "It's basically everything that Americans learn in the first six years of school."

"Why are you worried?" said Elder Brother. "We Chinese have much better memories than Americans do. I'm sure we'll both pass our exams."

"But most Chinese boys don't pass on the first try."

Elder Brother made a gesture like he was swatting away a fly. "Maybe you won't, but I will. This is easy compared to the Chinese classics."

※ ※ ※

One day Miss Julia told them she had received a letter from the Chinese Educational Mission office. "They want every boy to write an essay," she explained. "The Connecticut State Department of Education will choose ten essays to display at the Centennial Exhibition."

"Good!" said Elder Brother, grinning confidently. "I will show them."

But Miss Julia furrowed her brow. "I'll help you, but it won't be easy. Don't forget most of the other boys have been here longer than you have. Only the best will be chosen."

"And some of the boys have teachers who are men," Carson said in Chinese.

"We can still try," said Leon in English. "Can I write about the railroads?"

Miss Julia smiled. "Of course."

"I pick a better idea," Carson said.

Later, alone in their room, Carson announced, "I know my topic. I'm going to teach the Americans about Confucian values, obeying the emperor and your father and your elder brother. How wives obey their husbands. How daughters accept the husbands chosen by their parents. It's the right way."

"I think you should write about U.S. naval ships," suggested Leon. "Didn't Teacher Kwong tell us the emperor wants to modernize China's navy?"

Carson hesitated. "Naval ships?" It seemed beyond his imagination. Then his face hardened. "There's nothing about naval ships I can teach the people of America. Besides, I can do all my research in Chinese. I don't have to rely on that woman."

Leon decided he didn't want to teach the people of America anything. He decided to focus his essay on the Transcontinental Railroad.

To prepare, Leon got out the book Mr. Swann had given him, and Julia helped him read parts of it. He wrote down new words as he learned them. He learned that the railroad, from California to Omaha, Nebraska, was the longest in the world, over thousands of miles of harsh deserts and steep mountains. Construction had begun in 1865, when Leon was a baby, and it was completed ahead of time, in 1869. Just four years! Imagine.

Thousands of workers, including many from China, built it. It was a dangerous job. The workers had to blast tunnels through mountains. Many of them died. Sometimes the snow would block the line for weeks, and avalanches would wipe out the tracks. China didn't even have railroads, yet these brave workers had built this for America. Leon drew pictures to go with his report. All the railroad workers had black queues.

Mr. Swann had more books on this topic, but they were thick and hard to read. So several nights, after dinner, Mr. Swann invited Leon into his study and talked about railroads, which was also one of Mr. Swann's favorite subjects.

"Here's a date for you to remember," Mr. Swann said, "1830—write it down. That was the year the first true railroad opened in the United States, the Baltimore and Ohio. That's also the year I was born."

Sometimes Mr. Swann wrote down facts for him, tidbits he remembered from reading the newspapers during those years. One day he even took Leon to the public library and helped him look up information. When talking about railroads, Mr. Swann seemed animated and happy.

❋ ❋ ❋

One day, Miss Julia offered to drive Leon and Johnny to baseball practice. Leon was surprised that she knew how, yet she seemed comfortable with the reins. At the school, she hitched the horses to a wooden post and stayed to watch the boys play.

At first Leon objected. "I don't want to take up your time. We can walk home."

But quickly Leon noticed what was attracting Julia's attention. Yew-Fun's American brother, Thomas, was home from college for the whole summer. Thomas had decided to coach the local baseball team, and Julia's eyes were always on him.

That afternoon was cloudy, not too hot, perfect for long hours on the baseball diamond.

"Today we'll focus on pitching," Thomas said. "A team has only one pitcher, but everybody should learn how to throw—fast and accurate. First, everybody get down on one knee."

Some of the boys grumbled that they already knew how to throw, but Leon was glad to have a chance to learn from scratch. He listened carefully as Thomas showed them how to hold the ball. "Not too close to your palm," he said.

Leon had tried this many times, but the grip still felt awkward. He couldn't control the direction of his throws. He hated being so obviously behind the rest of the team in learning this skill. Even Charlie, only nine years old, could throw the ball farther than Leon could. He hoped Miss Julia wouldn't notice how bad he was.

Thomas stood behind him and held the back of his hand to show him the right motion. "That's right," he told Leon after a few good pitches. "Practice more at home."

A few weeks later, Thomas taught them the best way to put a spin on the ball and various strategies to make the batter strike out. At home, Johnny also gave Leon tips. Pitching was Johnny's specialty, and Leon felt lucky to have his help. As July turned into August and the sun shone hotter, Leon's pitching skills got better, and Thomas noticed. Sometimes he even let Leon step in as a backup pitcher for an inning or two, if they were playing against a poor team.

Soon Suffield began winning more games.

Thomas seemed to love coaching baseball, but the college man always found time to wander over to the spot where Miss Julia was standing in the shade of a tree, holding a parasol to protect her skin from the sun.

Miss Julia seemed less stern, prettier. She wore her light-brown hair brushed back neatly on the sides. Her curls, normally held back with bows, cascaded down her back. She seemed to shine from within. Still, Leon couldn't get used to the idea that young ladies could flirt in public with men who interested them, and it made him uncomfortable to watch Thomas and Julia. Young ladies in China, if they came from good families, had to be concerned about their virtue. Whatever happened to Julia's idea that Thomas was too good for her? He guessed that Thomas had talked her out of that.

One afternoon, after the game was over, Thomas got into the carriage with Julia, Johnny, and Leon. Thomas took the reins and sat up front with Johnny, while Julia and Leon sat in the back. Occasionally, Thomas glanced back at them with a smile of pleasure.

"My parents invited Thomas to dinner," Julia explained, a blush lighting up her cheeks.

Once they arrived, Thomas jumped down from the carriage first and offered his hand to Julia to help her alight. But other than that, he never touched her. Even on the cheek.

Mrs. Swann greeted Thomas warmly, and Mr. Swann talked with him at dinner about college life. Leon could understand most of the conversation now, and he listened for details, trying to imagine his own future life as a college man. At Yale, Thomas studied engineering, which was not as hard or prestigious as the classics, Latin and Greek, but Thomas said it was more interesting and practical. That was what Leon wanted to study, too, and the Chinese government had encouraged them all to learn about America's newfangled machines. Thomas talked a lot about baseball and football. The more he heard, the more Leon longed to go to Yale, too.

After dinner, they all sat in the parlor, where the men each drank a glass of sweet grape wine called port. Then Thomas left. He insisted he would walk home, since it was a fine night. Julia went out the door with him to say good night.

American courting habits were odd to Leon. Later, alone in their room, Carson commented on them in disgust. "She's acting like a loose woman," he said.

"I heard Mrs. Swann say she thought Thomas would make a good match," said Leon.

"Then they should arrange the marriage."

"What will happen to us if Miss Julia gets married?" Leon asked.

Carson shook his head. "She will move to that other family's house, until Thomas finishes college."

But what it would mean for them, Carson couldn't say.

"Anyway," said Elder Brother, "it's appropriate that the older sister should marry first."

Leon shivered. He hoped that Carson was not still thinking about Charlotte. Lately, he had noticed that Charlotte seemed annoyed whenever Carson spoke. She glanced at him and then looked away, at other people or even out the window. The more she ignored him, the more Carson tried to talk to her. Carson would speak faster, perhaps in an effort to sound fluent, but sometimes even Leon could not understand his brother's English.

As he fell asleep, Leon found himself praying to God that his brother would give up his ridiculous idea about marrying Charlotte. She was too young. Besides, he just didn't think Carson, with his anger and moods, would make a very good husband for Charlotte.

※ ※ ※

One Saturday, after baseball practice, Thomas accompanied them to the house again. When Leon came downstairs, after changing out of his baseball clothes, he saw that the door to Mr. Swann's study was closed. Mrs. Swann, Julia, and Charlotte were sitting in the parlor. Mrs. Swann was talking nonstop about the weather and cooling herself with her Chinese sandalwood fan. A book of poetry was open in Julia's lap, but she didn't seem to be reading it; instead, she was twisting her hands. Charlotte was sitting forward in her chair, eyes bright, as if expecting a treat. Carson sat next to Charlotte and watched her every move.

"What's going on?" Leon asked.

Elder Brother answered in Chinese. "The young man is speaking to the father in private. I think he's arranging to marry our teacher."

"Where are his parents?" asked Leon.

"Not here. The man arranges it himself. Charlotte told me they've been expecting it. I wish I knew what words he is using. But they wouldn't let me in the room."

Leon felt jealous that his brother knew more than he did about the family.

When they heard the door to the study open, they all sat up straight.

"Julia," Mr. Swann asked, "will you please come here for a moment?"

Looking nervous, Julia nodded and rose from her chair. Mr. Swann shut the door of the study behind her.

Leon couldn't get used to the way American families—especially fathers—used the polite word *please* when talking to their own family members. Even to women!

A few moments later, Mr. Swann, Julia, and Thomas rejoined the group in the parlor. Julia's face was lit with a beautiful smile. Thomas was grinning, too.

"We have some happy news to share," Mr. Swann said. "Thomas has asked for Julia's hand, and I have agreed."

Mrs. Swann let out a loud, happy "Aah!" Charlotte clapped her hands in delight. Thomas strode over to each of them, took their hands, and spoke a few words.

Leon could see that Miss Julia was thrilled. Still, he worried about how this engagement would affect his own future.

"I have told them to wait at least a year," Mr. Swann reassured the boys. "Thomas needs to graduate from college, and Julia needs to finish preparing our young Chinese friends for their school entrance exams."

"After that?" Leon blurted out.

Mr. Swann regarded him seriously. "After that, we shall see. I shall make sure you continue to have the best tutoring and guidance."

Leon hoped Mr. Swann would tutor them himself, yet that seemed unlikely. Mr. Swann was always so busy with his ministry.

"No worry," Carson said. "My brother and I, we pass exam this year. No need tutor."

Leon squirmed at his brother's poor English.

Mrs. Swann asked the maid to get everyone a glass of wine to celebrate the big news about Julia and Thomas. The whole parlor glowed with joy.

When the wine came, Carson took a glass for himself. Then he stood up, in front of the fireplace. Everyone stopped talking and looked at Elder Brother. "Very good for

Miss Julia," he said, holding up his glass. "Also, very good for Miss Charlotte."

Leon wished he could shout, "Elder Brother, stop it! Sit down!" but he didn't dare. He just hoped Carson would have the good sense not to ruin this happy moment.

But Carson's eyes glittered with determination. "Mr. Swann, I ask for hand of you daughter Charlotte. She marry me."

The joy turned to shocked silence.

Charlotte's eyes grew wide, and her face turned to stone. "Carson! What are you saying?"

"Good news for you," Elder Brother continued, smiling at her. "You say you want go China. Someday we go live there. You like it!"

Her face crumpled in misery. "No! No! Papa! Mama!"

Mrs. Swann looked horrified. "How dare he? The effrontery!" Her words were quiet, and Leon could barely hear them. He had never heard the word effrontery, but he got the message.

"Carson," Mr. Swann's voice sounded angry, "come with me into my study."

His face a mix of triumph and resolve, Elder Brother followed him,

After a split second of hesitation, Leon jumped up and followed, too. He couldn't stand the thought of staying in the parlor with the horrified women.

In the study, Mr. Swann gestured for Carson to sit down. Leon hovered behind Elder Brother's chair. His heart was thumping.

"Carson," Mr. Swann began. "You are only fifteen, too young to think about marriage."

"Oh, no," said Elder Brother. "In China, many man take wife at fifteen. We marry later, after I finish college."

Leon wished Carson would go back to his rigid quiet ways. What had gotten into him?

"Carson," Mr. Swann said firmly. "Charlotte is only fourteen. In this country, that is too young to arrange a marriage. I will not permit it."

Elder Brother smiled confidently. "Miss Charlotte. She like me. She wait for me."

Mr. Swann shook his head. "Charlotte likes everyone. From now on, you are not to spend time alone with her. Ever. If you try to see her alone, I will send you boys to another home. And I will report this to Mr. Yung."

Leon was furious with Elder Brother. Why hadn't he listened? How had he missed the obvious hints that Charlotte didn't return his affections? Leon and Carson had a nice home here, and the whole household had brightened lately, especially today. Now his brother had punctured the happiness. Why would Carson break the strict rule of not getting involved with American women?

Carson frowned. "No?" he asked, as if barely registering that Mr. Swann had turned him down. "You say no? My father has much money. Very rich man."

Leon flinched. That would never change Mr. Swann's mind!

"No." Now Mr. Swann's voice was firm, like a Chinese father's. "We will never mention this again. And there is to be no discussion of it outside this house."

That night at dinner, the mood should have been festive to celebrate Thomas and Julia's engagement, but the conversation was strained. Carson returned to his usual state of silence. Leon could sense his brother's slow burn. He felt certain Elder Brother would take out his humiliation on him. He braced his stomach for more punches.

# CHAPTER TWENTY-FIVE

# Summer Heat, Dark Clouds

—◇·◇—◆—◇·◇—

*W*hen the boys returned to their room after dinner, Carson's fuse exploded.

"Who do they think they are?" Elder Brother said in Chinese as Leon washed his face. "They own only two small fields. Our family owns much more land, with dozens of men working for us. They have only one hired hand on the farm, with his son."

Leon nodded, afraid to speak up.

"This man Swann!" Elder Brother continued. "He does no productive work. He just gives lectures once a week. All he can read is his *Bible*. Yet he thinks he is better than our father!"

"Elder Brother," Leon dared to interrupt. "It's not about our father. It's because we are Chinese."

"Chinese are better than Americans. Everybody knows that. We have three thousand years of history. They have only one hundred. We invented written language when their ancestors were living in caves."

Leon was glad Carson's English wasn't good enough to say such things to Americans. "They're good people, these Swanns."

"Good people!" Carson's face was red with anger. "Are you defending them?"

Leon's stomach tensed, but he went ahead anyway. "They took us into their home and treat us like family. They feed us and teach us."

Carson clenched his fists and came close to Leon. "Our government pays them to do this! Don't you remember all the gold we brought over? Why are you talking back to your elder brother? You are forgetting your Confucian values."

"My apologies," Leon mumbled, slipping into bed. Elder Brother was the one forgetting his values, forgetting the importance of obeying the rules set down by the Imperial Government for all the boys. But it was dangerous to argue with Carson when he was angry. And Leon had never seen him angrier.

Carson's fist slammed against the bedstead. "These Americans have no culture at all. They're stupid. Melon-headed ignoramuses." The wooden footboard shook with each blow.

Leon was glad it was not his stomach. But he was tired of his brother's outrageous behavior. Carson had gone too far this time, asking to marry Charlotte. He was the stupid one.

Carson extinguished the lamp and got into bed, too. "I don't want an American wife anyway," he raved. "Those revealing dresses they wear, showing off their bodies. Their eyes are such a weird, light color that they look empty. And American men—they all look alike, with their stupid beards and mustaches. It's almost impossible to tell them apart. And they talk too fast. They try to make it hard for us. A pox on all of them!"

Leon rolled over so that his back was to his brother. He tried to pretend he was asleep.

Elder Brother kept going. "And their religion! Unbelievably arrogant. They say only they will go to heaven and everyone else will go to hell. All the millions of people in China!"

Leon was surprised his brother had understood the sermons. Usually, Carson closed his eyes during church, and Leon had assumed he didn't catch any of the message.

"Ridiculous!" Carson continued. "So many good people in China. And all of them will go to hell because they don't believe in the Christian God?"

Eventually, Leon shut his ears to the ranting and fell asleep.

❉ ❉ ❉

The next morning, Leon could tell that Carson had barely slept. For the first time, Elder Brother refused to go down to breakfast. "Tell them I'm sick," he said.

Leon went to breakfast alone. The Swanns seemed relieved that Carson was not at the table, but the mood was still tense.

"You marry next summer?" Leon asked Julia.

She smiled at him. "I hope so. Thomas needs to talk to his parents about the details."

Leon noticed that her smile had a slight droop.

Carson did not come down for English lessons that day, so Miss Julia taught Leon alone. They spent extra time on his essay. He showed her the pictures in the book her father had given him, and she taught him more specialized words: *injector*, *hopper*, *conveyor*, and *spike*. She looked out the window, her hand to her throat, as he practiced writing each of these words ten times.

"What's this, in between cars?" he asked, pointing to a picture. Something metal was holding the cars together.

"That's called a *coupling*," Julia said. "Couple means two together. That piece joins two cars together." She blushed when she said this, for no reason Leon could fathom. Then she wrote it for him and helped him say it correctly. Clearly, her mind was elsewhere.

Carson did come to the table for lunch, but he said nothing as he ate. He stabbed his meat with his fork as if it were still alive and he wanted to kill it. He refused to look at Mrs. Swann or Julia or Charlotte. After lunch, he went back up to his bedroom, presumably to work on his Chinese. This time, Leon did not follow him. He was tired of working on his Chinese.

An hour later, Johnny showed up at the front door with the two little ones in tow. Paul and Polly ran over to Mrs. Swann, who hugged them and seemed to welcome the joyful distraction. Then Miss Julia drove Leon and Johnny into town for baseball practice.

The boys on the team greeted Miss Julia with applause and cheers. Thomas had told them that he had asked for her hand. Julia and Thomas beamed at each other, and Leon was glad they could enjoy their happiness without the shadow of Elder Brother's improper proposal. None of the boys knew about it, and Leon wasn't about to tell them.

❂ ❂ ❂

At dinner that night, Mr. Swann barely looked at Carson or Leon. He ate in silence, while Mrs. Swann chattered on about the children. Carson, too, was tense and did not look at Mr. Swann. Even Charlotte dropped her cheerful manner. She had no dimples when she didn't smile.

After dinner, Carson continued his rant while he and Leon were in their room getting ready for bed.

"That girl is no good. I think she already has a boyfriend."

Where did his brother get such ideas?

Then, before Leon could respond, Carson attacked him.

"Why do you insist on playing baseball?" Elder Brother demanded. "It takes away from your studies. Have you forgotten our mission, the reason the emperor sent us here? Not to learn some stupid game."

There was no point in defending himself, so Leon said nothing, but he listened closely. If Elder Brother explicitly said he could no longer play baseball, that would put him in an awkward spot. Fortunately, Carson did not say that. Yet. But his brother was acting so strangely these days. Leon sensed that the consequences for disobeying him would be higher now.

❋   ❋   ❋

The next day, Carson resumed his English lessons. Miss Julia was distant and cold, but Leon was relieved to see that Elder Brother wanted to keep studying hard to pass his school entrance exam. But Carson did not spend the afternoons in the parlor with Charlotte anymore. And each night, after dinner, he raged to Leon in Chinese, changing his opinion about Charlotte.

"American women have no morals! I hate how American men let their women run around on big feet and openly talk to men in public. Charlotte is different. She stays at home. She's the only decent woman in America. She wants to marry me, but her parents won't let her."

Leon could see that Carson was not just embarrassed and depressed but unhinged.

"I hate these people, these Swanns, these Americans," Carson said one night. "I hope they all go to hell! I'll never last fifteen years in this country. I'm going to go home."

Leon wished he could make things better. But he couldn't think of anything to do that would ease the tension Elder Brother felt—or smooth over the situation with the Swanns. He wished he could toss out a rope and pull his brother back to safety. But how?

❋   ❋   ❋

Finally, August 15 arrived. Miss Julia drove Leon and Carson to the schoolhouse in town so they could take the entrance exam. Johnny was not with them; his father refused to let him take the test. Johnny was a full-time farm worker now. Johnny didn't seem to mind.

Leon took the exam to get into seventh grade, and Carson went into another room to take a harder test to get into high school. Leon felt good after taking the written exam. Julia had prepared him well. After the written exam, a local teacher gave him an oral exam, asking him questions about grammar and geography. That went even more smoothly, although Leon badly mispronounced *punctuation* and *Gettysburg*. But the teacher smiled when Leon recited, in order, all the states the Transcontinental Railroad passed through. By the end, the teacher was nodding and smiling at Leon's answers. He said he was impressed.

But Carson seemed upset after the written exam. Leon and Julia waited on a bench when Elder Brother went in for his oral exam. When he emerged, his face was hard.

In the carriage, on the way home, Carson complained in Chinese to Leon. "That teacher! He spoke too fast. He has a different accent than Miss Julia, don't you think? I had to keep asking him to repeat. Didn't you think he spoke too fast?"

Leon nodded. But he hadn't thought so. "What about the written test?"

Carson looked out the carriage window. "It was easy. I'm sure I passed. I've decided to leave Suffield and attend high school in Hartford. It's a much better school. I can stay at the mission headquarters. I can't wait to get out of this small town with all its stupid people."

But his voice was flat. Leon sensed that Carson didn't think he had done well on the examination at all. Leon wished they didn't have to wait two whole weeks for the results. That seemed like forever.

# CHAPTER TWENTY-SIX

# The Centennial Exhibition

*A*ugust 21–25, 1876. Those were the dates Leon had memorized months in advance: the days when he would be in Philadelphia, with all the other Chinese students, attending the Centennial Exhibition. To him, it seemed like the culmination of his entire life.

In Suffield, everyone was talking about the Centennial. The world's fair sounded amazing. Frank had gone with his family the first week it opened, in May.

"You wouldn't believe . . . ," Frank told Leon and Yew-Fun, "sixty thousand exhibits! We saw only about a hundred. Maybe a thousand. And more than two hundred and fifty buildings! We spent most of our time in Machinery Hall. You would love it, Leon. Huge machines, loud noises."

"Look at this!" Mr. Swann said one night after dinner. "In the paper it says they expect ten million visitors to attend the fair over the next six months. That's 20 percent of the entire population of the country. Twenty-six states and eleven foreign nations have set up exhibits. Even China!"

Leon couldn't wait. After he returned from the exhibition, Leon knew, it would be time to get ready for the baseball play-offs, which had been delayed until September 2. But Leon stopped thinking about baseball. He stopped worrying about his exam results. He stopped thinking about the way Charlotte shrank back when Carson walked into the room. All he could think about was the excitement of going to Philadelphia for the huge event. He hoped his brother would return to normal once he was surrounded by Chinese boys.

Finally, the day arrived for their departure. Leon, Carson, and Yew-Fun took the local train the short distance to Hartford. There, for the first time, all of the boys of the Chinese Educational Mission gathered in one place. From scattered communities across Connecticut and Massachusetts, there were 113 boys—not the original one hundred and twenty. A few of the boys had died or been sent back to China. The Hartford headquarters building was nowhere near big enough to house them all. They had to stay one night in a hotel before leaving.

Several chaperones escorted the students, including the stern Teacher Chiu and the kinder Teacher Kwong, both bilingual, as well as several prominent Americans, including Connecticut's secretary of education, Mr. B. G. Northrop.

Among the chaperones were Miss Julia Swann and Mr. Thomas Travis, each of them assigned to supervise ten students. It was the first time Miss Julia had left New England, and even Thomas had not ventured farther than New York City. Leon had never seen Julia so lively, and he hoped Thomas could explain to him many of the mechanical inventions at the exhibition. Leon wanted not just to see those machines but to learn how they worked.

From Hartford, the boys traveled as a group by a chartered excursion train. Leon had never had so much fun in his life. Almost every passenger on the train was Chinese, chattering constantly in his familiar dialect. Leon pulled away from Elder Brother and looked for a brakeman or coalman to explain more about the marvelous workings of the Iron Horse. With better English now and a bigger vocabulary, he could ask detailed questions and understand the answers. But the fireman he found was busy shoveling coal and refused to take time to talk. Besides, Elder Brother came hunting for him and forced him to return to his seat.

"Behave yourself," Elder Brother hissed. "Don't ruin the trip for the rest of us."

Far bolder than Leon, Yew-Fun went off looking for the Connecticut secretary of education, to ask which students had been honored by having their essays on display at the state exhibit in Philadelphia. But he returned with no news. Mr. Northrop refused to reveal the names, only to say the state had chosen the work of ten Chinese students and displayed them with pride.

As the train pulled into Philadelphia, Leon could see it was a gigantic city. "Thomas told me it is twenty times bigger than Hartford," Miss Julia said. "Eight hundred thousand people." Instead of separate houses, Philadelphia had street after street of row houses, which were block-long buildings of three or four stories, divided into narrow, tall units, each with its own door to the street. On these hot summer days, people lounged about on the front steps.

When they started walking to their hotel, Leon held his nose against the terrible stench of horse manure in the cobblestone streets. Pedestrians, horse carts, mules, and wagons crowded the thoroughfares, including vendors shouting out the wares they were selling. It reminded him of Shanghai. Amid the strangers and the chaos, Leon felt small and unsafe, so he clung to his brother.

Fortunately, their hotel was just a short walk from the train station—and directly across from the entrance to the exhibition at Fairmount Park. The first thing Leon noticed about the Atlas Hotel was a large flag that hung over the main entrance. It was the dragon flag of China's Ching Empire! Their group had booked thirty-five rooms, on two long hallways. As the boys walked into the hotel lobby, a group of musicians began playing to welcome them. That night, and most other nights, they ate their meals at the nearby American Restaurant. It, too, flew the Chinese flag. Leon felt like an honored guest, part of a historic delegation.

When Leon got to his room, which he shared with his brother and two other boys, he found on his bed a custom-fitted outfit, with long trousers, a loose jacket, and thick cloth shoes. Every boy had one. Teacher Kwong explained that each time they visited the exhibition, the students were required to dress alike, in this special Chinese clothing made for the occasion. They were not to tuck their queues inside their shirts but to wear them outside, hanging down their backs, to show their pride in their native country. But instead of a skullcap, each boy had to wear a boater, a funny round straw hat with a rim and a maroon ribbon tied around it. This was the one item of American clothing included in the outfit.

"Who decided we had to wear this kind of hat?" Tik-Chang asked.

"No way I'm wearing this stupid thing," Carson grumbled. But they didn't have a choice.

That night in the hotel room, Leon could see the lights of the exhibition from his window and hear shouting and laughter from the street below. Everything he had learned about the Centennial kept racing through his mind. The next morning, the boys rose early and dressed in their dignified exhibition outfits. Leon thought the boater hat felt very strange. How would he keep it from blowing off?

After breakfast, as the Chinese boys left the hotel, the band struck up again. They walked across the street in two straight lines, in groups of ten, in good discipline. Each boy carried a notebook and pen. Their assignment was to take notes on everything they saw at the fair, so they could write an essay when they returned to New England.

While they were waiting to enter the exhibition, some American men and boys crowded around them.

"Where you come from?" asked one dark-haired boy.

"China," said an older boy.

"Chinamen! Chinamen!" Some smaller boys took up chanting.

"Look at their hair! Are they girls?"

"Hey, China boy. Are you a girl?" One young man sounded like he was picking a fight.

"Piggy, piggy pigtails!" shouted another.

"Everyone stay calm!" Teacher Chiu came over and stood with his back to the American hecklers. "Hold your heads high. Ignore them. We are scholars. Don't forget."

But it was hard, listening to those ugly words and seeing those leering faces. Didn't these boys have anything better to do, at this early-morning hour? Some were grown men, who should have known better. Leon stayed close to Carson, who was muttering Chinese curses.

"Hey, pigtails!" shouted one American boy who was standing near them. "You Chinee speakee Eng-a-lish?" The boy had a young face but was broad shouldered and rough-looking, twice as big as Leon.

Leon looked at Yew-Fun, normally good-natured, who had set his mouth in a firm line.

Suddenly, Carson lunged straight at the rough-looking boy. He grabbed his neck and started shaking him. Two other American boys began punching Carson.

Leon's breath caught in his throat. He wanted to jump in, but those boys were so big.

Fortunately, Thomas was walking just behind them. He stepped into the fray and grabbed Carson and the American boy by their collars. "Stop it! Now!" he shouted. Tall and muscled, Thomas commanded respect. The other American boys melted away. "Watch your manners!" he yelled at them. "Back in line!" he shouted at Carson, who rejoined Leon.

"Turtle's eggs," Elder Brother muttered, rubbing his arm.

A bad feeling washed over Leon. Elder Brother was totally transformed since their arrival in America the previous winter, when he had criticized Leon for lunging at an insulting boy. What else might his brother do to ruin the visit to Philadelphia?

Once inside the exhibition grounds, they went straight to the Chinese exhibit, in the fair's main building. Leon wanted to go directly to the Connecticut exhibit, to see which essays were displayed, but the chaperones decided they should wait for that.

The entrance to the Chinese exhibit was an ornate gate, like the entryway to a Chinese temple. Above the gate, in Chinese calligraphy, were the words "Great Ching Empire." Inside were displays of precious porcelain vases, rare ivory carvings, and decorative silk screens. A year ago, Leon would have been impressed, but now he found them boring. They made China look fabulously wealthy but not modern at all.

Staffing the exhibit were Chinese men dressed in traditional clothing, the long gown and short jacket with knotted buttons up the center. When Elder Brother saw these men, he eagerly began talking to them. In fact, a crowd of students gathered around each of them. Some of the men spoke Leon's southern Chinese dialect, and they were happy to answer the boys' questions about the latest news from China. The men also asked them about their experiences in America. What kind of homes did they live in? Did they find English difficult? Did they miss their families? One of the men reminded Leon of his uncle. It felt good to have a connection to home.

The rest of the day, the boys toured other exhibits in the main building. It was, Leon learned, the largest building in the world, although only temporary. Towers stood at the four corners, and tall glass windows let in light. A broad avenue ran down the center, with displays on each side. The German exhibit showed modern machine guns, which fascinated Leon. Mexico displayed a four-thousand-pound block of silver. The boys gathered around it, trying to guess its value.

The British display showed something called a bicycle, with a huge front wheel and a small back wheel. A man sat on a seat about six feet off the ground and rode the contraption around in circles, making it move by using his feet to push pedals. It looked like it would tip over any minute.

"So dangerous!" Miss Julia said. "Imagine if he fell!"

"That will never work on dirt roads or cobblestone streets," commented Thomas. "It's just a toy for the rich."

But Leon wished he could learn to ride on one. It looked like fun!

Outside the main building, a narrow-gauge railroad took visitors from one part of the park to another. There was also a train that ran on just one rail, called a monorail, which linked the halls of horticulture and agriculture. Leon wished their group could stop rushing long enough for him to examine how these two railways differed. But they were nothing compared to the glory of the Transcontinental.

That night, back at the hotel, Teacher Chiu took Carson aside and gave him a lecture about his aggressive behavior. "Be careful. I'll be watching you." he said. Afterward, Elder Brother complained of a headache and refused to go to the restaurant for dinner. Leon brought back some rice, which his brother devoured hungrily.

Something was wrong with Carson, and other people were starting to notice.

# CHAPTER TWENTY-SEVEN

# Over the Edge

———◇·◇——◇——◇·◇———

*O*n the second day, the boys got to visit the most popular attraction, Machinery Hall. The huge building stretched over fourteen acres, with nineteen hundred exhibitors.

Right at its heart was a gigantic steam engine, called the Corliss Centennial. Its clattering and clanking were so loud, Leon couldn't hear anyone's voices when he stood near it. It seemed two or three times as big as a rail locomotive, and several men were continually shoveling coal into it. Miss Julia put her hands over her ears.

Leon stood in front of it in awe. He could recite many facts about this Corliss steam engine, although no one would have heard his voice in its shadow. It produced the power of fourteen hundred horses! Its fifty-six-ton flywheel could spin at thirty-six revolutions per minute! It provided enough power to run nearly all the other machines in the huge building.

Other exhibits in Machinery Hall amazed Leon, too, and he took lots of notes. Otis Brothers demonstrated a hoisting device that could lift heavy loads straight up. In the

Hydraulic Annex, a gigantic system of water pumps provided power to a motor that could run machines. A newly invented compressor could keep things cold inside a box, like a mechanized icebox. Leon saw a mechanical printing press. An electromagnetic generator. A machine that could be used to type English words on paper.

At another display, they saw something even more astounding: a telephonic receiver that could transmit voices from far away! How was this possible? Imagine being able to stand in America and talk to his father in China! He had not heard his father's voice in over a year. Tears popped into his eyes at the thought, but he wiped them away before anyone saw.

Leon couldn't find words, in English or Chinese, to describe the way he felt, standing along the rope line, staring up at these huge machines. They were made of metal and moving parts, not alive, yet he loved them. They could transform lives, bring people together, mass produce things people needed every day. He wished he could jump the rope and touch them, feel the heat and vibration, turn them on and off, open them up and examine how the moving parts worked together. Math problems on paper left him cold, but the idea of understanding and perhaps inventing machines— that was a dream life!

China needed these machines, not porcelain vases and ivory carvings. And he was one of the lucky ones, one of the chosen few, who would have a chance to learn about American machines and take them back home to China. If he could keep out of trouble, study hard, and pass his exams, he could unlock the magic behind this machinery.

The future belonged to America. That seemed to be the theme of the whole exhibition. But Leon could imagine past that. Someday, China would wake up from its slumber. Someday, China would be a modern nation with railroads and machines. With all its learning and brilliant minds,

China could embrace technology, too. And Leon would be part of that great enterprise.

"Stop that! Don't touch me!"

A woman's voice broke Leon's reverie. Some American men were shouting, too, over at another exhibit.

"Ka-Leong! It's your elder brother!" Yew-Fun said urgently, pulling Leon by the elbow.

They ran across the aisle to where the commotion was. It was at an exhibit showing machines that sewed clothing, the one invention that Miss Julia had wished to see. Four pretty young American women were demonstrating how the machines worked.

Several of the older Chinese boys were clustered there, and Leon guessed that it was the girls, not the machines, that had attracted them.

"He pinched my arm!" One of the young women was pointing into the crowd of Chinese onlookers.

Leon's heart squeezed tight as he saw the accused. His brother was standing in front of the others, defiantly leering at the young woman, who was wearing a dress that accented her large bosom and small waist.

This time it was Miss Julia who intervened. She talked to the girl, trying to calm her down, saying "I'm so sorry. Please forgive him. I'll talk to him. He didn't realize . . ."

But Carson's face showed that he did realize it was wrong to pinch the American girl, and he took delight in it. Leon knew exactly what his brother was thinking—that the girl had no business wearing tight clothing like that in public, talking to strange men. She had asked for it. A few of the other Chinese boys were laughing, but others seemed embarrassed.

Miss Julia took Carson firmly by the arm and led him away, lecturing him. Leon knew he should stand by his brother, but he chose not to. How humiliating. Their instructors and chaperones had given them many guidelines about proper behavior at the exhibition. No one had ever said, "Don't pinch the American girls." But it should have been obvious. What had made Carson even think of that? And why was he openly flouting the rules?

Carson never got into trouble. That was what Leon did. But things were changing, and Leon did not like these changes. Not at all.

❋ ❋ ❋

That evening, back at the hotel, Thomas took Carson aside and gave him a tongue-lashing. From across the large room, Leon could hear the severe tone but not the exact words. Carson refused to answer any of Thomas's questions. He just stared at the ceiling. When Carson came back to the group, he wouldn't look at Leon, and the other boys stayed away from him.

When the group had gathered in the dining room for their evening meal, Commissioner Ngeu stood up.

"Silence!" Teacher Chiu said.

Commissioner Ngeu cleared his throat. "I have very good news. Tomorrow afternoon, we will have an unexpected opportunity. We will get to meet the president!"

The boy's voices burst out in a flurry of excitement.

The president of the United States of America, Ulysses S. Grant, was visiting the Centennial Exhibition. The next afternoon, he would hold a reception in the Judges' Hall. He had invited all the students of the Chinese Educational Mission to meet him there!

Leon could scarcely believe it. He would see the president! Maybe even shake his hand. President Grant, Leon knew, was the general who had won the War Between the States, keeping the country together. He was the greatest man in America.

Carson, sitting next to Leon at the table, had no reaction. Leon decided that during the meeting with the president, he would stand next to Carson, near the door, and be ready to grab him if anything went wrong.

The chaperones went into a tizzy. That evening, they inspected the outfit of every student and cleaned all the spots off. The boys had to look like proper Chinese scholars, representing the dignity of the Great Ching Empire.

The thrill of the announcement drowned out the shock of Carson's behavior. But Leon did not forget. Anxiety created a knot in his stomach, and he watched his brother closely in the next bed until Carson drifted off to sleep.

The following day, before the big event, the boys finally visited the Connecticut state exhibit. It was extra large because the former governor of Connecticut, Joseph Hawley, was the president of the U.S. Centennial Commission. Mr. Northrop greeted them as they arrived, and he immediately showed the boys where their work was displayed. A big sign announced that this was the work of Chinese students educated in Connecticut. There were written exercises, essays, and exam papers, as well as maps drawn by the students and small sketches.

"Ka-Leong! Look!" Yew-Fun sounded thrilled.

There, pasted on the wall, was Leon's essay about the Transcontinental Railroad. His breath caught in his throat, and his heart pumped like a steam engine. He had submitted a map of the United States showing the route of the railway and a sketch of a steam engine locomotive. Leon had worked long and hard on that map and sketch, and he grinned with delight when he heard the other boys compliment him on it— especially the older boys, who had been in the United States for four years already. Two of them had already been accepted into college. His essay was short and simple compared to the other essays, but under it was posted a sign: "Woo Ka-Leong arrived in the United States less than nine months ago."

Tik-Chang and Yew-Fun gathered around him and slapped him on the back.

"*Kung hei, kung hei,*" they said, congratulating him in his dialect.

Leon looked for Elder Brother, who was examining all the essays on the wall, but his was not among the ones displayed. Like Leon, Carson had worked hard on his essay, writing it in Chinese first and then translating it, using big words and long sentences. But he had not created a sketch or map, and Leon suspected that other boys could write better long essays.

Elder Brother did not congratulate Leon. He stared for a long time at the long essays that were chosen, as if trying to figure out why they had won. Then he walked away and pretended to look at a nearby exhibit. Leon could tell by the rigid look on his brother's face that he was upset. But there was something different about Carson, beyond disappointment. His whole body seemed tense, like a coiled spring. Still, Leon was tired of worrying about him. He wanted to talk about his own small victory.

"That locomotive you drew is almost perfect. What books did you use?" one of the older Chinese boys asked Leon. His name was Jeme Tien Yow, known by his American nickname, Jimmy. Leon had heard that he was one of the smartest students.

Thrilled, Leon told the older boy about his American father and the books and the library, how he had found a picture to copy. Several other boys crowded around, listening to their conversation. Leon's heart swelled. Jimmy had seen that book and knew of several others. Clearly, he knew a lot more about trains than Leon did. Leon used his notebook to jot down the name of two books the older boy recommended.

Suddenly, Teacher Chiu's voice interrupted: "Woo Ka-Leong! Where's your brother?"

Elder Brother had disappeared.

# CHAPTER TWENTY-EIGHT

# More Consequences

—◇·◇——◇——◇·◇—

*W*ith more than one hundred students, even their chaperones could not always keep track of all the boys at every moment. Although Teacher Chiu had said he'd be watching, it was Miss Julia who had realized that Elder Brother was missing. She told Thomas, who told Teacher Chiu, who was furious.

Leon stood still as a rock in a stream as others flowed about him. He scanned the crowd, expecting to spot Carson's familiar face, but all he could see were straw boater hats, maroon ribbons, and neat black queues. Being short has its disadvantages.

"Elder Brother!" he shouted in Chinese, wishing his familiar voice might draw Carson back. But he had a sinking feeling in his chest.

He watched as Thomas and Teacher Chiu rushed off to look for Carson. The other chaperones gathered up the rest of the students and made them stand together in a less crowded part of exhibition hall. Miss Julia stood behind Leon, with her hands on his shoulders, as if he might disappear, too. Or maybe she was trying to keep him from falling over.

"What got into him?" Jimmy asked Leon. "Is your brother always like this?"

Leon looked at the floor. He was embarrassed and worried at the same time. No, his brother was not always like this. It seemed as though a gear had slipped in Elder Brother's brain, sending him careening off into dangerous territory.

*Elder Brother, come back*, Leon said inside his mind, trying to project his thoughts out into the busy hall. *Everything will be all right. Just come back. I'll be good.* His hands were shaking. Miss Julia crossed her hands over his chest and pulled him closer.

After a long wait, Thomas returned, his brows just as tense as before. "We haven't found him," he said to Miss Julia and the other chaperones. "Look. It's almost time for the big visit. Teacher Chiu and I will stay here and keep looking around this area. You all go ahead."

They could not be late for the grand reception with President Grant. In two straight lines, they filed out into the Judges' Hall. Lined up by height, Leon walked next to Tik-Chang, but his mind was with Elder Brother, wherever he was. Was this deep shame the way Elder Brother felt, all those times when Leon misbehaved as a little boy?

At Judges' Hall, the teachers arranged them in four rows. Tik-Chang and Leon were in the front, with the shortest boys. Commissioner Ngeu stood in front of them. "Stand straight!" the commissioner barked, and they did. Leon didn't think he could stand so straight and still for so long. He glanced nervously at the door, certain that Elder Brother would burst in, shouting strange things in poor English.

"Did you hear?" Leon could hear Jimmy say from two rows back. "President Grant is the one who turned on the Corliss engine on opening day!"

"Silence!" said Commissioner Ngeu.

Several other groups of people came into the room and stood at attention in similar clumps. Most of them seemed to be European, but one group had similar features to their own—dark hair and small noses, but with no queues. Leon wondered if they were Japanese.

Finally, after what seemed like an hour, another door opened and several American men in military uniforms marched in. They formed two rows, facing each other. A small band began a martial tune. Then a stout man strode into the hall, between the soldiers, who saluted as he passed. The man had a high forehead, craggy eyebrows, and a graying, well-trimmed beard. He wore a shiny black suit over a stiff, white shirt, with a black bowtie.

So this was the president of the United States! If the soldiers had not saluted him, Leon would never have known. He looked like an ordinary man, not dressed in yellow robes like the emperor. Still, he had an air of authority as he stood on a podium.

"Ladies and gentlemen," the president began, "it is an honor and a privilege to welcome you to the United States of America. Although our country is much younger than most of your countries . . ." The president said quite a few words, but Leon could understand only about half of them. Apparently all the other people in the hall were foreigners, too. Most were adults.

Finally, the president stepped off his podium and came toward their group first. He shook hands with Commissioner Ngeu, who said a few words to him in well-rehearsed English. President Grant smiled and nodded at the boys. Then he went to one end of their group and extended his hand. The boy at the beginning of the line looked confused but stuck his hand out, too. The president shook it, said something, and quickly moved to the second boy. Leon's hands were sweating. The emperor of China, the Son of Heaven, would never deign to greet ordinary people as equals, especially from another country. Elder Brother would have said the behavior was undignified. But Leon admired it.

When it was his turn, Leon put out his small hand, and President Grant grasped it and shook it, looking straight into his eyes and saying "Welcome." A wave of warmth washed over Leon. It was a moment to remember for a lifetime.

It wasn't until the president had reached the end of their group that Leon thought again about Elder Brother. He glanced nervously at the door, but Carson did not appear.

Neither did Thomas. As eager as Leon had been to meet such a powerful and famous man, a new surge of anxiety tightened his chest.

Where was Carson? Maybe he had been kidnapped. But probably not. Everyone knew his brother acted strangely. No one doubted Carson had run away.

After all the thrills of the Centennial Exhibit, after the ultimate honor of meeting the president of the United States of America, the boys left the fairgrounds that day in a somber mood, talking quietly and glancing at Leon with pity. At least, that's how it felt to Leon. His face burned.

❋ ❋ ❋

When the group returned to the Atlas Hotel, Teacher Chiu was standing in the lobby.

"I found him," Teacher Chiu told the boys in Chinese. "You can all relax now. Go to your rooms."

A tight band across Leon's chest loosened. As the other boys trooped up the stairs, Teacher Chiu pulled Leon aside.

Just then, Thomas burst into the lobby from the street. "Did you find him?"

"Yes," Teacher Chiu answered in English. "We found him at the China exhibit," the teacher explained in English.

Thomas's shoulders eased and a look of relief lit up his face. "What was he doing there?" Thomas asked.

"He was begging the men there to take him home with them. He said that life in America was terrible. He was miserable. He said that American people jeered and spit at Chinese people. He even said that his host family insulted him. He wants to go home to China."

Thomas looked shocked. Leon had heard these complaints before, but he never guessed that Carson would say all this in public. He wished Teacher Chiu hadn't told Thomas. "What did the men say, those men at the China exhibit?" Leon asked.

Teacher Chiu shook his head. "They seemed relieved when we took him away."

"Did they agree to take him home?" A whole new scenario stretched out before him.

"I don't know."

"Leon," said Thomas, "please don't tell Miss Julia about this, all right? I'll talk to her."

Leon nodded. "Where is Carson now?"

"Commissioner Ngeu took him to your room. Your brother was acting very wild. It was hard to get him to leave the exhibit and come back with us. Now he has gone silent."

"Should I go to him?" Leon didn't want to, but he wasn't sure what a younger brother was supposed to do.

"It's probably better that you don't. Apparently he is saying crazy things about you, too."

A shiver ran up Leon's spine. Had his brother actually gone crazy? It sounded as though a monster had taken up residence inside his brother's head.

That last night at the Atlas Hotel, Leon shared a bed with Tik-Chang in another room, half afraid his brother would find him in the middle of the night and beat him or spout crazy words.

The next morning at breakfast, Leon did not see his brother. But when he was sitting on the train, he saw Carson board with Teacher Chiu gripping his elbow. The teacher pushed Carson into a window seat and sat next to him the whole journey, not allowing Carson to talk to the other boys, not even Leon. Some of the boys whispered that Teacher Chiu had tied Carson to his wrist with a rope, although Leon did not see this. Even Carson's friends acted like they had never liked him.

Tik-Chang sat with Leon, and they talked nonstop about the Centennial Exhibition—about everything they had seen and done there. About everything except Elder Brother. No one knew what to say about him. Least of all Leon.

At Hartford station, most of the boys got on other trains or went home with their families by horse carriage. Thomas relayed a message to Leon: he was to proceed to the headquarters building, with Teacher Chiu and Elder Brother. Leon's insides were shaking as he said good-bye to his friends and walked toward his brother and teacher. What would happen to them now?

As they waited for the carriage to pick them up, Carson stared off into the distance. He didn't even acknowledge Leon. When the driver arrived, the three of them climbed aboard. Only after it started moving, once they were surrounded by the noise of the streets, did Elder Brother speak.

"We're going home to China," he said, quietly so that Teacher Chiu would not hear.

Leon's gut twisted. "Why?" This was just what he had feared. As the elder brother, Carson had the right to speak for both of them.

"These barbarians smell like garbage." Carson said this so quietly Leon could barely hear him. Was this really his brother speaking—or the monster that had taken over him?

As the carriage bumped along the cobblestone streets, Leon's mind reeled. He missed home, but he dreaded the thought of going back now, with his brother, in disgrace.

His mind bounced back and forth like a ball. According to Confucian rules of Chinese society, Leon was supposed to obey his elder brother and go along with his plans. But he wanted to stay with the Swanns in Suffield, to go to grammar school, to play baseball in the play-offs. Yet if he openly defied his brother, that would be seen as "too American." What could he do?

Could he defy his brother's wishes—and centuries of tradition?

❂  ❂  ❂

At the headquarters, Leon and Carson were ushered into the sitting room, where one of the teachers and a servant watched them closely. Leon felt like a prisoner. Did these people think Carson would jump up and run away? Well, of course, he had done just that.

Finally, the boys were summoned to the formal reception room. Mr. Yung sat in the leader's chair, frowning at them. Leon was glad it was Mr. Yung and not Commissioner Ngeu who would decide their fate. He knew that Mr. Yung wanted the Chinese Educational Mission to succeed. He would need to take strict action about Elder Brother to save the program from criticism at home.

The two boys took off their boater hats and stood at attention before the official.

"Woo Ka-Sun, explain your behavior in Philadelphia." Mr. Yung spoke in Chinese, his voice harsher than Leon had ever heard it.

Elder Brother lifted his chin in defiance. "I wish to return to China. Immediately. This country is not fit for civilized men."

"I repeat: explain your behavior."

Leon could sense the power struggle between them. He had never seen his brother defy authority before. No boy could win a struggle with an imperial official.

"Commissioner Yung," Carson said, acknowledging Mr. Yung's higher status, "please do not forget who I am. During the train robbery, I saved the gold for this educational mission. But I am not the right person for your mission. I want a traditional Chinese education. At the exhibition, all I did was go to the representatives of my country and ask them to help me go back to China. Now, I respectfully make my appeal to you."

"Explain your reasons for this request."

"Well, first, my father needs me at home. My eldest brother recently died."

Mr. Yung's eyes clouded. "I recall that. But you did not discuss this with me."

Carson went on. "Also, I've discovered that these people, these Americans, are . . ."

Leon held his breath. Carson shouldn't be saying this.

"They are barbarians," Carson blurted. "They know nothing of rules and rituals."

Leon thought of Charlotte, and Miss Julia, and the Swann parents, and Thomas. Barbarians?

"They are ignorant of the classics. We have nothing to learn from them."

Leon thought of Machinery Hall, of the huge steam engine, of the sewing machines, the bicycle, the talking machine. He thought of the Transcontinental Railroad.

"Their exams test for the wrong things. Their machines are silly, useless toys."

Leon squeezed his eyes shut, wishing he could shut his ears, too. Of the more than one hundred students on this mission, only his brother was saying such things. And Elder Brother was saying this directly to the man who had made it his life's work to ensure that China sent students to learn the advanced technology of America.

"Their young men waste time with stupid games. Their women dance with men and wear dresses that show their bosoms."

Elder Brother's voice veered into a high pitch. It didn't even sound like him. Was this the same person who had wanted to marry Charlotte, just a few weeks earlier?

"In the home where you placed me," Carson went on, "a young woman threw herself at me and begged to marry me." Leon swallowed a gasp. Did Carson really think that? "All of us should be able to return home, to the Middle Kingdom, to our civilized country," Elder Brother continued. "At the very least, I request permission for my brother and me. We cannot stay here one more day. Please . . ." Here, his voice cracked. "Please, Commissioner Yung. Send us home." *Us.*

Mr. Yung allowed a few moments of silence before responding. "Woo Ka-Sun, what can I do to make your stay in America more agreeable?"

Leon thought this reply very mild considering the way his brother had been ranting. For the first time since they came into the room, he looked up, hoping to see reason return to Carson's face.

For a few seconds, Carson hesitated. What would make Elder Brother's stay more agreeable? Leon wondered. If he could be accepted at the high school in Hartford and live at the headquarters. Maybe Mr. Yung could make sure that happened.

"Nothing." Carson's voice was firm. "My father needs us at home. Please book us on the next train west."

Mr. Yung now turned to Leon. "Woo Ka-Leong, do you wish to return home?"

By reflex, Leon glanced at his brother. That was a mistake. Carson's frowns always intimidated him. Especially now. Why would anyone care to know his opinion? But Mr. Yung had asked. This might be his only chance to say what he wanted. "I wish—"

"My younger brother will do as he is told, as a younger brother should. His duty is to his father and his family. Woo Ka-Leong returns home with me."

Leon snapped his mouth shut. Once his brother had spoken, Leon could not defy him.

"Woo Ka-Sun, I will speak to you again after dinner, to give you my decision. You may go to your room now. Woo Ka-Leong, you are to remain here a few minutes longer."

Elder Brother bowed once to Mr. Yung and then shot a look of warning at Leon as he turned and left the room. Not until the door closed after him did Leon's breathing begin to slow down.

Mr. Yung looked at Leon but said nothing.

Leon wiped his forehead, rubbed his eyes, and twisted his hands in a knot. He did not know how to answer the question he knew was coming again. When he looked up, Mr. Yung was regarding him with pity. Leon dropped his eyes quickly, examining the rug.

"I realize you are a good Chinese son who obeys all the Confucian edicts about loyalty to your elders. I commend you for obeying your brother. But I need to ask a few questions about your elder brother, Woo Ka-Sun. Tell me, when did he begin acting strangely?"

Leon could not even move his hands. Yes, Elder Brother was acting very strangely, but Leon could not admit that. When had it started? Was it when the bandit knocked his head with that pistol? Or when First Elder Brother died? Or when Charlotte turned him down? He couldn't say. He looked up at Mr. Yung with pleading eyes, thinking, *Please, don't make me answer that question!*

Although Leon had said nothing, Mr. Yung seemed to read his expression.

"Did you like the machines in Machinery Hall?" Mr. Yung asked.

Leon exhaled heavily. He had not realized he was holding his breath. "Oh, yes."

"Which machine did you like best?"

Leon's hands unfroze and began to move. "The biggest one. The Corliss steam engine." He answered in English because he didn't know the name in Chinese. An image entered his mind of the gigantic machine, smooth and powerful—as if muscles could be made of metal. He wished he were made of metal.

"I hear you've been playing baseball," Mr. Yung continued in English.

"I have." Leon blushed in embarrassment. Mr. Yung was the one who had recommended he try baseball. Did he dare admit to him how much he loved the game?

"What position do you play?"

"Third base, sir."

"Have you tried pitching?"

Leon's face reddened at the memory of the snowball. "I . . . I've tried. I'm getting better."

"When are the play-offs in your town?"

"They . . . they promised to delay them until Yew-Fun and I got back."

"Any chance your team will win?"

"Maybe. We're ranked second now. Enfield is ranked first. We'll play them on September 2."

"That's next week."

Leon looked down at his hands.

"Woo Ka-Leong, would you like to play in the play-offs?"

"Not for myself," Leon said.

"What?" Mr. Yung's thick eyebrows rose in surprise.

"For my father. I mean—not my father. For Reverend Swann. You see, he lost his son."

Leon examined Mr. Yung's face, desperately hoping to see understanding in his features. Surely Mr. Yung, who understood America better than any of them, could see his point.

Mr. Yung frowned. "He lost his son?"

"I mean . . ." Leon felt he was on shaky ground. "My father lost a son, too, but he has two more. Mr. Swann lost his only son. He has only daughters left. His son loved baseball. He died before we came. When he was just ten."

The Chinese man's eyes glistened. "His only son?"

"So, you see. I have to play one last game, before I leave. It's the last game of the season. It may be my last game ever. We wouldn't have to leave for China before then, would we?" Leon didn't like the way his voice sounded squeaky, like a little boy. At such an important moment, why was he whining about baseball?

Mr. Yung cleared his throat. It seemed to take him a moment to regain his composure. "Woo Ka-Leong, I understand that your essay was chosen for display at the exhibition. That you wrote about the Transcontinental Railroad. Congratulations."

Leon nodded a humble acknowledgment.

"You have been here less than a year. But if you were to stay in America, what would you study?"

Leon shook his head, with sadness. "My elder brother has commanded me to return home with him." His dream would never happen now.

"What if your elder brother changed his mind and commanded you to stay?" Mr. Yung continued, switching back to Chinese.

If only. That would be so wonderful.

"If he commanded me to stay . . ." Leon examined the thought in wonderment. He remembered his dream, which he seldom mentioned to anyone. "I would study railroads. Yes, railroads. I would try to get into Yale, like you, Commissioner Yung. I would apply to the engineering school, to study trains and engines and compressors and machines." His words spilled out, half in English, half in Chinese.

He paused, and Mr. Yung nodded, encouraging him to continue.

"I would learn about steam engines. How they work. How to build them. How to drive them. How to repair them. And about building railways. How to design a railroad. Not just a small one, like at the exhibit, but a long one, like the one that goes across America."

Leon no longer saw Mr. Yung's face or the formal room where they were sitting. He had a vision in front of him. "China could have railroads, across the whole country. From south to north, so people from my hometown could get to the capital overland, without going by ship. From east to west, so people from the inland areas could get to the coast. Up and down, all over. Wouldn't that be wondrous? Wouldn't it?"

Leon had never said so many sentences in a row in any language, certainly not to a man of high stature, far above his own humble station in life. Suddenly, he realized he might have said too much.

Mr. Yung's eyes were flooded with tears now, and they were overflowing, down his cheeks. Leon had never seen a Chinese man weep. It frightened him.

"Commissioner Yung! I'm sorry! I meant no harm! Please forgive me! I said too much. I should keep my mouth closed. Elder Brother is always telling me that."

Mr. Yung put up his left hand, as if to say, "Stop talking." With his right hand, he wiped his eyes.

"Woo Ka-Leong," he said at last, "you are the reason I started this mission."

# CHAPTER TWENTY-NINE

# Good News, Bad News

—◇·◇— —◈— —◇·◇—

Elder Brother did not ask Leon what he had discussed with Mr. Yung. Instead, as they ate a small dinner of fried rice and sliced pork with Chinese pickles in the students' dining room, he raved about how wonderful it would be to return to China. "I'm sure Father will agree to give me a classical education now," Carson said. "Maybe you, too. Learning English is a waste of time."

Leon shoveled rice into his mouth and just listened for a long time. His brother was either silent or talkative. Never normal. Finally, he asked his brother, "What if Mr. Yung says no?"

Carson shook his head but looked worried. "I think I explained myself well, don't you?"

Leon nodded and picked out a thin strip of pork.

After dinner, Mr. Yung called the two brothers into the reception room again.

"I have made a decision," he said in Chinese. "Woo Ka-Sun, I deny your request to return to China. The Imperial Government chose you for this program and expects you to complete it. Your obligation to the emperor is higher than to your family. Sometimes we have to make personal sacrifices for the good of our country. You need to learn how to eat bitterness and prevail. Both of you must return to Suffield tomorrow and continue your studies. I do not want to hear any such request from you again. Do you understand?"

Elder Brother's face froze. He stared blankly and refused to answer.

"We understand, sir," said Leon. This was the outcome he wanted. But he couldn't imagine how Carson could return to Suffield and resume his previous life, after all this. If Elder Brother snapped once, he could snap again. "We will both do everything as you command," Leon said, a little louder, hoping that saying the words in front of Elder Brother would make it so. Carson had been taught to obey his elders. Maybe all it took was a firm order from a man in authority. Maybe.

That evening, Elder Brother said almost nothing to Leon—just two sentences: "We're going back. I'll find a way."

The next morning, Teacher Chiu took them to the Hartford train station and bought three tickets. He accompanied them for the sixteen-mile journey to Suffield. Leon knew the teacher's role was to ensure that Carson did not run away again. But Carson showed no signs of rebellion. In fact, he showed no signs of life. He shuffled along and did as he was told, with no expression. He said almost nothing, even to Leon. What was going on inside Elder Brother's mind?

Miss Julia and Mrs. Swann greeted them at the door, glancing at one another, as if uncertain what to say. Leon wondered how much Thomas had told them about the incident at the exhibition. But the Swann women warmly greeted Teacher Chiu and invited him to stay the night, since there was no train until the next morning.

Carson ate dinner with the family, moving like a machine, but did not respond to any questions. It was as if he had gone deaf and dumb. After Mrs. Swann excused them from the table, Carson went straight up to his bedroom.

Leon trudged up the stairs behind him, afraid what might happen behind that closed door. He clenched his stomach. Surely Carson would blame him for Mr. Yung's decision. But that didn't happen. After closing the door, Leon stood next to it, his hand on the doorknob. But Elder Brother didn't even look at him. He washed his face and went straight to bed in silence. Leon slipped into his own bed and lay like a board under the sheets. A breeze blew the shimmery curtains. The onslaught did not come. Carson's breath slowed to a regular pace, but Leon remained stiff a long time.

The next morning, after breakfast, Teacher Chiu asked to speak to each of the boys individually, in the Swanns' parlor, before he left. He insisted that Leon come first.

Leon stood before his teacher, expecting to hear orders about how to behave and how to watch his brother.

Teacher Chiu cleared his throat. "Woo Ka-Leong, I have good news. You passed the entrance exam and can begin seventh grade in September."

A pulse of power surged through Leon's heart, and for a second his troubles and fears sizzled and evaporated. He passed! He could go to school with the other boys! He wouldn't have to stay at home all day and . . .

But Teacher Chiu was not finished. "Your elder brother did not pass his entrance exam, though. He will need to study at home for another year."

Leon's euphoria collapsed like a rail trestle under too much weight. Oh, no. That wouldn't work. Carson, at home with Miss Julia? Elder Brother would never accept that. And Miss Julia was hoping to get married soon. But Leon had envisioned this possibility.

"Teacher Chiu, if I may." The teacher's eyebrows rose, but Leon continued. "Could my elder brother move to Hartford, to live at headquarters with you and study English there? I think he would do better."

Teacher Chiu cocked his head, as if he had not imagined this possibility. "That's not what the Mission House is for. And he wouldn't learn much English, living with us," the teacher said. "You don't think he could handle it, staying on here?"

Leon shook his head. "My elder brother will do whatever you recommend."

Teacher Chiu nodded. "We think staying with families is the best way to learn English, but moving to Hartford might be good for your brother, at least for now. I will discuss this with the commissioners. But don't tell your brother about this possibility. I don't want to get his hopes up. You may go now. Tell your brother to come in here."

Leon waited outside the door, afraid he would hear his brother blow up and spout curses in Chinese. But when Elder Brother emerged from the parlor, his face was pale and blank. He brushed by Leon and climbed the stairs without a word.

CHAPTER THIRTY

# Elder Brother

The play-offs were a week away, and school would start the following Monday. As soon as he could, Leon rode into town with Mr. Swann and rushed to Yew-Fun's house to tell him the good news about school. At practice, the other boys on the team slapped him on the back and congratulated him. Leon relaxed. It felt so good to be away from his brother.

Back at home in time for dinner, Leon asked Miss Julia if she had heard from Teacher Chiu, but she hadn't. He still hoped his plan would be approved, for Elder Brother's sake.

All day, every day, Carson remained in his room, writing Chinese characters over and over again. Miss Julia stayed home to keep an eye on him. Every few hours, she knocked on his door and brought him a cup of tea or a small plate of food. She told Leon that she offered to give Carson English lessons, but he refused. She let it go, since late August was vacation time, and the weather was too hot for studying.

Leon watched his brother closely. He sensed the anger and humiliation churning below the calm surface. Carson seemed strangely empty. What was he thinking? Something was brewing inside Carson's mind, Leon was sure of it. And a little afraid of what it might be.

On Sunday, Elder Brother refused to go to church with the family. "Why should I go?" he said to Leon in Chinese. "I learn nothing there."

Leon considered staying at home with his brother, but Julia told him that Thomas had asked the team to meet with him after church to talk about the big game. So he went with the Swanns. He had an uneasy feeling, leaving Carson alone in the house. Would he run away again?

After the service, the Swanns ate dinner with the Travis family, as usual. The whole time, Leon fidgeted. He was itching to get home and make sure Elder Brother was all right.

Finally, the dinner ended and the Swanns got back in their buggy and headed home. As they pulled into their own driveway, a strong wind picked up. Trees thrashed against the house.

"Feels like a summer storm," said Mr. Swann.

Leon suddenly got a sour feeling in the depths of his stomach. He remembered the summer storms at home, called typhoons. They could be very damaging.

The minute the carriage stopped, Leon jumped out and ran in the front door before Mr. Swann could get down and help the ladies out. "Elder Brother!" he called out.

Carson was not on the porch and not in the parlor. Leon ran up the stairs to the bedroom. The door was shut. Locked. That meant Carson was inside. A terrible image occurred to Leon, one with blood.

"Elder Brother!" he shouted, rattling the knob. "Open the door!"

No sound came from within.

"Elder Brother!" Leon's voice was higher, shriller. "Are you all right?"

Leon stopped for a moment. His heart was pounding

against his ribs. No sound came from within the room. Had Carson jumped out the window? This could not be happening.

Miss Julia ran up the stairs and stood behind him. Leon put up his hand to silence her.

At last he heard a soft sound from within the room.

Leon's heart beat faster. Why had he left Elder Brother alone? What had Carson done in his absence? Had he hurt himself? Leon had been selfish; he'd thought only of himself. He didn't care enough for his elder brother. What did the Swanns matter, or the Suffield baseball team, compared to his own flesh and blood?

Footsteps crossed the floor. Wooden planks squeaked. Elder Brother was coming toward the door. He was alive, but something was wrong.

Leon could barely breathe. It felt like a giant screwdriver was twisting his guts.

Finally, the lock shifted. Leon dropped his hand from the doorknob. The knob turned.

*Please, let Carson be all right.* If Elder Brother wanted to go back to China, Leon would go with him. No questions asked. *Please, God,* he thought. *Please, Christian God. Please, Kuan Yin, goddess of mercy. Please, all gods everywhere. Let Carson be all right.*

The door opened. Carson stood there. Whole. No blood. Under his eyes, the circles were darker than before.

Leon did something he had never done before. He grabbed his brother and hugged him. Hard. Harder even than Mrs. Swann had hugged him that first day he had met her.

"I'll do anything you want. I promise. I'll be good," Leon gushed. He looked up at his brother's face. Carson's eyes were glassy.

"What have you done?" Leon asked him.

Carson smiled strangely.

Then he turned his head. Behind his neck, his black hair stuck out weirdly.

Leon sucked in his breath. Elder Brother's queue was gone. Carson lifted his left hand. In it was the long, black braid that had once hung down his back. That had always hung down his back. His loyalty to the emperor, to China, to his homeland. To their homeland. His ticket back to China.

Carson raised his right hand. In it was a pair of scissors.

"Your turn," Elder Brother said, waving the scissors in the air.

Leon backed up. As usual, his queue was tucked inside his shirt. Still, Leon grabbed the back of his neck to protect it.

"I can't. You can't. We can't."

Carson wasn't allowed to cut his own queue. That was high treason. But he had. What shame this would bring on Carson! On their whole family! On Mr. Yung Wing. On the entire Chinese Educational Mission.

"Stand still," said Carson. "I will do it now." He waved the scissors, his eyes glinting.

Leon stepped back again, stumbling against the open door.

"No." Leon spoke firmly. "You will not do that to me!"

He turned and ran right into Julia, with her huge skirts, who had been standing behind him, at the top of the staircase. "Pardon me." Leon brushed past her. He galloped down the stairs and toward the front door, past the gaping stares of Mrs. Swann and Mr. Swann, who was holding Charlotte.

Just as he was about to dash out the door to safety, he heard Julia scream.

He turned and looked back. Had he put Julia in danger? Was his brother truly mad?

Mr. Swann set Charlotte down on the hall floor. Then he loped up the steps, three by three.

Through the banister, Leon could see what was happening. Mr. Swann pushed Julia aside and grabbed the scissors out of Carson's hand. Then he grabbed Elder Brother's arm and twisted it behind his back. A sharp cry of pain shot out of Elder Brother's mouth.

"Come with me, young man." Mr. Swann could sound fierce when he wanted to. He marched Carson down the stairs and into his private library. Then he slammed the door shut.

Leon could hear an angry lecture going on behind the closed door.

Julia, he could see, was safe though undoubtedly startled by the sight of Carson, with his wild eyes, brandishing scissors.

Leon backed up against the wall and slid down to a seated position, next to Charlotte. He began crying uncontrollably.

Charlotte put one arm around his shoulder and pulled him close to her, like an elder sister. Her voice was soft and sure. "Shhh. It's all right, little brother. Take it easy."

# CHAPTER THIRTY-ONE

# Leon Decides

—◇·◇——◇——◇·◇—

"*I*'ll do anything you want. I promise. I'll be good."

Those words had shot out of Leon's mouth in desperation, when he feared his brother had hurt himself. Now they pounded inside his head, like a hammer. *What if Elder Brother gets sent back to China now and insists I go with him? Would I really do anything he wanted?* He had never gone back on a promise.

"No. You will not do that to me."

Leon had also said that. Those words, too, knocked the insides of his skull. For the first time in his life, Leon had openly defied an elder in his family. Did that mean he had rejected all the good values of his upbringing? Once on the outside of his family, could he ever get back in?

He couldn't believe what Elder Brother had done. It was like spitting in the emperor's face. Of course, they would send him back to China. What would that mean for Leon?

After what felt like an eternity, Leon heard the door to Mr. Swann's study open. Leon kept his forehead buried in his arms, not wanting to face whatever came next. Mr.

Swann's shiny black shoes tapped across the wooden hallway floor and stopped in front of Leon.

"Leon. Come into my study." Mr. Swann's voice was gentle and sympathetic.

Charlotte squeezed his shoulder and handed him her handkerchief. Leon wiped his nose and stood up. He could face Mr. Swann but not his brother. He dragged his feet as he followed the man into the study and jerked at the harsh sound of the door slamming behind him.

Carson was sitting in a chair, his eyes still gleaming, an odd, exultant smile glowing from his face. Around his neck, his black hair stuck out like the tail feathers of a cock—an ugly distortion of the way a Chinese man should look.

Taut as a clothesline, Leon walked over and slipped into a chair next to his brother.

"We're going home," Carson said to him in Chinese, his voice nearly shaking with incredulous joy. "I'm sure of it."

A vision flashed into Leon's head: his entire baseball team, in their positions on the field, looking at him expectantly, waiting for him to fill the empty spot at third base. They had delayed the play-off game for him. They were counting on him.

Mr. Swann's expression was hard to read. "I will notify at once the commission headquarters in Hartford that your brother has cut his queue. I understand this is strictly forbidden. I trust they will send instructions."

Back in their bedroom, Leon looked around nervously for the scissors, worried that his brother would again try to cut off Leon's queue. But Elder Brother hummed softly, as happy as Leon had ever seen him. He opened up the huge trunk and began packing his things.

Leon's heart still churned with contradictory feelings. Rebelling in his own, small way, he refused to pack. Instead, he went straight to bed, exhausted. When his brother was not looking, he tucked the baseball mitt under the covers, next to his belly, and curled up with it. He wished he could keep it, but he would not need it if they were sent back to China. And he was sure Mr. Swann would not want to part with it.

A few hours later, in the blackness of night, Leon awoke and could not go back to sleep. He imagined Father's reaction: fury at the shame Carson had caused. What kind of future would they have in China? He also rehearsed, in his mind, what he might say to Mr. Yung Wing. All the words he could think of sounded wrong. Mr. Yung would make the decision for him.

❖ ❖ ❖

The next morning, Mr. Swann and the two boys were sitting in the parlor opposite Mr. Yung Wing over steaming cups of milky tea. Mr. Yung's face hardened when he saw Carson's hair. Mr. Swann gave a brief explanation, in English, of what had happened. It was clear to Leon that the Swanns had no idea how unhinged Elder Brother had become in the past few months—or why. Elder Brother's face remained passive until Mr. Swann reported that Carson had asked to marry Charlotte. Then it reddened.

"This caused great distress to my young daughter," the minister said, "and to our whole family. Although he is a fine young man, my daughter is too young to consider marriage. I had trusted these two boys to act like brothers, not suitors, to my two daughters."

Leon stared at his fists, clenched in his lap, when he heard these words. He wondered how Mr. Yung's American father-in-law treated him.

Finally, Mr. Swann stood. "With your permission," he asked politely, "I would like to take my leave now. I am sure you have much to discuss in your language. Before I do, though, may I add one point? The younger of these two brothers has shown exemplary behavior while living in my household. The decision is yours, of course. But if you decide to keep him in America, I would be happy to let him continue living here with us."

Leon's heart swelled.

After Mr. Swann left the room, a heavy silence fell. Then Mr. Yung let loose a torrent of angry words in Chinese, directed at Carson. "Do you realize what disgrace you have brought on yourself? And on your fellow students! On the entire Chinese Educational Mission. And on the emperor, who trusted you."

Leon's stomach knotted as the tirade continued. All of it was directed at Elder Brother, but as a member of the Woo family, Leon was shamed, too. The outburst seemed out of character for Mr. Yung, who had been so lenient when Leon had thrown the snowball. But maybe this was different. Maybe Carson cutting his queue endangered the whole Chinese Educational Mission. It was an act of defiance, not a stupid mistake.

Still, Leon hated to hear these harsh words. Back in China, Leon's father had sometimes yelled at the boys and beat them, but these words were sharper and more painful than a beating. Bruises heal, but condemnation festers.

Carson, who had always prided himself on loyalty and obedience, sat stony faced. Leon stiffened in his chair, horrified.

Finally, the tirade ended. "Woo Ka-Sun," said Mr. Yung, "we have no choice but to send you back to China in disgrace. You may never wear the scholar's robes again."

At these words, Carson cried, "No, not that!"

"That's part of the penalty," Mr. Yung said. "You have lost the privilege of studying to become an official. Surely you knew that."

Carson fell to his knees and began sobbing. Finally, it seemed, he realized how thoroughly he had shattered his own dream.

Leon wanted to kneel beside his brother and comfort

him. But he knew that such outward signs of sympathy would imply that he condoned his brother's actions.

Leon tried to imagine Carson's future in China. A man without a queue could be thrown into jail for treason. Father would have to hide Carson for years in the house, or get a wig for him. But everyone in the village would know.

"Now," Mr. Yung concluded, "roll out of here!" That final sentence, in Chinese, was a deep insult, almost a curse.

Carson stood erect. His tears ended abruptly. He nodded once, turned, and left the room.

Leon stood up to leave, too, but Mr. Yung ordered him to sit down. Echoes of the angry curse continued to bounce off the walls, and Leon realized he was shaking, from his very core.

After a few moments, Mr. Yung stood and walked over to him. He put his hand on Leon's shoulder, but Leon wished he could swat it off.

*For the rest of my life,* Leon thought, *I hope I never again witness such a degrading scene. Whatever my brother did, he did not deserve such humiliation.*

Leon could not look Mr. Yung in the face. No one should treat his elder brother that way. It felt as though this official was attacking his whole family, their upbringing, everything they had ever valued. Leon knew that the right thing was to keep his fury to himself. It was not appropriate to express anger to a superior. But he could barely contain it.

"Woo Ka-Leong," Mr. Yung began at last, speaking in a soothing tone. "I know you would like to stay in America. You do not need to follow your elder brother."

Leon swallowed hard. These words did not reassure him. This was the same man who had berated his brother and forced him to grovel like a criminal.

"My elder brother," Leon repeated, still shaky and uncertain what words would come out. "My elder brother, Woo Ka-Sun, is"—he had to take a breath—"very smart. The best. In Shanghai, he ranked number one. He can recite not only the *Three Character Classic* but dozens of Tang poems." Leon's voice grew steadier. Mr. Yung's face registered surprise, but a tight coil of fury in Leon's stomach was unwinding. Emboldened by his resentment, Leon sat tall. He took a deep breath. "If my brother had stayed in China, he would have passed all the national exams—every one! He would have become a high official—a big shot! It wasn't his idea to come to America to study English. My father ordered him to do so, and he obeyed. But he couldn't"—*how to say this?*—"he . . . he didn't like it here. He begged to be sent back to China, months ago."

Leon was veering close to the edge now, blaming the commissioners. Leon knew that was bad. But his outrage drove him on.

"My elder brother, Commissioner Yung, has made some mistakes. But you know what? He is a true Confucian gentleman. He obeys his father. He reveres the emperor. He wants to go back and serve his country."

Leon's words reverberated in the study. Mr. Yung regarded him evenly.

"Your elder brother, Woo Ka-Leong, has not just made mistakes. He has insulted the emperor and his fatherland." Mr. Yung's voice, too, was firm. "When he cut off his queue, he knew the consequences. Now he will face them. My question is for you. You have a choice. You can follow your brother, in disgrace, back to China. Or you can stay here and finish your studies. It's up to you."

Leon clasped his hands tightly in his lap. He had a choice. Would he be loyal to his brother? Or would he follow his heart?

"My elder brother . . . he says I am becoming too American."

Those words, "too American," seemed to echo in the room, like the shrillest notes of a Chinese opera singer.

"And what do you think?" Mr. Yung asked.

"Well, maybe he's right. I have American friends. I like speaking English. I love playing baseball." Leon hesitated. Did that make him too American? "But I'm proud of being Chinese! We have the best civilization, the longest history. I know that. But I also love modern things—railroads, engines, machines. These Americans have invented some wonderful things that can help China." So was he too Chinese, or too American?

"That's who I am. But if you really give me a choice . . . ," he hesitated again, examining the older man's eyes, "then I want to stay here and go to school. That's why the emperor sent us here, isn't it?"

The wise man regarded him in silence, his expression hard to read.

"But," Leon continued, "I respect my elder brother. I hope he can be given a second chance."

This time, Mr. Yung smiled. "Woo Ka-Leong, you're a good man."

# CHAPTER THIRTY-TWO

# Good-Bye

—◇·◇—◇—◇·◇—

*T*he next morning, Leon sat next to his brother as they ate their scrambled eggs.

His brother was talkative again. "I'm already packed. I'll go back to Hartford with Mr. Yung today. Then, next week, I'll leave for China. Teacher Chiu will travel with me. So will one of Commissioner Ngeu's wives. Did you hear? She can't stand the horrible food in America. I agree. When I get home, I'll have rice porridge for breakfast every day."

Leon brought a forkful of eggs to his mouth.

"Father will be disappointed in you," Carson continued. "Ah-Ma will cry when she sees you didn't come back."

*Father will be even more disappointed in you*, thought Leon, but he didn't say so. Father wanted them to finish their schooling in America, not come home in shame. At least Carson had stopped insisting that Leon go back with him. *The emperor will also be disappointed in you*, Leon thought. *We were supposed to—*

Carson interrupted his thoughts. "I will tell them how it is here. How these Americans try to make us act like them. You really should stop playing that foolish ball game."

Leon chewed a piece of bacon and swallowed.

"You're becoming too Americanized. All the boys are. I'll tell them that."

Leon hoped no one would listen to Elder Brother's opinion. Who would listen to a boy who had cut off his queue? Still, Leon worried that other people would report the same thing. Surely, the Imperial Government would never end this educational mission because of reports that the boys were becoming too Americanized. It was too important for them to learn about America's modern technology and take it back to China.

After breakfast, the two brothers stood in the front hallway of the Swanns' home. Leon could barely look at his brother, with those stiff hairs sticking out from his neck.

"Good-bye, Carson Woo," Rev. Swann said, shaking Elder Brother's hand. "Best of luck for all you do in the future, back home in China."

Elder Brother just nodded, not saying good-bye or thank you for all the Swanns had done for him in nine months. Then he turned to Leon. He did not hug him or shake his hand, in the American way. He just bowed his head. Leon bowed back, hardly believing this moment had come.

"I'll see you when you get back home," Carson said simply, as if that event were not fourteen years in the future.

"Give my greetings to Father and Mother," Leon replied. He had tried to write a letter for Carson to take home but could not think of the right words. "I promise to keep up with my Chinese so I can write letters."

Carson did not smile. "You'll have to get someone to help you."

There was nothing else to say. Leon watched as Elder Brother walked out the door. He ran out to the front stoop to wave, but Elder Brother did not turn back.

Leon blinked away a few tears. He would now be in a distant foreign country, without a single family member on the continent. But he was relieved not to have to answer to Elder Brother anymore.

Leon chased after the carriage, but it quickly disappeared. He took a long walk around the field and along the familiar road, thinking hard. China's rules were too rigid, he believed. Loyalty and patriotism should be measured by what was in the heart, not by the queue hanging down the back. But America's ways were too free. If young people were given too many choices, the whole society could fly apart, as if spun by centrifugal force. In America, ignorant boys mocked Chinese queues. They acted like they were superior to learned scholars from China. But in China, high officials scoffed at modern Western technology and refused to build railroads. Maybe he, Leon, could be a bridge.

For the first time, Leon fully understood the courage of Mr. Yung Wing, who had spent years in Peking and Shanghai, trying to convince high officials that China needed to learn from the West. One misstep in China and no one would ever listen to you. How had Mr. Yung achieved this, getting China's government to send one hundred twenty boys to study in the United States?

Why couldn't Carson adapt to life in America? Was something wrong with him? It was beyond Leon to figure it out. But already he missed his brother. He had never spent a day without him in his life.

Leon turned and headed home.

CHAPTER THIRTY-THREE

# The Play-Offs

—◇·◆·◇◆◇·◆·◇—

*T*wo days later, on Saturday, Leon woke up alone in the bedroom he had shared with his brother. He let his fingers rest briefly on a stack of books Julia had bought for him, books he would need at school when he started seventh grade the following Monday. They had hard leather covers with gold letters embossed on them. *School.* He couldn't wait.

But this was the big day. The championship game. Suffield versus Enfield. Leon's team had defeated every other team, but Enfield had a crackerjack pitcher, who made it hard to hit the ball at all, let alone get a home run.

"Thomas says there is a good chance you'll win," said Miss Julia as she stepped up into the carriage.

"Thomas has trained them well," Mr. Swann said. He lifted Charlotte up to the seat beside Julia.

"I'm sure he'll bring his porch chair to the game for me," Charlotte added, her voice lighter than ever. "He always finds the perfect spot for it."

Leon stretched and curled his fingers, practicing for a catch, happy and nervous at the same time. He wanted to punch his mitt, but Mr. Swann was holding it in his lap.

As the horses jerked the carriage into motion, Charlotte patted him on the knee. "It'll be okay, little brother! Whatever happens, we're behind you!"

Leon decided he liked it when she called him that, but he wondered where his brother was this minute.

When they arrived at the diamond, Mr. Swann handed him Owen's old baseball mitt. Leon thought he detected a smile but wasn't sure. He laced up his spiked shoes. Yew-Fun was stretching his legs in preparation for the game. Johnny was loosening up his pitching arm.

The Enfield players arrived with their families in a convoy of horse carriages. They jumped out eagerly and ran to the baseball diamond. The afternoon sun beat down, making the air almost unbearably hot and humid. Still, it seemed the whole town came out to watch.

Thomas and the Enfield coach tossed a coin to see which team would go to bat first. Enfield won the toss. The coaches clapped their hands and the players took their places. Leon ran to third base. Sweat dripped down his back, and his nerves felt tight. Win or lose, he would start seventh grade next week.

Win or lose, he would stay in Suffield. He had already weathered the storm that mattered. But it sure would feel good to win. Suffield had not had a winning season for four years, since before Yew-Fun arrived in town. This year would be different.

From Johnny's opening pitch, Leon knew this would be a close game. Enfield's first batter reached first base. Leon could feel the sweat dripping down his sides. Enfield's second batter hit a long drive into the outfield, and their players started to round the bases. The outfielder threw the ball to Leon at third, but the ball soared past him. Leon could not get to it in time to tag the players out. He was mad at himself. If he were taller or had longer arms, he would have caught that ball. Enfield scored three runs in the first inning.

Enfield's pitcher, who was on his third season, struck out the first two Suffield batters. Yew-Fun, third at bat, made a two-base hit. Young Charlie got to first.

Then Johnny was at bat. Leon wiped drips of sweat from his forehead and then held his breath as he watched. Johnny was their best player, but he seldom had faced a pitcher like this one. Could he do it?

Johnny whacked the ball, and it soared through the sky over the heads of the Enfield boys. Leon and his teammates cheered as Yew-Fun and Charlie crossed home plate and Johnny ran all the bases to home. Leon's team and their supporters jumped up and hugged each other. Their cheers sailed up to the summer sun. At the end of the first inning, the teams were tied, three to three.

For the next few innings, both teams played well. Enfield took the lead again, Suffield pulled ahead, then Enfield. Leon struck out his first time at bat, then hit a double and drew a walk. Johnny's pitching improved, and he struck out several of the Enfield players.

Finally, the last inning arrived. The teams were tied, six to six. Then Enfield got one run. Pulling his hat low over his eyes to cut the sun's glare, Leon focused on the next batter, who hit the ball high into the air, almost straight at Leon on third base. A pop fly. Leon lifted his mitt and prayed he would catch it. He did! That ended Enfield's half of the inning.

His teammates slapped him on the back as they gathered at the bench.

Now the Suffield team was at bat. To win, they needed two runs.

Johnny slammed the ball deep into the outfield, and the boys cheered. The Enfield left fielder dove for the ball but dropped it. Johnny got all the way to second. The next Suffield player got tagged out at first, while Johnny ran to third. The next batter struck out. Two outs.

Leon stepped to the plate. His nerves were jangling.

He had struck out many times during the season. He just couldn't end this game by striking out again, no matter how tough that Enfield pitcher was. If he could get Johnny in, they would be tied at least. Maybe another player could get Leon in. That would do it!

Leon wiped his hands on his pants and spit, as he had seen Charlie do. He held the bat just as Johnny had taught him and focused hard on the pitcher. He had to at least get to first.

The ball came curving in at him. Thomas had told him many times how to hit a curve ball. He remembered his coach's words and held off on his swing until the ball neared the plate.

He swung. *Crack!* He hit the ball. It bounced past the third baseman, just inside the line. He ran to first. He had a stitch in his side when he got there. But he made it!

Leon turned around just in time to see Johnny stumble on his way to home plate. The Enfield catcher caught the ball and tagged Johnny out.

The game was over. Suffield had lost nine to eight.

All the air went out of Leon's lungs.

Still, their team had played well, all the way to the finals. And Leon had not caused the final out. At least, not directly.

The Enfield boys cheered. Johnny looked devastated. Yew-Fun patted him on the back, wordlessly.

Thomas told their team to huddle, so they gathered in a circle, arms tossed over one another's shoulders, backs soaked in perspiration from the merciless sun.

"You played hard and well," Thomas said. "All of you. I'm proud of you."

With Johnny's arm on one of his shoulders and Charlie's on the other, Leon melted into the warmth of his team. He belonged.

The huddle broke up, and the boys turned to their families. Mr. Swann was standing behind Leon, who glanced up at his face, expecting to see disappointment. Instead, he saw joy.

"Well done, my son. Good game," Mr. Swann said.

He had called him "my son"! Leon gazed up at him in amazement.

"My Chinese son," Mr. Swann said, with a smile.

That was even better. Now Leon knew that not only was he accepted into the Swann family, but they valued him for who he was.

Somewhere, Owen's ghost was smiling.

Mr. Swann smoothed down some of Leon's hair, which was escaping from his queue, then put a fatherly hand gently behind Leon's neck as they turned to walk together toward Julia and Charlotte.

After the game, all the Suffield boys, with their families, crowded into Yew-Fun's house, where Thomas's mother had made a big cake for them, covered in chocolate icing. Johnny refused to eat at first, until Miss Julia brought him a piece. Leon ate a big piece, savoring the sweetness that had once seemed too overpowering. Around him, the boys were laughing and talking in English. Leon understood every word. Well, nearly.

They had lost the game, but you would never know it. They were a team, already planning for the next season.

# Epilogue

$\mathcal{L}$eon and his brother, Carson, are fictional, as are the people they met in Suffield, including the Swann family. However, the Chinese Educational Mission to the United States was real.

The emperor of China did send one hundred twenty Chinese boys to study in America. Ranging in age from eleven to sixteen, they arrived in four contingents of about thirty boys each, from 1872 to 1875, and they stayed with host families in Connecticut and western Massachusetts. They learned English, attended grammar school and high school, played baseball, went skating and sledding, and generally lived like American boys, except that they were not permitted to cut their queues or join a church. The few who did were sent home in disgrace.

As a group, these boys visited Philadelphia for the Centennial Exhibition in 1876, where they shook hands with President Ulysses S. Grant. One contingent experienced a train robbery by the infamous Jesse James and his gang. Most of these Chinese boys learned English quickly and became good students. At a time when less than two percent of American young people attended college, many of these boys were accepted into such universities as Yale, Columbia, Rensselaer

Polytechnic, and the Massachusetts Institute of Technology. The Chinese government supported them financially and arranged for them to continue studying Chinese during their stay so that they could fit in when they returned.

The Chinese Educational Mission was the brainchild of a forward-thinking man named Yung Wing, who graduated from Yale in 1854 and then returned to China to convince Tseng Kuo-fan (Zeng Guofan), a high imperial advisor, to send more than one hundred students to the United States to obtain a modern education. The plan was that the boys would stay in America for fifteen years to acquire technical skills and knowledge and then return home to China to help modernize and strengthen their homeland.

In 1881, the program ended abruptly. The emperor issued an order that all of the boys return to China immediately. This cut short the mission before most of them could graduate from college, let alone earn advanced degrees. One reason was China's anger that the United States government refused to allow any of the Chinese boys to study at the U.S. Military Academy at West Point or at the U.S. Naval Academy at Annapolis, although these academies had admitted students from Japan. Another was China's irritation with the rising tide of anti-Chinese sentiment in America, directed mainly at the flood of low-wage Chinese laborers in the western states. In 1882, the United States passed a law banning immigration of all laborers from China. But the main reason cited by the Imperial Government was that the boys had become "too Americanized."

The boys, now young men, returned to China as ordered. On their way home, in San Francisco, a group of them played one last baseball game, against a local Oakland team. According to an article in the *San Francisco Chronicle*, they won by a score of eleven to eight.

After the young men landed in Shanghai, they were locked up and treated shabbily at first. The winds in China had changed, and anyone with a foreign connection was viewed as suspicious. Many of the men spent years in obscurity at low-level jobs. But in later years, some achieved positions of power and prestige in the government of China. One of them, Jeme Tien Yow, spent thirty-two years building railroads in China; he designed and supervised the construction of the first railway built entirely by Chinese engineers and is revered as the father of China's railways. If Woo Ka-Leong had been real, he would have worked by his side, helping to build railroads and modernize his country.

Liang Yu Ho and Tong Shao Yi, two of the youngest boys in the program, both 12 when they left China in 1874. Courtesy of Thomas LaFargue Papers, 1873-1946 (id. 2-1-15), Manuscripts, Archives, and Special Collections (MASC), Washington State University Libraries.

Six boys from the first group of the Chinese Educational Mission (CEM) after arriving in San Francisco, 1872. Courtesy of Thomas LaFargue Papers, 1873-1946 (id. 2-1-5), MASC, Washington State University Libraries.

Identified in Shanghai Tower as the first group of 30 CEM students, in uniform, sent to the United States in August 1872. Courtesy of Thomas LaFargue Papers, 1873-1946 (id. 2-1-13), MASC, Washington State University Libraries.

The "Orientals" baseball team at the CEM headquarters, Hartford, 1878. One of them is Jeme Tien Yow. Courtesy of Thomas LaFargue Papers, 1873-1946 (id. 2-1-11), MASC, Washington State University Libraries.

The schoolroom at Chinese Educational Mission headquarters, Hartford. *Harper's Weekly*, 18 May 1878.

"Visit of Chinese Students from Connecticut to the Centennial Exhibition."
Daily Graphic, 31 August 1876.

# Resources

—◇·◈·◉·◈·◇—

*J*n English, the best sources about the Chinese Educational Mission are the following:

Lee, Yan Phou. *When I Was a Boy in China*. First published 1887 by D. Lothrop Company. Reprinted from the collections of the University of California Libraries.

LaFargue, Thomas E. *China's First Hundred: Educational Mission Students in the United States, 1872–1881*. Pullman: Washington State University Press, 1987. First published 1942 by Washington State College Press.

Leibovitz, Liel, and Matthew Miller. *Fortunate Sons: The 120 Chinese Boys Who Came to America, Went to School, and Revolutionized an Ancient Civilization*. New York: W. W. Norton, 2012.

Rhoads, Edward J. M. *Stepping Forth into the World: The Chinese Educational Mission to the United States, 1872–81*. Hong Kong: Hong Kong University Press, 2011.

Yung, Wing. *My Life in China and America*. Hong Kong: Earnshaw Books, 2007. First published 1909 by Henry Holt.

http://www.cemconnections.org/, a website set up by some descendants of the Chinese Educational Mission scholars.

# Acknowledgments

———◇·◈·◇———

M̲any thanks to Peter and Betty Tonglao, who first told me about the one hundred and twenty boys of the Chinese Educational Mission to the United States. Peter's grandfather, Tong Shao Yi (Tang Shaoyi), was one of the real boys sent to America in the 1870s, and he later served as the first premier of the Republic of China in 1912. Hearing this story sparked my imagination and sent me off to do research on the history of the mission and how it fit into U.S. and Chinese history. Peter's wife, Betty, and his daughter and granddaughter, Lynn and Anna, read the manuscript and encouraged me.

I am deeply grateful to Edward J. M. Rhoads, author of the most authoritative and meticulously researched book on the Chinese Educational Mission, for his helpful comments and corrections, as well as Scott D. Seligman, author of *The First Chinese American*, and friends Nancy Kennan and Gary Duberstein, for their careful reading of the manuscript. I also appreciate my critique-group friends, all excellent and prolific writers for children and young adult readers: Brenda Z. Guiberson, Kirby Larson, David Patneaude, and Conrad Wesselhoeft. They improved every chapter with their invaluable insights and advice. I'd also like to thank

Carla Jablonski and Meredith Bailey, who applied their editing skills to make this story shine.

Likewise, this book would never have reached readers if it weren't for the confidence of Brooke Warner and Lauren Wise of SparkPress and the skills of Liane Worthington and the publicity team at BookSparks. Many thanks from me— and, I hope, from countless readers of all ages who will love this book.

# Questions for

# Classroom Discussion

1. What differences did you notice in this story between Chinese attitudes and American attitudes?

2. What are Confucian values, and how do they affect the way Leon responded to his emperor, his father, and his brother?

3. What are Victorian values, and what did you notice about the way Americans acted in the 1870s, compared to today?

4. Why do you think Mrs. Swann objected to Carson's proposal? What do you think she meant when she said, "How dare he! The effrontery!"? Do you think Carson was wrong to do this?

5. Which of the two brothers is more like you?

6. How do you think Carson's personality changed during the story? What might have caused this? Did it disturb you? Do you think he would have been understood better in today's America?

7. Why did Carson have a harder time adapting to America than Leon did? What were the differences in their basic personalities and life experiences? Why do some people adapt better than others to life in another country or culture?

8. Try to imagine moving to a country where people speak a different language, without your parents. What would it be like for you?

9. Elder Brother says he thinks China's traditions are better. But did he benefit from those traditions, back in China? And does he believe in and honor those traditions?

10. In your opinion, why does Elder Brother really want to go back to China?

11. When during the story did you feel most worried? What surprised you the most?

12. What can you tell about the role of women in America in the 1870s? How does it differ from today? How was it different from the role of women in China?

13. How much choice did kids have in those days, compared to now? How much choice did Johnny have, and how did that contrast with some of the other boys in town? Do you think Leon would really have been given a choice about whether or not to go back to China?

14. In the 1870s, America had more advanced technology and machinery than China did. Is that still true today?

15. How did you feel at the end of the book?

16. Why do you think the Chinese government was so worried about the boys becoming "too Americanized"?

17. What do you think happens to Carson after the book ends? To Leon?

# Fun Facts

Baseball was invented in the United States and became widely popular in the New York area in the 1850s. The rules and ball size were not standardized until 1876.

Although baseball is very popular in Taiwan, it is relatively unknown in mainland China.

In 1875, the United States had more than 74,000 miles of railroad tracks, connecting the East Coast to the West Coast. China had none. The first two railroads built in China were dismantled at the orders of the emperor. The first one to endure was built in 1881.

The first U.S. transcontinental railroad was finished in 1869, when two major railways connected in Utah. At first, it took at least seven days to travel from New York to San Francisco.

More than 10,000 Chinese laborers worked to lay track and build tunnels for the western portion of the first transcontinental railroad.

One group of boys on the Chinese Educational Mission really was stopped by a train robbery, in 1873, by the notorious bandit Jesse James and his gang.

For thousands of years of history, Chinese people lived by Confucian values, which required strict obedience to emperor, father, husband, and elder brother.

The 1876 Centennial Exhibition showed the world how advanced American technology was, with a gigantic steam engine, sewing machines, typewriters, a monorail, and even the first telephone invented by Alexander Graham Bell.

Author Mark Twain met with President Grant to ask him to write to the Chinese government to persuade them to let the boys continue their studies in the United States.

# About the Author

*D*ori Jones Yang is a Seattle-area writer with extensive experience making personal connections across boundaries of culture and time. Raised in Ohio, she lived and worked in Singapore and Hong Kong and covered the opening of China as a journalist for *Business Week*. Married to a Chinese man, she has traveled widely throughout Asia.

Her previous books include *Daughter of Xanadu*, a young-adult historical novel set in China at the time of Marco Polo, and *The Secret Voice of Gina Zhang*, an award-winning middle-grade novel about a girl from China who begins fifth grade in Seattle only to discover she has lost her voice. After studying Chinese for many years, Dori knows what it feels like to struggle to express your thoughts in an unfamiliar language.

Learn more at www.booksbydori.com.

*Author photo © Chris Loomis/SparkPoint Studio*

# SELECTED TITLES FROM SPARKPRESS

SparkPress is an independent boutique publisher delivering high-quality, entertaining, and engaging content that enhances readers' lives, with a special focus on female-driven work.
Visit us at www.gosparkpress.com

*Colorblind,* Leah Bowron, $16.95, 978-1-943006-08-3. The time is 1968. The place is Montgomery, Alabama. The story is one of resilience in the face of discrimination and bullying. Using the racially charged word "Negro," two Caucasian boys repeatedly bully Miss Annie Loomis—the first African-American teacher at the all-white Wyatt Elementary School. At the same time, using the hateful word "harelip," the boys repeatedly bully Miss Loomis's eleven-year-old Caucasian student, Lisa Parker, who was born with cleft palate and cleft lip. Who will best the bullies? Only Lisa's mood ring knows for sure.

*Huskers,* Strat Warden, $15, 978-1-940716-99-2. Huskers follows a group of young boys on a quest who confront their individual flaws, conquer their personal demons, and discover the values that will guide them the rest of their lives.

*The Red Sun,* by Alane Adams. $17, 978-1-940716-24-4. Drawing on Norse mythology, *The Red Sun* follows a boy's journey to uncover the truth about his past in a magical realm called Orkney—a journey during which he has to overcome the simmering anger inside of him, learn to channel his growing magical powers, and find a way to forgive the father who left him behind.

*Kalifus Rising,* by Alane Adams, $16.95, 978-1940716848. Sam Baron just freed Orkney from the ravages of the Red Sun—but now, imprisoned by Catriona, leader of the Volgrim Witches, Sam finds the darker side of his half-god, half-witch heritage released, and he fears he might destroy what he saved. As Sam's friends rush to save him, other forces are at work in Orkney's shadows—forces that could help free Sam, or condemn him to the darkness forever.

# About SparkPress

—◇·◇—◇◇—◇·◇—

SparkPress is an independent, hybrid imprint focused on merging the best of the traditional publishing model with new and innovative strategies. We deliver high-quality, entertaining, and engaging content that enhances readers' lives. We are proud to bring to market a list of *New York Times* best-selling, award-winning, and debut authors who represent a wide array of genres, as well as our established, industry-wide reputation for creative, results-driven success in working with authors. SparkPress, a BookSparks imprint, is a division of SparkPoint Studio LLC.

Learn more at GoSparkPress.com